She sensed that danger lurked nearby

Allie sat for the longest moment on the bare mattress, listening as his footsteps descended the stairs. An engine started in the parking lot below. A car squealed out onto the street. Then she began thinking about the people who were chasing the man. Who were they? What would they do to her if they found her here, where he was supposed to meet the blonde called Liz?

All of a sudden she shuddered with fear. She had to flee. Why had she waited? But just as she stood, there was a sound, a sound that echoed in Allie's mind like an explosion. . . .

ABOUT THE AUTHOR

Although Jan Michaels is from Kentucky, she
considers herself a transplanted Yankee and
has called Chicago home for most of her life.
In addition to being an author, Jan is a wife,
mother, volunteer, registered nurse and
unregistered chauffeur—not necessarily in
that order. She has been published under the
pseudonym Jan Matthews and believes
there's no finer mix than cops and robbers
and romance. Jan enjoys hearing from her
readers, and letters will be forwarded to her if
sent to Harlequin's New York office:
300 E. 42nd St. N.Y., N.Y. 10017.

Books by Jan Michaels

HARLEQUIN INTRIGUE
32–PURSUIT IN THE WILDERNESS
71–THE ONLY WITNESS

Red Dog Run

Jan Michaels

Harlequin Books

TORONTO • NEW YORK • LONDON
AMSTERDAM • PARIS • SYDNEY • HAMBURG
STOCKHOLM • ATHENS • TOKYO • MILAN

This one is for Matt,
who hasn't had a book of his own yet.

Harlequin Intrigue edition published May 1988

ISBN 0-373-22089-8

CAST OF CHARACTERS

Alanna Martin—She was swept into a maelstrom.

Reeve Chandler—He needed papers to spare his brother from torture.

Curt Chandler—He was double-crossed by a CIA agent gone haywire.

Liz Hernandez—If she had shown up, who knows how events would've unfolded?

Paul Sammison—He relished stalking an old rival.

Zane Younger—A Denver policeman with more on his mind than crime.

Tom Biner—A juicier prank he could not have devised.

Two East German agents—All they wanted was to stay in this country.

Danhi and Jean—Their Navaho reservation provided safe harbor—briefly.

The mob—If they couldn't get their mark, who could?

Frank, the reporter—His fatal flaw was in knowing the *wrong* people.

Chapter One

Alanna Martin froze as the cold metal of the gun pressed into her temple. Although it was peripheral to her vision, she could see that it wasn't an ordinary weapon, such as a tiny handgun or a revolver, but a big, dark, ugly thing that would leave an exit hole the size of a crater. The man holding the gun wasn't ordinary, either. He was as big and dark and menacing as the pistol leveled against her head.

Ordinarily Alanna would have screamed. She had never seen a gun before, at least not one like this, except perhaps on television. Sonny Crockett carried one like it on *Miami Vice*. So did Hunter. And Dee Dee. But they weren't desperate. Alanna had never seen a man this desperate, either. Desperate enough to kill.

"Okay, lady," he rasped in her ear, crushing her tight against his length, "don't move a muscle."

More than desperate. Dangerous. Menace laced his voice, darkening the low, husky tone of his commands, and it was in the stance of his body, which, despite her fear, she could feel pressed against her, every muscle tight, coiled for instant action. And Alanna knew without his telling her that this wasn't a scene from *Miami Vice* or *Hunter*, and if she did scream, she was as good as dead.

"Just relax now and cooperate," he went on, "and everything will be fine. I'm not going to hurt you."

Famous last words. They were hardly soothing, particularly since he kept one hand clamped over her mouth as he snaked the other one around her rib cage, pressing tight just below her breasts. He pulled her backward, toward the bathroom. Since she didn't have much choice, she stumbled along, tripping over his feet. The gray designer suit with the pencil-thin skirt that she had scrimped and saved to buy twisted up around her thighs, probably ruined. She'd heard it tear.

"You're early, but then I figured you would be," he said as he flicked on the bathroom light, releasing her mouth only long enough to quickly pull the string. "Good dye job. No roots."

Apparently he was expecting a bleached blonde. Alanna was a natural blonde, but she didn't say anything. How could she talk now, when his fingers clamped her flesh and his arm held her like a vise? He nestled the gun against her hip. Besides, she couldn't have formulated words even if she'd tried. All that came from her throat was the harsh sound of her own breathing.

Paralyzed by fear, she focused on the light. The bare bulk swung back and forth, illuminating the room beyond in a crazy tilting pattern. She could see the dresser, and the light swung back. She could see the bed, and the light swung back. She could see the table, and the light swung back. Everything was old and well used, nicked and torn. The bed sagged in the middle. This was a first-rate motel?

Alanna supposed she should have been more alert, more dubious. Certainly she had placed too much trust in her boss, Tom Biner. The man was notoriously cheap, and he'd made her reservations himself. When the taxi had dropped her off a few minutes before, she'd thought the ancient two-story structure just outside of Denver, Colorado looked run-down. It was tucked in a densely wooded area, probably to hide the paint that peeled from the siding. Even from the outside, the rooms had looked small and dingy, but Alanna had been so excited about being in Denver, in the Rocky

Mountains, that she'd ignored the less-than-luxurious accommodations. In all her life she'd never been west of the Mississippi, and the experience had at first seemed promising. The sun had bathed her face in soothing warmth, and the air had felt so cool and clean. Not at all like Chicago.

"Now," the man holding her captive said, as though everything had been settled, "what's your name?"

Since he was still pressing his hand over her mouth, Alanna doubted he was truly interested in her answer. Yet he jerked her tighter against his body. The air went out of her lungs in a rush.

"I said, what's your name?" he snarled nastily.

"Nancy," she murmured from around his fingers, trying to catch her breath. She didn't know why she lied. It just seemed a good idea. Maybe she should bite him. So far she hadn't struggled at all. She'd walked into the motel room and into his arms, and there she had stayed, quiet as a church mouse.

Shocked.

Numbed.

She needed to do something. She could sink her teeth into the fleshy part of his fingers. Or she could kick him. She was wearing three-inch spike heels. They could damage a man's foot as well as a woman's. And in fact many times when in pain, she had wished that she could dig her heel into the instep of the person who'd designed them.

If she fought back, then what? The light still swung, and she could see the bed again. And a shadow. Her and the man and the gun. And she could see herself dead, tied up on the bed with a bullet hole through her brain. Her palms grew cold and clammy; sweat beaded on her forehead. She'd always been a chicken, since the day she was born. She'd come out with a whimper instead of a lusty cry. Nothing had changed. She chickened out now, too. So why in the world had she tried to lie?

"I thought it was Liz," he said. He loosened his fingers.

Her name. "Yes, Liz," she answered. "I'm sorry, I forgot."

"Your name?"

A bad move. "What do you want it to be?"

There was a moment of silence. "I said I wouldn't hurt you, lady. Don't you believe me?"

"No." She hadn't needed to think twice there.

"Can't say that I blame you, considering the people you work for." He jerked her tighter, making her teeth snap together. He then loosened his grip on her mouth. "Okay, Liz or Nancy or whatever you call yourself, enough stalling. Where is it?"

"Where is what?"

"The briefcase."

Her briefcase? "It's over there," she said. She flicked her eyes to the door.

She'd placed it there when she'd come in, along with her luggage, intending to turn on the light. The room had been dark, the draperies drawn. But the man had grabbed her from behind. She couldn't help but wonder what she had stumbled on. If this was a television show it would be a drug case, and he would be the bad guy. But what in the world did he want with her briefcase? *Her* briefcase! All she had in it was her presentation that was scheduled for the next morning. She'd flown to Denver as a representative of Fantastic Foundations. She was to meet with several companies and show them her designs.

Her designs! Suddenly she wondered if this wasn't all a trick. Things like this didn't happen in real life. Rough-looking men didn't hide out in dark motel rooms and grab women coming through town. But what if someone was trying to steal her designs? Someone like Mable Hill, her co-worker. Ever since Alanna had started at Fantastic Foundations, the woman had acted underhanded, all because Alanna had better designs. Would Mable go this far?

Or, Alanna thought, the more likely culprit might be her boss. Not to steal her designs, but to hire a man with a gun

to scare her. Tom Biner was a prankster. Last Halloween
he'd sent a costumed gorilla to surprise her, and for Christmas he'd mailed her a card with a Santa who popped out
and went "ho, ho, ho" when she opened it. Then he'd
laughed just as hard. But this was going too far. This was
too frightening. And if it *was* Tom's idea of fun, when she
got back to Chicago she would hang him by his fingernails
and ram his joke—and his first-rate motel room—into the
ground. Now that her eyes had adjusted to darkness, she
could see the room clearly, and the place was a dump.

"I'm going to let you go now," the man said. "But don't
make any fast moves. Hear me?"

She nodded. "Yes."

And yes, she was going to enjoy giving Tom Biner his
comeuppance. Or Mable Hill. She was so convinced now
that the entire episode was a spoof, or an attempt to sabo-
tage her work, she lunged for her briefcase the moment the
man released her. She refused to let him get his hands on it.

But her action was a mistake, a dreadful mistake. The
man lunged for her, and he was faster than she. He caught
her by the arm, and twisted it to her back, then thrust her
against his body. If she hadn't realized it before, she noticed now that he was built like a brick wall, tough and
strong and unbending. She felt as though she'd run into
stone.

"You don't hear very well, do you?" he snarled and
poked his face a few inches from her own. His eyes were
cold and hard, a deep sapphire blue, that glinted as cold as
the gun he held in his hand. He had clicked off the safety.
The sound was soft, but it echoed in the room like a shot.
His hand, cuffed around her wrist, held her still as he glared
at her—a killer, she was sure.

Alanna swallowed hard, and her heart began to pound in
her chest. This was the real thing. Certainly neither Tom nor
Mable would go to such lengths to scare her.

"I'm sorry," she murmured, hoping that if she apolo-
gized he wouldn't hurt her.

"I'll just bet you are." With agility the man shoved her to the bed and knelt beside her, still holding her wrists in one hand and the gun in the other. Pinning her hands above her head, he peered at her. "Are the papers that important? Were you supposed to get them back? If Sammison thinks you can outmaneuver me, then he's a fool."

Certainly the person called Sammison wasn't alone. Considering her rash behavior, Alanna had fallen into the same category. Why had she tried to fight? All she could do was stare at the man glowering above her. Her first assessment of him had been accurate. He was desperate. The room was dark, but the light from the bathroom played on his features. Aside from his eyes, which she had already noticed were an unusual shade of blue, his hair was the darkest she'd ever seen, a true jet black. Thick and straight, it grew longish in back, curled along his neck and framed a face that was so hard it could have been carved from granite. His eyebrows were an angry slash across his forehead, and his jaw was set in a determined thrust. His complexion was almost bronze, darkened further by a harsh stubble of beard. Apparently it had been several days since he'd shaved.

If Alanna had been pressed, she would have sworn that he'd emerged from a cigarette commercial. Rugged—that was the term that described him. All he needed was a horse and a campfire and a woman at his side. Earlier she'd noticed the blue chambray shirt that stretched taut over broad shoulders, the well-worn jeans that rode low on his hips, the brass belt buckle with an Indian lance etched inside, wispy feathers floating on the wind.

Even under ordinary circumstances he'd be a difficult man to deal with, Alanna thought, for there was something wild about him, something untamed. She didn't know him at all, and yet she knew in an instant that he was a hard-drinking, hard-riding, hard-loving man; all heartache.

She frowned, shaking her head. She had to be crazy, thinking crazy, to romanticize him. The man was dangerous, and she was in deep, dark trouble. "Listen, mister," she whispered, finding her voice as she tried to make sense of everything he'd told her. "I think you've got the wrong person."

"Sure."

He didn't believe her. "I'm not kidding."

"Neither am I."

Unfortunately that was painfully obvious. "You wouldn't consider letting me go, would you?"

"No."

She hadn't really thought that he would. She frowned. Now what? She had to try another track. "Who's Sammison?"

The man flashed a derisive grin. "Gonna play dumb, huh, and pretend not to recognize your boss? Okay. No problem. I like dumb broads. They're easier to deal with. Where's your weapon?"

"I don't have one."

"Mind if I check?" he retorted sarcastically.

Before Alanna could object, he placed the gun aside and shifted his weight so that he could frisk her, quickly and efficiently running his hand up and down her body. Even though the gesture wasn't sexual, it was demeaning, and Alanna cringed, her flesh shuddering involuntarily as he patted along her breasts and thighs. She felt helpless and at his mercy, and she knew somehow that this man was merciless. When he killed—and she had no doubt that he had—he would do it without compunction. He would pull the trigger with no regrets, no second thoughts, and he would walk away from the battle like a gunslinger from the wild, woolly West, nonchalantly blowing the smoke from the barrel of a six-shooter, and strolling right into a woman's arms.

"Anything under your skirt? A thigh holster?"

"No," she said again, lying very still. He was practically on top of her. Her arms ached where he held them stretched above her head, but she didn't move, fearful that he would harm her. Would he rape and plunder? "I told you I don't have a weapon. I'm not who you think I am."

"Really?" His tone was still mocking, disbelieving. "Tell me then, if you're not who I think you are, what are you doing at the Rustic River Inn with a brown briefcase?"

"Everybody has a brown briefcase."

"Not at the Rustic River Inn," he said, hauling her up from the bed with a quick tug on her arms. "And particularly not tall blond women coming to room 210." Letting her go, he stepped back and held the gun on her. It was already cocked and ready to fire. She'd heard the telltale click several minutes earlier. All he had to do was squeeze. "Okay, like I said before, no quick moves. Now suppose you sashay your pretty little behind over there and get that briefcase. Set it on the bed and open it for me."

"Look, mister," she started again, wanting to convince him he had the wrong person, "you're making a mistake."

His glance told her that he wouldn't tolerate objections. "I've made mistakes before. Lots of them. Just do what I say, and you won't get hurt. Now get the briefcase."

"There's nothing in it." At least nothing that would interest him, she mused.

But he became angry. He glared at her and gripped the pistol ominously. "You better hope the papers are there, sweetheart."

God, he was serious. How could she convince him that she wasn't this Liz, this ambassador of someone called Sammison? She'd handled everything wrong. She should have told him right away that he had the wrong person. Instead she had acted liked a scared rabbit. But she'd been so frightened. Although not as frightened as she was at this moment. Clutching her hands in front of her, she walked slowly to the briefcase and picked it up. "You're going to be disappointed."

"I hope not," he answered. "Or you and your boss are both in trouble. I don't like double crosses."

She could imagine what he would do to her. He was the type of man who would be big on revenge. Hanging by the neck until dead, whiplashes on her body, little knife nicks. Full-blown, painful torture, nothing subtle or simple as bamboo shoots under the fingernails. Maybe even Indian torture. She pictured the buckle he wore, bearing the lance and feathers. What did Indians do to people?

Alanna had watched a movie once where a band of Apaches had buried a man up to his neck in sand then spread honey over his head. The ants had marched across the dessert and swarmed over the helpless victim, who had screamed out in agony. She shuddered. Had she been dealing with this man, she wouldn't have double-crossed him, not ever. Just the look in his eyes was enough to make her obey. How could she have fantasized about him before? He wasn't a gunslinger from the old West. Hadn't she already decided that he was a murderer? A hired killer. Or a hunted killer. She didn't know which was more dangerous.

Carefully she placed the briefcase on the bed and pressed the clasps open. The snap made them both flinch. She gulped down her rising fear. No sense telling him he was going to be upset. She'd have to await his fury. Closing her eyes, she flipped open the top and waited for him to react to the lacy bras and garter belts that spilled out of the case. The first outfit was red, trimmed in black, as racy and sexy as the limits of her imagination. The garter belt was a peekaboo affair bordered by little black bows, and the bra plunged practically to Australia. Lord, what would he say?

But silence greeted her. The only sound she could hear was her blood roaring in her ears. Swallowing the lump of fear in her throat, she opened her eyes and looked at him. He was staring at the briefcase as though it were an alien from outer space.

"Want to try them on?" she said in a crazy attempt at humor. Maybe he would let her go now.

He didn't laugh. He didn't even smile. Slowly he lifted his gaze to hers. "Aren't you working the wrong side of town?

I thought high-classed hookers concentrated on the convention hotels.''

"What!" Alanna gasped. For a moment she didn't believe her ears. He thought she was a hooker?

But he didn't elaborate. "Damn!" he exploded, slamming his fist against a nearby dresser so hard the wood nearly splintered. "Damn Sammison to hell!"

If Alanna had thought the man was frightening before, it didn't compare to now. His face looked like a mask of wrath. Had something been lying on the floor she felt certain he would have booted it across the room and against the wall with the force of an atomic bomb. She was glad her briefcase was out of harm's way.

She suspected the people he'd called Liz and Sammison weren't exactly innocents in this little caper, but she almost felt sorry for them as she gazed on the man. When he caught up with them, they would have more than their share of trouble.

"I know I've mentioned this before," she murmured softly, trying not to aggravate him further. "But I—I think you've got the wrong person."

He grunted agreement. "No kidding. Not even Sammison would be stupid enough to send a broad with lingerie." He paced the room for a moment, stomping across the faded purple-and-gold flowered carpet with long, angry strides. Matters were complicated enough without running into some dizzy dame toting around fancy red underwear. What the hell was he going to do with her? Reeve Chandler had a mountain of problems, and this woman standing in front of him was trouble he didn't need. Suddenly he whipped his attention back to her. "Okay, lady. Let's hear it. If you're not Liz, just who the hell are you?"

Alanna was surprised by his sharp tone. Just who the hell did she think *he* was? He had accosted her and suddenly he was acting as if the whole scenario were her fault. *He'd* accosted *her*! And for the past twenty minutes she'd been trying to explain to him that there had been a misunderstanding, a mistaken identity. Had he listened? No! He'd tossed her around the room, scared her to death, accused her of assorted crimes.

"I'm a representative for Fantastic Foundations," she said archly. "In case you haven't guessed, it's a lingerie company. I design and sell lingerie."

He didn't think that was funny, either.

"I tried to tell you."

"What's your name?"

A familiar question. There was no reason to lie now. And really, she couldn't have told a falsehood if her life depended on it, not to this man who still looked as though he were ready to embark on a murderous rage. "Alanna. Alanna Martin." She paused, adding lamely, "People call me Allie."

This time he stared at her and not her briefcase, directing his gaze to her as though she were the lowest life-form on the evolutionary scale. "What the hell does your nickname have to do with the situation?"

"Nothing." She clutched her hands tightly together. If only she wasn't so scared. "I'm just nervous."

"Take off your dress."

She glanced at him. "Pardon me?"

"You really do have a hearing problem, lady. Take off your dress."

God, he was going to...she couldn't say it. And just moments ago she'd dared to smart off to him. "I—please don't—don't make me do that," she pleaded, her heart hammering full speed.

"Off," he said, his voice laced with menace.

"I'm not wearing—" She took a calming breath and gestured at her clothes. "This is a suit," she said. A designer suit that had cost her half a week's salary.

From the look on his face, he thought she'd sunk even lower. "Then take off your *suit*."

"I'm not a hooker," she blurted out.

He just glared at her. "Let's go, lady."

Unfortunately he wasn't talking about leaving. She didn't have much choice. Slowly, with trembling fingers, Alanna reached for the bow at her neck and untied it. She couldn't help but fumble with the buttons. They were tiny and delicate, like the blouse. It was a deep, rich, red silk, and she was wearing a red camisole under it, one of her designs. One of her racy, sexier creations.

The garment was meant to seduce. Not that she did much seducing. She'd had only one lover in her life, and that had been while she was young and impulsive, a college kid hell-bent on losing her virginity. She just liked sexy underwear. On top she wore expensive but demure, straitlaced designs, paralleling her demure, straitlaced life-style. Hell, the last man she'd dated had given her a broom for her birthday. A *broom*, for God's sake! She hadn't known whether he was telling her she was a witch, a shrew, a good housekeeper, or all three.

"I said, let's go, lady."

Alanna jumped when he spoke. God, how this man could scare her. He pointed the gun at her again, motioning her to increase her speed. "Hurry up."

"I can't," she murmured. Why was this happening to her? What had she done to deserve such treatment? "I can't do this. Please don't make me."

"Look, sweetie." Moving close, he poked his face into hers. "You've got a choice. Either you take off your dress— and fast—or I do it for you."

Alanna opened her mouth to speak, but no words would come out. Paralysis had gripped her again. What was there to say, anyway? Her orders were fairly explicit. She glanced toward the door.

"Don't even think it."

She looked back at him. Briefly. Then, before she realized what she was doing, she bolted toward the door. She could make it outside. She was in good shape. She could get away. Why hadn't she tried before? Because she was basically a smart person. She'd been meaning to join the health club, but hadn't. She realized how significant that was when he effortlessly caught up with her, encircled her waist and bent her backward over his propped-up leg. She stared at him from upside down. "You hear all right, lady," he said. "You just don't listen."

"Please let me go."

"Not on your life."

"Don't...you aren't going to...?" She still couldn't say the word. "Please don't touch me."

He just laughed, a brusque, mocking sound. "This may surprise you, lady, but regardless of your kinky underwear, I have no interest whatsoever in your body. I'm sure you'd be great in the sack, but I'm in a hurry. I don't have much time, and I sure don't have time for games. So take off your clothes," he ordered. *"Now."*

When he let her go, Alanna stepped away with her back to him. She couldn't prevent the flush that spread over her face as she unbuttoned, then peeled off her blouse. She let it slide to the floor. He was a man, after all, and she didn't know whether or not to believe him about wanting her, but his tone brooked no argument.

"Turn around."

No, please no, she pleaded silently. "Am I—"

"Come on, lady," he cut in, apparently at the end of his patience. He spun her around to face him, then stepped backward. "Will you get your clothes the hell off? I already told you I'm in a hurry. This isn't a striptease."

"I didn't think it was," she retorted sharply, growing angry again. First he had insinuated she was a hooker, and now he was calling her a stripper. "I'm going as fast as I can. Do you think I want to upset you?"

He frowned, as though surprised by her outburst. She was surprised, too. She was a stone-cold coward, and right at that moment she wanted to cut out her tongue. Sometimes she was worse than a fool. Yet he just glared at her. "Move it, and you won't upset me."

Despite her fear, some innate stubbornness must have surfaced to allow Alanna to defy him. She stood stock-still, her eyes averted, hoping he wouldn't force her to go any farther. Surely he had made her suffer enough. Finally he said, "Excuse me, but what are you waiting for?"

"What should I do now?" she asked, her eyes still lowered.

She knew she'd made another mistake when he swore crudely. "What the hell?" he rasped, gritting his teeth so tight she could hear them grind together. "Do you need lessons?"

"No, I just—"

"Take off your skirt!"

This time she didn't dare disobey. Although she wanted to go faster, her fingers seemed frozen, stiff and lifeless, and she worked the zipper just as awkwardly as the buttons on her blouse. She wiggled the wool-blend skirt over her hips what seemed like hours later. For a moment she stood in just her half-slip and camisole top. While the lingerie covered her breasts, rather than plunging low, it was alluring, and she knew his gaze was on her. Would he change his mind? Mortified by what he was forcing her to do, she closed her eyes as she reached for the straps, intending to lower them.

But he stopped her. "That's far enough. Get your clothes and your luggage, and put them in the bathroom."

Relief pulsed through her in a thankful rush as she folded over to gather the items. Only—what if he had some weird fetish he would only do in the bathroom?

"Get the bed linens, too," he ordered.

Still afraid to refuse, Alanna scooped up the items, crumpling the sheets into a ball along with her clothes, and walked toward the small room, grateful for the reprieve. If necessary she'd lock herself inside.

He must have guessed her intent. "Toss everything on the floor and lock the door," he instructed her. "Then close it— without going in."

The Rustic River Inn was an old motel, and the bathroom lock was one of those that locked from either side, but only unlocked from the inside. Once closed, she wouldn't be able to get to her clothes. Or anything else with which to cover herself. He clicked on the bedside light while she dumped all the items in a heap.

When she pulled the door together, he motioned her back with the gun. "Sit on the bed."

"Are you going to tie me up?" She didn't want to be tied. It was demeaning enough, having to undress and not having anything to cover herself with.

He stared at her for a long moment, taking in her curves. But he wasn't looking at her at all, she realized. She could have been made out of wood for all he cared. Or air. She could see the wheels turning in his head. What was he thinking? Finally he muttered, "Damn! I could use a stiff drink."

Alanna was about to suggest room service, but somehow she didn't think he'd appreciate her gallows humor. She didn't understand it herself, except that it seemed to be a release valve for all that was happening to her. If she didn't joke about the situation, she would go stark, raving mad.

The man remained serious. He stalked to the window and pushed the draperies slightly aside to glance outside. A slice of light pierced the room. Reeve sighed again and dropped the curtain in place. Even though he knew he'd been double-crossed, he half expected Liz to knock on the door at any moment. After all, Sammison had gone to the trouble of registering her in the room, probably a ploy to get Reeve here and off the trail of his brother. Now he had a lingerie designer—a broad who sold bras—and he'd held a gun to her head. Stupid woman. Yet this wasn't her fault, he reminded himself. He couldn't trust her. He couldn't trust anyone, but he supposed he could give her some sort of explanation for the ordeal he'd put her through, an accounting. She was sitting there looking so confused and forlorn.

She was a cute little blonde. Too bad she wasn't his type. Despite being a bit ditzy, she seemed bright.

"I need to buy some time," he said.

At last he'd told her something significant. She was making progress. "There are people looking for you?"

"Yes, and I'm looking for people."

People who would be coming to this motel. People who were supposed to meet him and give him papers. A bleached blonde with a brown briefcase. Liz. A man named Sammison. "What are you going to do with me?"

"Lady, every instinct I have screams to me that you're trouble. You're going to run scared. Broads like you always do." He sighed again as if he were unhappy about his decision. "Look, I'll leave you untied if you promise not to call the cops."

"I won't," Alanna nodded gravely. "I promise."

He smiled, and oddly it was a gentle expression that softened the lines of his face. Under ordinary circumstances he might even be termed handsome, she thought. If you liked the big, broad-shouldered type. And Alanna didn't. She didn't even like Sonny Crockett on *Miami Vice*, although she watched the program. Or Hunter. Not anymore. They were dangerous men, like this one. And *he* was definitely dangerous. More dangerous than anyone she'd ever met or even heard about on a television program.

"Sure," he said. "The minute I'm out of here you'll run crying to the law. You know, lady," he went on without waiting for her answer, "you've stumbled into something crazy, something you can't handle. If I were you, when I got my clothes back, I'd get the hell out of here."

She didn't need him to tell her that. She had already gathered that she had walked into the wrong place at the wrong time. She had every intention of leaving the motel as soon as possible. Of leaving Denver. The West entirely. If she had to, she'd run all the way back to Chicago. The city had its share of smog, corrupt politics, and muggers running loose on the streets, but there wasn't anything as frightening as this man and whatever he was involved in. "Right. I will."

"Don't call the front desk, either."

"I won't."

He reached for the phone cord and ripped it from the wall. "Insurance. By the way, who's your boss?"

Why did he want to know that? "Tom Biner."

"He own the company you work for?"

"Yes."

"He's booked you in a dump."

"I know," she said.

"Just give me ten minutes to get away."

"I will."

Her responses were reflexive and out of fear. But since she'd given her word, she'd have to stick to it, coward or not. Even as a child, she took a vow of silence literally. Once she'd gotten into trouble because she'd promised not to tattle on her brother for breaking a church window. He'd thrown a baseball through the expensive stained glass, shattering it to bits. Because she was the one caught sneaking into the church to retrieve the ball, everyone blamed her, including her father, a stern taskmaster. She'd ended up paying for the darned thing, from her weekly allowance and later from a job. But she hadn't told, not even the next night, when her brother had put a frog in her bed as a prank.

The man opened the hotel room door, and Colorado sunshine poured in. The sun was setting to the west, bathing the room in a rosy glow. Tall mountains rose majestically in the distance.

"Oh." Starting to leave, he paused and glanced back at her. "Just out of curiosity, did you design that garter belt in your briefcase?"

She nodded. "Yes. Why?"

"I thought you'd like to know, it needs another bow. Right here." He pointed to an area low on his midsection

and winked at her. *Winked.* "That is, if you're trying to interest a man. Good luck, sexy lady," he added. "Be sure and
go home."

Chapter Two

Sexy lady! Damn the man! Alanna was so angry she threw a shoe at the door.

She meant to keep her promise, she really did. After her display of temper she sat for the longest moment on the bare mattress, listening as his footsteps descended the stairs. An engine started in the parking lot below. A car squealed out into the street. Then she began thinking about the people who were chasing the man. Who were they? What would they do to her if they found her here, where he was supposed to meet the blond woman called Liz?

Suddenly she shuddered with fear. She had to flee. She had to get her clothes and go. Why had she waited? But just as she stood up to inspect the lock, someone knocked at the door. The sound echoed in Alanna's mind like an explosion. She froze, staring at the wooden structure as though it were alive and ready to strike.

"Are you there, Miss Hernandez?" a voice called. "It's the bellhop. I need to check something in your room."

Totally ignoring her state of dress, or rather, of undress, just thrilled that it wasn't the person called Sammison hunting her down, Alanna ran to the door and flung it open. What could she have done to cover up anyway? Her clothes were in the bathroom, entwined in sheets and blankets. The draperies looked a bit difficult to rip down. And at this point she wasn't going to be impeded by false modesty.

But she regretted her rash decision immediately when a freckle-faced kid of about nineteen, dressed in jeans and boots and a well-washed work shirt, stood framed in the doorway, staring at her. A smile spread across his face as he took in her scantily clad body. "Hi."

"Hi," she said back.

"The front desk asked me to come up," he went on, apparently memorizing the lacy pattern at the V of her breasts. "Something's wrong with your phone. It's blinking an out-of-order signal on the switchboard."

The phone! Alanna turned to glance at it. "I caught my foot on the cord and pulled it from the wall," she said, looking back at the kid. Why was she lying? Oh, yes, she'd promised. "Can you fix it?"

"Probably," he answered. "Is something wrong, lady?"

Why would he ask that? "No." Suddenly she paused. "What did you call me?"

"Lady?"

"No, before. What did you call me when you knocked on the door?"

"Miss Hernandez. That is you, isn't it?" Glancing down, he checked a card in his hand. "Let's see, room 210. It's registered to a Miss Elizabeth Hernandez."

Liz.

"Oh, God." Alanna closed the door in his face and leaned against the back of it, breathing hard. Panic clutched at her throat. How had they gotten that name?

"Miss Hernandez?"

Damn! She pulled the door back open. "Call the police."

"Huh?"

"I have to speak to a policeman," she said hurriedly. "There was a man here."

"Oh, yeah?" The boy's face lit up with interest, and he glanced beyond her into the room. Then he smiled at her again. "You new in town?"

"Excuse me?"

"Did you have fun?"

Alanna glared at him. At least he turned red. She wanted to grasp his arms and shake him, but she supposed that, considering how she looked, his erroneous assumption was logical. "A man tried to accost me," she said slowly and distinctly. "He held a gun to my head and threatened me."

"Sure, lady, whatever you say." The boy didn't believe her any more than the man who'd threatened her earlier had. "Look, this ain't a classy joint," he went on, "but if you call the police they're going to bust us for prostitution."

"I'd like to speak to the motel manager," she said quietly.

But the manager didn't believe her, either, nor did the detective who arrived over an hour later. She could tell that as far as all three men were concerned, either she was making up the entire story to cover up a clandestine affair, or she had lost her mind.

"Could you describe the man again?" the detective asked, flipping open a pad of paper.

He was obviously bored. When he'd arrived at the motel he'd introduced himself as Zane Younger. He was the image of his name. He was young, too, although not as young as the bellhop, and he was quite attractive, rugged looking, like the other man, the dark stranger who had held Alanna hostage. Only this man had pulled a cowboy hat low over his forehead and wore jeans, boots and a string tie laced around the throat of a western-style shirt. Over that he had slipped on a tweed jacket with suede elbows. Someone had unlocked the door to the bathroom, but Alanna had left her clothes inside, under the crazy notion that the evidence would prove her story. She'd had to ask for a blanket to drape around her shoulders, and she sat on the bed huddled in the scratchy brown garment.

"Miss?"

"He was big," she answered.

"Big, how?"

"Tall."

"Any identifying features? Scars? Birthmarks?"

She frowned, trying to remember. "No. He had dark hair. Very dark."

"Ever seen him before?"

"No."

"Sure?"

"Yes," she said testily. "I'm sure." Of course she didn't know the man!

The detective paused. "You say your name is Alanna Martin?"

Say? Alanna frowned again. "Yes."

"Allie?"

She nodded. "Yes."

"The man knocked on the door?"

"No, he was waiting inside when I opened it."

"How'd he get in?"

She shrugged. "I don't know."

"Was the door locked?"

"Yes."

"And?"

"And what?" she asked, beginning to chafe at his line of questioning.

"And what happened?"

"I told you, he grabbed me."

"How?"

"Around the waist." She gestured to her body. "He put his other hand over my mouth and dragged me into the bathroom."

"What did he say?"

"He told me he wouldn't hurt me."

"Did you believe him?"

"No."

She glared at the detective, but he wasn't even looking at her. He was scribbling on a pad, and continued questioning her in a bored tone. "Did you register at the front desk before you came up to your room?"

"Yes."

Finally he looked up. "Then why is Miss Elizabeth Hernandez registered to this room?"

"I have no idea," Alanna answered brusquely. "Maybe they gave me the wrong key."

"Do you know Miss Hernandez?"

What did he mean by that? He was acting as if she were under suspicion. "No," she said simply.

"Then how do you know the name?"

Surely he didn't think she was that stupid. "The man *mentioned* her name."

"Miss Hernandez."

"No, he called her Liz," Alanna said, growing more and more exasperated. Was he deliberately trying to trick her? "The man was supposed to meet someone named Liz here, in this room. Liz works for Sammison."

"Who is?"

At that, the anger that had been brewing inside Alanna spilled over. "If I knew, I wouldn't need you!" She stood up and started to pace across the room. "Look, you don't seem to understand. A man accosted me. He put a gun to my head and—"

"Any bruises?" the detective cut in.

Surprised by his question, Alanna paused and glanced at her wrists. She wasn't hurt. Yet she could still feel the stranger's strong, hard grasp. "No. No, I'm not hurt."

"Do you want to be examined by a doctor?"

As she looked up again, she realized what he was referring to. She flushed. "He didn't...he didn't do anything to me."

"I thought he held a gun to your head."

Damn the man! Both men! Only this one was deliberately misunderstanding, provoking her! "He did," she said. "He didn't do—"

"Right," he cut in again. "Okay. Once again, how'd the room get registered to Miss Hernandez?"

Alanna's patience was all used up. "Once again," she snapped, purposely mimicking him, "how in the world am I supposed to know? Why don't you ask the manager that question? I'm a guest at this motel."

Apparently he didn't realize she was angry. Or else he didn't care. "I did," he said. "They took the reservation by phone." He scribbled something on his pad of paper. "Do you have any other identification on you, Miss Martin?"

He'd already checked out her driver's license and social security card. What more did he want? "Why don't you take my fingerprints if you don't believe me?" she sneered. They'd already decided they wouldn't be able to dust for the man's fingerprints. Too many people had poured through these motel rooms. But they could take hers. "Or do you want me to swear out an affidavit? I could even make it a blood vow, if you wish. We'll slit my wrists. Or how about a sorority pledge?"

"I believe you."

That couldn't be proved by the questions he was asking. "Then why do you want more identification?"

"Just doing my job."

Alanna sat back down on the bed. Someone flipped on the lights beside her as the detective tipped his hat back to reveal a shock of sandy, curly hair. He glanced at her, for the first time actually taking her in as more than a silly complainant. She shifted uncomfortably as his gaze raked over her body. Even wrapped in the blanket she knew her curves were visible. And why not? She was wearing one of her push-up, push-out brassieres that emphasized her shape, and because she was angry, she'd allowed the blanket to slip while she'd been talking, revealing a thin, red strap. She yanked the blanket tighter around her shoulders.

"Well—" suddenly he smiled charmingly "—of course, I *could* check out your company through the computer. That is, if you'd like to come down to the station."

More than a bit piqued by his change in attitude, Alanna glared haughtily at him. "Why do you have to check out my company?"

"Precaution, Miss Martin, just precaution," he explained, going to the window as the man had an hour before, and glancing outside. At least he wasn't staring at her anymore. The bellhop whispered something in his ear, and he grinned, then dropped the drapes and turned back to Alanna. "In these cases we have to check out everything, including the complainant. If you do decide to come down to the station we could kill two birds with one stone. You could take a look through the mug shots and try to identify the man who was here while I run a computer check on your company. We may find out exactly what happened."

She hesitated. Maybe she'd imagined his skeptical looks. He certainly seemed nice and understanding now. "Do you believe me? I was accosted."

"I already told you I believe you."

"I'm not a hooker," she said, feeling compelled to defend herself.

He smiled again, gently. "Sorry about that. It's hard to tell these days."

"I design and sell lingerie."

"Nice stuff." His eyes glinted at the sight of the open case on the bed.

"Thank you," Alanna said. "I have a presentation to give in the morning. I hope my buyers like it, as well."

"I don't think you can miss." He flipped his pad closed and splayed his legs apart. "Why don't you get dressed? We'll go to the station, and then I'll help you get settled in a new motel. I don't imagine you'll want to stay in this motel tonight."

She didn't. And she wanted a *hotel* this time, a good one. But she was surprised by his offer of help, and was thankful. "Do you have time to do all that for me?"

He nodded. "I'll be off duty soon. I'd be glad to help you. You've really had a hard time of it, and I'd hate to leave you with a bad impression of Denver. Just call it western hospitality. By the way, how was your flight out?''

"Great," she said. What had happened *after* her flight was the problem.

"Ever been to Denver before?"

"No."

"Good. I'll give you the ten-cent tour after we visit the station." He gestured toward the bathroom, indicating she should start dressing. "Take your time."

"Nice of you to be so helpful," the manager remarked to the detective as she sprang from the bed.

Zane Younger just laughed. "I'm a nice guy."

"Sure," the manager responded in neutral tones, not wanting to challenge the detective.

A bit skeptical of that declaration herself, *and* of his new attitude, Alanna headed to the bathroom and locked the door behind her. Yet if you couldn't trust a cop, who could you trust? After all that had happened to her she was probably being paranoid, thinking everyone was out to get her. Earlier, when the detective was being nasty to her, he had been doing his job. And he hadn't really looked at her in an odd manner. Had he?

Sighing, she let the blanket fall to the floor and pulled her suit back on. She was thankful the skirt wasn't ruined, as she had feared earlier, and the blouse was only a bit wrinkled. She glanced in the mirror and thrust out her tongue at her image. Denver had turned out to be quite an adventure, particularly for a woman whose idea of danger was doing her nails on a Saturday night, and whose sense of fun was sipping wine during the intermission of a ballet. Funny, she didn't look like someone who had been scared out of her wits. She was pale, and most of the makeup she had applied this morning had worn away. But she appeared surprisingly unperturbed, despite the rude greeting. Who was the dark man who had accosted her? Where had he gone?

Running a brush through her hair, she turned from the mirror. Who cared, as long as he was gone! She was safe and sound, and the police were here, helping her. That was the important thing. She buttoned her soft gray jacket together and opened the bathroom door. On impulse, at the last minute, she turned back and ran a splotch of red lipstick over her mouth.

"Ready?" Zane Younger asked when she came back into the room. Reaching around her, he picked up her suitcase.

"What about the bill?" the hotel manager said.

The detective smiled at him. "Under the circumstances, don't you think you could waive the bill? Miss Martin has had quite a traumatic experience here. She could make things difficult for you regarding security and all."

The manager nodded as though he hadn't thought of that aspect until it had been pointed out to him. "Right. No problem." He smiled, too, but it was phoney. "Have a good stay in Denver, ma'am."

"She will." Taking her elbow, Zane guided Alanna down the steps and across the parking lot toward an unmarked brown sedan.

As they walked outside, the bright sunshine still bathing the western sky blinded Alanna, and she shaded her eyes with one hand. Although she had relaxed considerably, she couldn't help but glance around at the other cars, wondering if Sammison or the man, or even Liz would come barreling into the parking lot, guns blazing. All she saw was two men arguing heatedly in another language, German perhaps. Both of them were short and stocky, and they wore dark suits and skinny little ties.

After a few minutes one of them noticed Zane and Alanna. The two grew suddenly quiet. "Were they here before?" Zane asked.

"Do you think—"

"No," he said.

"Tourists?"

"Probably. Or itinerant farm workers."

Since when did itinerant farm workers wear suits? But she shrugged. "You have quite an effect on people," she remarked, assuming he was the cause for alarm.

"Cops usually do."

"How can they tell you're a cop?"

He laughed down at her. "We all act alike. It's the swagger." He seemed to sense her unease and softened his tone. "Don't worry, the man who visited you, and his anticipated guests are long gone, Miss Martin."

She smiled at him as he opened the front door of the car and watched her climb inside. He was certainly easy to talk to, and he was gracious. On top of that, he flashed a cute western grin. She was almost sorry she'd snapped at him.

She mused over his words. "Do you really think they're gone?"

"Why stick around?"

He had a point. "Thanks," she said, grateful for the comforting words. He slammed her door. She needed to relax and forget everything that had happened to her. "And please, call me Allie."

"Sure thing, Allie. I'm willing to bet this whole mess was a case of mistaken identity, plain and simple," he continued, slipping into his side of the car.

"Do you get very many cases of mistaken identity?"

"Not in Denver. We have one of the lowest rates of violent crime in the nation. Sometimes it gets downright boring around here."

She laughed, and he looked pleased. "What kind of crime *do* you see?"

"Oh, the usual, just not a lot of it. Robbery, assault and battery, loitering." He started the car and pulled away from the curb, turning onto a street that lead directly into the bright sunshine. "A little cattle rustling now and then."

"Still?" This was, after all, the twentieth century.

"Raising cattle's big stuff out this way," he said. "Why, there's a feed lot up near Greeley—that's northeast of here—that houses over two hundred thousand head of cattle and uses computers to figure out how much feed to store, by gauging the age and weight of each cow. So rustling's a fact of life. Nowadays we worry about it being accomplished electronically. Sometimes thieves can steal the entire herd, sell it and collect the money from a computer terminal. The worst part of it is that usually the whole scam is operated from here, in Denver.''

That had to be odd, a mix of the old ways and new technology. "Do they get caught?''

"Not always.''

He had pulled out onto a highway, a scattering of tall buildings in the distance. From this view the mountains were even more magnificent, off in the clouds. "Are you from Denver?'' she asked.

"I'm what they call a seminative,'' he answered. "I've been here a long time and consider myself a native.'' When she frowned, he explained, "It's a long-standing feud among Coloradoans. Not many people who live here were actually born here. How about yourself? Are you from Chicago?''

She nodded. "Yes. I'm a city girl, born and bred. But the mountains are lovely.''

"They're prettier up close,'' he said. "You ought to take a drive out to them if you're going to be here a few days.''

"Maybe I will. Is it hot in the mountains?''

"It's cooler than in town, but it depends on where you go. Hiking's tough. What, don't you like heat?''

"I detest it. And truthfully, I can't imagine myself off hiking in the wilderness.'' She was too citified, too pampered by city comforts to relish a hike of any sort, she supposed.

"It's not so bad, once you get used to it.''

She shook her head. "No, thank you. I'll take cement any day.'' She flexed a foot as if to test her footwear. "Besides, I'd ruin my high heels.''

He laughed. "Well, there are plenty of sights here in Denver, too, less strenuous things to do. If you don't want to hike, you could always sprawl out by the hotel pool and get a tan. It's great. Without the humidity, you don't sweat."

"Sounds heavenly."

"Sounds like Denver."

She smiled, amused by his pride in the town. It *was* a lovely city, she decided a few minutes later as he pulled into a wide parking lot in what she assumed was the downtown section. Tall, stately trees lined both sides of the street, quite different from most of the landscape they'd passed, which had looked sparse and somewhat barren.

"Here we are," he said. "Law enforcement, western style."

The tall building was quite modern and not particularly western in style. Cavernous and somewhat dark inside, on the ground floor, people manned state-of-the-art telephones, handling the hustle and bustle of police work. To Alanna, brought up on TV precinct houses, the whole place seemed amazingly empty. No drunks fought in a corner; no hookers lounged against the clean walls. Two uniformed officers manned a central reception desk, and a guard controlled access to the elevators. Apart from these three officers, Alanna and Zane were alone in the massive entrance lobby.

Seating her in a private room, Zane placed several large album-type books in front of her. "Mug shots. Let me know if you come across anyone familiar."

"Where will you be?"

He winked. "Checking on you."

She smiled again as he sauntered away. He could be quite charming, this officer of the law. Interesting. Unlike the other man, who could be more than interesting. Would she find him in the photos? She glanced down at the stack of books and opened the first one.

PAUL SAMMISON KNEW something had gone wrong the moment he picked up the phone. A spiel of angry German greeted him. Peeking around the door to see if his secretary had noticed the accent when she fielded the call, he closed his office door and let the man swear at him. Outside, a horn blared. This time of day, Washington, D.C. traffic was awful. At least it was summer. Then again, the exhaust smelled bad. And it drifted in through the air-conditioning ducts. Damned cheap government. When the German had calmed down, Sammison said, "Hans, I told you not to call me here."

"Where am I supposed to call you?" he said in a German accent.

"Anywhere. Not here."

"You screwed up, Sammison."

Funny, how odd American slang sounded in another language. With the emphasis on the *c* and *w*. "Hans, if anybody screwed up, it's you and your buddy. Where's Chandler? I told you that if you wanted to stay in this country, you better take care of him."

"He was gone when we got to the motel."

Paul Sammison much preferred to do his own dirty work; mistakes happened when you let inept people try to handle it. Hans, however, was supposed to be top-notch in his field. "Where did Chandler go?"

"I don't know. There was a woman there with a brief-case. Did you double-cross me, Sammison? Does she have our names?"

"You know I wouldn't do such a thing."

"I know no such thing."

What was that old saying about honor among thieves? But he wasn't exactly stealing. More like murder, or more correctly, termination. And these men were in on it. "I'm telling you I didn't cross you," Sammison said. "Whoever the broad was, she wasn't from my office. There was a mess-up at the registry desk."

"We'll see."

"Look," Sammison said, "everything's still on. Chandler will call me. He wants his brother. I'll get back to you."

"When?"

"Soon."

"I'm telling you, Sammison, I don't want no double cross. I want to stay in America."

"Yeah. Yeah, I know. You all want to stay in America."

"I have roots here. A daughter."

Didn't he have roots in Germany? Of course, he was from East Germany. Communist roots. "Yeah. I'll take care of it. Don't call me here again."

"I would kill you if I thought you were lying to me."

"Oh, hell, just kill Chandler," Sammison answered. "That's what you've got to do."

Although he'd remained calm on the phone, Paul Sammison slammed the receiver down on his final note and threw a pencil against the wall. Damn Reeve Chandler to hell and back! Elusive bastard. The man had stuck in his craw for the past ten years, and for the past two years he'd had to put up with the kid brother. Curt Chandler had the same warped sense of right and wrong. But where Curt was brutally honest, Reeve was also dangerous, savvy. Hell, he was brilliant. For weeks he'd flitted around like a proverbial ghost—here one moment, gone the next.

This time he would take care of the man himself, Sammison thought, and once and for all. The Germans would be on his tail, but so would he, Sammison. He wasn't going to let anyone mess up his plans. Not this time. And certainly not Reeve Chandler. He hated the man with a vengeance normally reserved for archrivals. He laughed, but it was a bitter sound. They were archrivals, and they had been since they'd worked together down in that steamy, sweaty, insect-infested jungle in South America training guerrilla soldiers. They'd found those treasures in a cave—hundreds of thousands of dollars worth of gold relics. Paul had wanted to take a few back, just a few, and live on easy street, but Reeve had notified the government, and they hadn't gotten one red cent. Not a lousy dollar for their troubles. Paul had endured yellow fever and syphilis both, on top of

it. The damned whore he'd taken to bed had slept with the
entire city of Rio. He'd taken penicillin and quinine for
months. There were nights he still sweated, nights he came
down with the chills. Yellow fever never left the body. And
it was all Chandler's fault. Chandler, who had women instead of sore-laden whores; Chandler who got all the pro-
motions, the commendations, the recognition; Chandler,
who'd escaped the jungle unscathed. The doctor had told
him that, even treated, the syphilis might affect his brain.
Hell, maybe he was already crazy, but he detested Reeve
Chandler.

And now he'd get back. Maybe not this moment, but
soon. Soon. In spades. In a way, he was glad the Germans
had screwed it up. It was time to take care of Chandler
himself. Then again, he had his ace in the hole. More than
the Germans were following Reeve Chandler, and before he
packed his bags, maybe he ought to find out how the others were doing. He picked up the phone and dialed a number, leaning back again in his leather chair as the number
rang. What the hell. Why was he worried? If his ace card
hadn't panned out, he'd play another. All he had to do was
wait for Chandler to call. Sammison knew he'd be in contact any day now—in fact, any moment. Chandler knew
Sammison's assorted phone numbers by heart.

ALANNA LEAFED THROUGH the pictures for what seemed
like hours. It amazed her that so many people were either
criminals or ex-criminals or suspected criminals. The books
contained thousands of photos, each person more evil
looking than the last. Bearded, scarred, tattooed and whis-
kered men, women and debatables, they all glared at her
from their places on the pages. But none of them looked like
the man who had held a gun to her head at the Rustic River
Inn.

She sighed and rubbed the back of her neck wearily. Zane
had dropped into the room several times, bringing her a cup
of coffee or a soda, offering encouragement. Several other

detectives had also stopped by, smiling or signaling thumbs-up. She was ready to give up when she heard Zane at the door speaking to someone, another detective she assumed. She closed the book she'd been studying and walked toward them.

"Is that the broad with the lingerie everybody's been talking about?" the other man said, poking Zane in the ribs. "She's quite a looker."

"You should see what's underneath that prim gray suit," Zane's voice answered. "She's got on the sexiest red underwear I've ever seen."

"I can imagine. Have fun tonight, man."

"That's my intention."

Although they had whispered, she heard every word, and fury shot through Alanna like a sagebrush fire in high wind. So that's why Zane had been so nice to her, so helpful. He was going to have a good time. And she'd thought he was charming. Apparently when he'd looked at her in the motel room, he'd liked what he'd seen, as far as the red underwear went. Damn! Damn all men to hell and back! No, let them stay in hell. Each and every one of them. First she'd been accosted by a madman who thought she was a hooker, and now she'd been duped by a cop who assumed she was easy. Well, she'd show this one a thing or two, starting with her temper, of which the other man had only gotten a brief glimpse.

Swinging on her heel, she marched back across the room and grabbed her jacket from a chair just as Zane stepped inside.

"See anyone you know yet?" he asked, flashing that cute western grin.

She glared at him. Cattle rustling, indeed. He probably told that story to every city girl who came through town. "I've decided not to look anymore."

"Feeling tired?"

"Feeling sexy, actually," she snapped. "Wanna find that hotel?"

His mouth dropped open. "What?"

"You knew this was impossible, didn't you?" She gestured angrily at the mug shots spread across the table. "You knew I wouldn't be able to find a picture of the man who attacked me. What was next? Dinner? A little tête-à-tête in my hotel room?" She picked up her suitcase in one hand and her briefcase in the other, lifting her chin defiantly. "For your information, I am not promiscuous, dammit! I happen to be a respectable citizen who was wronged in your fair city. I'll say one thing for the man who held me captive in that motel room. He may have put a gun to my head and made me undress, but at least he was honest." With that, she stomped her spike heel into Zane Younger's instep as she walked away.

"Allie!" he called after her, hopping around on one foot.

"It's *Miss Martin* to you from now on!" she flung over her shoulder.

"Al—Miss Martin, wait," he cried.

Everyone in the police station turned to stare. For a moment Alanna thought she might be in trouble. After all he was a cop, and she'd deliberately injured him. But he'd injured her, too. If he tried to prosecute, she vowed she would press charges against him for sexual harassment.

"Miss Martin!" he called, limping behind her down the hall toward the front door. "What about finding the man?"

"Forget it."

"What about a hotel room?"

"I can find one myself."

"Be careful," he said then, a genuine note of concern in his voice.

She spun around with that. What did he know? Was she in danger? "Why?"

At least he was honest now. Hobbling toward her, he shrugged. "No reason."

"You haven't found out anything about the man, have you?"

He shook his head. "Truthfully, Allie—Miss Martin," he corrected softly, his voice a low murmur. "Up until now I didn't believe there was a man."

Alanna stared at him in disbelief. Surely he wasn't saying— "All this was for..." She choked back her fury. "Just to seduce me? How could you?"

"Sorry."

"Sorry?" she echoed. *"Sorry!"*

"What did you expect me to think?" he said. "I find you at a sleazy dump wearing the sexiest underwear I've ever seen, with a story that's so wild, it's incredible."

He had a point, she admitted grudgingly. Her story was wild. "I wasn't lying."

"I know that now." He shrugged again, wincing and nursing his instep. "No harm done?"

While it was true that, with the exception of her pride, Alanna hadn't actually been damaged by the episode, a crime had been ignored. A man was on the loose, a dangerous man. But even if the police had believed her, they wouldn't be able to catch him. Zane Younger probably knew that as well as she did.

"If you want, we can have an artist sketch the man's face and put out an all points bulletin on him," Zane said.

"Would it do any good?"

"Probably not."

"Do you think he's after me?"

"No, like I told you in the motel parking lot, even though I didn't believe he existed, there'd be no reason for him to stick around. He'd risk capture."

"What about the people he was supposed to meet?"

"They never showed up. At least no Liz ever checked in. The hotel manager believes the clerk forgot to register your name in Miss Hernandez's place when she didn't show up and you did. The guest in the room originally assigned to you decided to stay on, and the motel—as well as every one in town—is overbooked. Several big conventions take place this time of year. They put you into the first available space.

If Miss Hernandez eventually showed, the manager said, they would have used the same ploy... You see, I'm not all opportunist," he went on to explain with a rueful grin. "I'm a fairly decent detective. I did check."

Although she nodded, she was unwilling to forgive so easily. "So essentially I'm safe?"

"Essentially." Another grin lit his face. "Miss Martin, someone who looks like you is never safe."

She just turned away. The other man hadn't thought that, the dark, mysterious man. He'd ignored her, even when she'd undressed.

"Have a good presentation tomorrow," Zane called.

"Yeah." She glanced back and, despite her anger, smiled. "I'll think of you."

His laugh echoed across the room. "Call me if you decide to go to the mountains."

"Right."

Fat chance of either happening. She wasn't going to set foot in those mountains, or any other mountains for that matter. Or anywhere hot and physically taxing. And she was swearing off men as of this moment! *All* men. Or she was going to swear at them. She could hardly wait to call her boss and tell him exactly what she thought of him. Looking back, this was all Tom Biner's fault. He'd booked her into a cheap motel. They'd messed up the registry.

Allie pushed open the heavy entrance door. Once on the street she had no idea where to go. Unfortunately Denver didn't compare to Chicago. There was hardly any traffic and even fewer people milling about. She didn't see a single taxi. She started to walk toward some tall buildings. There had to be a hotel here somewhere.

To compound her problem it had gotten dark outside, and although she'd put on a brave front in the police station, she wasn't exactly comfortable being in a strange city all alone. With every step she took, her nerves screamed that someone was following her. Someone tall and dark. Someone dangerous. Desperate. She glanced behind, over her shoulder several times, but no one paid any attention to her.

Relief flooded through Alanna when she came to the first building. The fact that the place was a hotel and several stories high made it even more appealing, not to mention the fancy chandeliers and plush carpeting in the lobby. Her luck was holding up when she learned that, despite the heavy convention season, several rooms were available. She checked in and charged the room to her company without even inquiring about the price. The hell with being conservative. Good old Tommy boy was going to pay for more than a few nights at an expensive hostelry. He was going to pay, in spades, for what he'd put her through at the Rustic River Inn and here, on the streets of Denver—one of the safest cities in the world.

The bellhop, properly attired this time in green-and-gold livery and wearing a tiny hat with tassels, escorted her to her room, carrying her luggage. She kept her briefcase.

After the stoic-faced man had turned on the lights, including the one in the bathroom, and left, Alanna locked and chained the door and went to draw the window shades. For a moment she thought she saw the tall, dark man standing under the streetlight across the road, watching the hotel. Panic crowded her stomach as the light gleamed on his hair. But he moved on, and she yanked the shades down, telling herself it wasn't him. She'd always had an overactive imagination, and considering what she'd been through, it was only natural it was operating full tilt.

And she didn't need to think about men. Not now. Not ever, and particularly not that one. Zane was right. The dangerous gunslinger was gone, and so were his friends, or rather, his enemies. Given another minute, she'd be seeing the men in the parking lot, too, the ones she was sure were speaking German.

Alanna turned away. Forget it. Forget the man, forget the people. She had to concentrate on her meeting tomorrow and her designs. She started to unbutton her blouse, but she paused, staring across the room at the window. She had to admit, the dark-haired stranger *had* been fascinating in a perverted sort of way. Interesting. Handsome. Even sexy, maybe.

Dangerous, she reminded herself.

And crude. He'd sworn at her. A disgusting suggestion. Although not so disgusting with the right person.

My, what was her problem!

Leaping up from the bed, Alanna realized she was romanticizing him again. She stripped off her clothes and shrugged into a nightgown, deliberately blanking her mind. Yet, as though drawn to him, compelled by something she didn't understand, she glanced back at the window. Where was he? Was he out there watching her? Suddenly, spurred into motion, she tucked a chair under the doorknob and scooted the dresser in front of the drapes, huffing and puffing with every shove. The hell with this nonsense. Six stories up or no six stories up, she wasn't going to take any chances. Colorado dreaming.

Or was it Colorado fear?

Chapter Three

Reeve Chandler pulled his hat low on his head and hunched down in the car seat, watching as Alanna Martin marched into the hotel. He'd followed her all the way from the police station, and earlier, from the Rustic River Inn to the station, waiting for someone to approach her, someone other than a cop. When he'd left the motel that afternoon, he'd intended to get to a phone and contact Paul Sammison, using the agent's message service. But just as he'd barreled out of the parking lot, he'd noticed another car coming in—a car with two men inside. They were both short, wearing suits and old-fashioned ties, and they were arguing in German. Agents?

Perhaps they were looking for names, too. The same names he wanted, names that would get his brother out of that stinking hellhole in East Germany called a jail. For the past three months Curt had rotted away, while the United States government had denied any knowledge of his existence, leaving it to Reeve to rescue the kid. And Reeve knew he was running out of time. He knew the East German secret police, and he knew his brother. They gave a prisoner about three months, using that time to see if the government would push to make some prisoner exchange or some other trade-off. They also used less harmful means to extract information from a prisoner. But after a time, if both the government and prisoner, were intractable, they turned to bloodier means. First a toe, then a foot, then the entire leg would go.

Reeve was beginning to get anxious, very anxious. He knew the clock was running down. And he was growing tired of being deceived. So far he'd been led on a wild-goose chase, and it was time to trust his instincts. Certainly these two men were closer than Sammison, who was sixteen hundred miles away in Washington, D.C., using strange setups to trick an old foe.

His decision made, Reeve had whirled the Jeep around and roared back to the motel. But the two agents—if in fact that's what they had been, and not hired assassins—had gotten nervous and had disappeared in the foray. The police, and the blustering, steaming manager had scared them off. For the moment. Reeve had elected to stick with the blonde, figuring if he'd been cheated by Sammison, so had others, and they'd find her later, when she was alone. All he wanted were the papers that would free his brother, who perched precariously on a dangerous phase of his incarceration. Innocent or not, Alanna Martin seemed a likely lead. In a way he owed it to her to stick around and see what might happen, he mused. Thanks to him, everyone was hot on her trail.

Everyone except the police. Reeve couldn't help but wonder what had gone wrong at the station. Moments before, when she had left, she had burst through the doors like a fire-breathing dragon, and had stomped down the street gripping her briefcase so tightly, she looked fit to be tied. Coming upon the hotel, she'd sailed inside so blithely she might have owned the place. He had to give her one thing: she had verve. Clumsy verve. But still something. He just hoped that since she hadn't been smart enough to leave town, she had enough sense to stay put and lock her damned door. He hadn't noticed anyone dogging her footsteps yet, but he knew they were there, just as they knew he was there. Sooner or later they would show themselves. And he had to make sure they didn't maim that sexy butt of hers. Or worse. He'd seen them leave worse remains behind.

Foolish woman.

And he'd make sure they didn't do the same to his brother.

After parking the Jeep, Reeve leaned against a street lamp and watched the entrance to the hotel. A few minutes later he moved to the shadow of another building. As much as he wanted to phone Sammison, he didn't dare leave this outpost. Around dawn he noticed a cowboy going inside. A cowboy with squeaky boots.

RED WAS ALANNA'S favorite color. It just so happened that it was also her most complementary color. A long time ago she'd had her seasons done and, despite the fact that she was a blonde, she was a *winter*, and she could wear jewel tones. Alluring, flamboyant tones. She walked toward the full-length mirror mounted on the hotel room door as she cinched a wide, white belt around the red-and-white polka-dot dress she was wearing and slipped into the matching bolero-style jacket. Everything was coordinated, including her red spike heels, wide-brimmed hat and pale red fingernails.

Everything except her briefcase, she thought, turning to lift it. It was made from real leather, and it was deeper than average and a tad wider. Her uncle had given it to her four years ago, when she'd graduated from college, specifically for hauling her designs around town. Sometimes her family, particularly her father, was appalled at the bras and garter belts she designed, and at the fact that she was perfectly happy creating lingerie instead of saving or defending lives. But the money was good, and she was moving up in the fashion world, becoming a name brand. Fantastic Foundations, as well, was a young, aggressive company and Tom Biner, despite his penchant for second-rate motels and cheap travel arrangements, was a super boss.

Last night he'd been sincerely sorry about all the trouble Alanna had gone through. He'd laughed when she'd told him the reason the Rustic River Inn wasn't rated by triple AAA. Neither did the name make any sense. There was no rustic river nearby, unless you counted the Colorado or the Arkansas, and they roared no closer than twenty miles out of town. In fact, the only river she'd managed to pinpoint in the city proper was the South Platte. But it meandered through town hardly wider than a creek and joined up with another river somewhere near the Continental Divide, miles away.

She'd explained about the mix-up at the check-in desk. That a Liz Hernandez was booked by phone, and when she didn't show up, the clerk put Alanna in her room. The motel was overbooked because several conventions were taking place in town at once. Tom had roared, exclaiming that truth devised better pranks than his imagination ever could.

By the time she had made telephone calls to her buyers and touched base with Tom Biner last night, Alanna had almost forgotten about her rude experience. She'd wandered around the hotel room looking at brochures and maps, marveling at all the places to visit here in Denver. There were tours of the mountains. Old gold-mining towns. Hang gliding. Not that she wanted to do any of it, much less hover in the air under an oversize kite. But they'd given Denver an aura of glamour, of possibilities. In themselves, the activities looked either too hot or too strenuous. She was more interested in the tamer sport offered by the hotel's pool. After she marketed her designs that morning, she would take Zane Younger's suggestion and enjoy the facilities for a few days. Then she would head back to Chicago rested and refreshed. Even her boss had admitted that she deserved a vacation.

With a final glance at her reflection in the mirror, Alanna readjusted her hat and opened the door, locking it carefully behind her. She couldn't erase her traumatic experience from her memory yet. After yesterday she wasn't taking any chances.

The hallway was empty except for a couple of people, but the elevator going down was crowded, men dressed as cowboys chatting with each other, women laughing and talking. A few children fidgeted excitedly as they watched the numbers flash past on the board above their heads. Intending to have the doorman call her a cab, Alanna sank to the first floor and crossed the lobby with purposeful strides. The place was busy, even at this time of the morning. People were coming and going, registering and checking out. Luggage littered the area.

Dodging an incoming guest, Alanna hurried into the fast-circling revolving door. One of the cowboys—the thin, wiry one who had got on the elevator with her on her floor—ducked in behind her, still conversing with his friend. Out on the street the sunshine was blinding, the day bright and new. A gentle breeze lifted her hair. Pausing near the curb, she held down her hat and glanced toward the mountains, enjoying the spectacle. Too bad she didn't like outdoor activities. The peaks looked challenging as well as beautiful, almost compelling in the early-morning light.

Still holding down her hat, Alanna stepped off the curb. The next thing she knew, someone had lunged into her. At the same time something hit her over the back of her head, something hard and unyielding. She blinked, unable to believe that this was happening to her. *What* was happening to her?

She half turned, still in a state of shock while the cowboy who had ridden down with her in the elevator wavered before her eyes, his purple-and-green shirt growing fuzzy and distant. Before her eyes closed completely, she had a vision of a short, heavy, light-haired man maneuvering away, pushing through the crowd. He resembled one of the men in the parking lot of the sleazy motel yesterday. But that was silly, she thought. Those men were itinerant workers. Or tourists. She couldn't remember which.

Yet another one of them grabbed her briefcase and shoved her to the ground. And the cowboy had a gun now. He cocked it and fired, running after the men. Everyone stood staring after the trio. The doorman shouted, and a car squealed in the street, and from somewhere she heard a high-pitched scream. Was it her own voice? Alanna couldn't tell. But suddenly she was grabbed around the waist and pulled inside an open Jeep, the force of the vehicle toppling her inside. She had barely fallen into the seat than the vehicle took off again, doing a U-turn in the middle of the block. She heard tires screech on the pavement, and she smelled the scent of burning rubber. Somebody else ran down the block after the careening Jeep—the other cowboy?—shouting and screaming.

"Hold on," a familiar voice said beside her, "unless you want to fall out. And you better duck," he added. "One of those bullets might hit you."

So many gunshots rang out that Alanna thought they had entered a war zone. Yet, hardly flinching, the dark stranger she'd met the day before—the very one she'd thought was so fascinating last night—careened the Jeep down the street. The vehicle tilted and lurched, reeling around corners and cars. Alanna held on for dear life, clutching the seat and the roll bar above her as though they were lifelines. There weren't any doors on the vehicle, and she was afraid she might fall out any moment. She could feel the sensation of blood oozing slowly down her head. It was sticky, ticklish, but she didn't dare relax her grip on the Jeep for a second, not even to stop the bleeding.

The man tore through town as if chased by demons, swerving from one road to another, up and down side-streets, weaving through traffic, until he merged with a bunch of cars again, suddenly braking to a slower pace.

"You can get up now," he said to her at last.

She hadn't realized she'd sank to the floor. Cautiously she extricated herself from under the dashboard and touched her head. Her hand came away red, streaked with blood.

"You all right?"

"I'm not sure," she answered, feeling like swooning. "I could probably use a few stitches." She still felt stunned. She'd lost her hat somewhere along the way, and her nylon stockings were ripped and torn. Fortunately her stockings matched her dress, a sleeve torn and flopping in the breeze. One knee was scraped and bleeding, and dirt encrusted her white jacket. But at least she was alive. Yet she didn't know whether to thank this man for rescuing her, berate him for injuring her or cower in fear. She could see the outline of his gun under his pant leg, where he'd tucked it into his boot. What kind of man carried a weapon as a matter of course?

"You can get to a hospital later," he said. "They'll take care of your head."

"I suppose."

"There's a seat belt there. Maybe you ought to put it on."

Alanna ignored his suggestion. At the moment a seat belt was the least of her concerns. She had to control her trembling. "I know this might sound a little redundant," she said, "considering our discussion yesterday, but maybe you could tell me what's going on?"

The man shot her a brief glance. To make matters worse he looked as forbidding as he had the day before. In fact rougher, if that was possible. His beard had grown heavier overnight, and he appeared tired, as though he hadn't slept in days. Still there was a breathlessness about him, a reckless abandon that was appealing. On the other hand a woman would be foolish to fall in love with him.

"That's what I was going to ask you, lady," he answered. "You must like to live dangerously."

"Me!" Incredulous, Alanna touched her hand to her chest. Wasn't that akin to the pot calling the kettle black? Every time she saw him he seemed to dance a step closer to the edge of a precipice.

"I told you to get out of town last night," he went on. "Why didn't you?"

"I moved to another hotel."

"That's not leaving. I told you to leave."

His brashness amazed her. She stared at him in disbelief. "Well, excuse me, sir. I hadn't realized you'd issued an order."

"It wasn't an order." He glanced in the rearview mirror and turned down another street, going at such a leisurely pace now that it was wearing on her nerves. They could have been out for a Sunday drive. "Just a smart thing to do. What'd you tell the police last night?"

How had he known about that? "Nothing."

"Nothing?"

The way he phrased the single word made her regret even mentioning him to Zane Younger. She shifted uncomfortably. She'd forgotten about the torture, how he would extract revenge. "Not much," she corrected.

"What?"

"I—I described you."

"How?"

"Generally."

He shook his head, obviously exasperated. "Lady, not only can't you hear, you aren't very smart, either."

The man went from bad to worse. Now he was insulting her. Alanna glared at him. "And just what's that supposed to mean?"

"I told you not to say anything to anyone."

"I was scared," she explained, her mouth a pout. "I didn't mean to say anything. The police came, and I—"

"Yeah," he cut in. "I figured as much."

"I didn't mean to tell," she repeated in her defense. "It was an accident."

"It's been my experience that nothing's ever an accident. You were rash, lady."

For the life of her, Alanna failed to understand how he had arrived at that conclusion. She'd come to Denver to show potential buyers a line of racy underwear, and so far, in less than twenty-four hours, she'd been accosted by him, propositioned by another man, terribly inconvenienced all around, then hit over the head by still another man. *She* did rash things?

All right, so she'd told the police about him, but what had he expected her to do?

"Pardon me, for my imperfections," she muttered, sagging into the seat and staring straight ahead. "I hadn't realized how rash I'd been."

"You're pardoned."

"Why, thank you." Brash was a conservative description for him. What had happened to the man who had teased her about being sexy? This one was all business, and she stared at him in continued disbelief.

"Like I said, you should have left town yesterday."

"Obviously I didn't," she answered. "And now I suppose I should be grateful to you for saving my life."

"Not necessarily. Or at least not yet." His eyes were glued to the road.

"Excuse me?" He talked in puzzles.

"We're not out of the woods yet." He tilted his head to one side in a nod, indicating their situation.

They weren't through town, either. Forgetting their argument, Alanna glanced around, feeling suddenly vulnerable. Being roofless and doorless, the Jeep was so open they were like moving targets. Turning off the road, he headed up an expressway ramp. Where it hit the pavement, the morning sun was blinding. How had he gotten away from the people chasing them? Assuming he *had* gotten away. The police should have been shortly behind them since he'd been speeding. But then, so had a lot of people, and unless a squad car had noticed, they'd gotten away with it. Yet surely someone had reported the incident at the hotel. There'd been gunshots fired. Of course this was cattle-rustling country. Gunshots could be a way of life. The point being, there was no one of authority behind them.

"So," she said conversationally, hoping she could penetrate the curtain of secrecy enfolding him. It would be nice to find out exactly what was going on in this wild game of mistaken identity. "Now that we've got everything clear, were you just hanging around the hotel today, or were you there for a reason?"

"I was watching you."

Another surprise. She glanced back at him. "How did you find me?"

"I never lost you."

"From the Rustic River Inn? You followed me?"

"Yes."

"I thought you had to get away."

"I did."

He was a regular fountain of information. "You watched me all night?" He *had* been the man outside her window. And the other men had been there, too, watching her activities, waiting for their chance.

"And all morning," he confirmed.

"Why?"

"It's better that you don't know."

"Oh, really?" She smiled sweetly, falsely. "How nice of you to make that decision for me. Tell me, do you happen to know those men who hit me over the head and stole my entire fashion line?"

"Yes."

"But you're not going to tell me who they are."

"No."

It figured. "Could I ask why?"

"Sure."

But he didn't say anything more. "I get it," Alanna said, nodding understanding. "I can ask, but you're not going to answer."

"Right." He passed a car full of people, laughing, happy people. "I told you, it's best that you don't know."

"Oh, yes, for my own good, as you say."

She had to be crazy, she thought, or else she was suffering from a concussion. *Something* had to be wrong. She was sitting here discussing the situation so calmly she might have been remarking on the weather. *Nice day out.* Lovely. *The sun's so bright.* Isn't it though? *Do you get this kind of weather often?* Often enough. *Oh, by the way, why did those men accost me and you nearly kill me yesterday?*

She touched her head. At least the bleeding seemed to have stopped. "Well," she said, almost philosophically, "who do you suppose they were shooting at, you or me?"

"Probably me," he answered. "If they had wanted you dead, they would have just slit your throat before they took your briefcase."

Alanna flinched, thinking of her throat being slit. There would be blood all over, and it would hurt. "Nice people."

"I've been telling you that for two days now."

"Then why did you rescue me?"

"Because I wasn't sure they wouldn't change their minds."

"And still slit my throat?" Jolly, she mused, and involuntarily placed her hand at her neck. "Since they took my briefcase, I assume they were after the same thing you were after yesterday."

"Seems likely," he agreed. His eyes continued to dart from the mirror to the road.

"Papers," she suggested.

He nodded.

"From a bleached blonde named Liz."

He nodded again.

When they opened the case and lingerie spilled out, they were going to be as surprised as he had been the day before. Would they come back to slit her throat? Was that why he'd rescued her? "How did they find me?"

"They followed you."

It appeared that everyone had followed her. She may as well have been the Pied Piper winding her way around Denver. She could have lured *all* the rats from the land. What was this man into? Not drugs. Well, maybe drugs. She supposed people needed papers with drugs. Did men slit throats over them?

"At least the cowboy helped me," she remarked.

"The guy behind you?" he asked, turning at last to peer at her. "He wasn't a cowboy. He's an FBI agent."

"FBI?" Alanna repeated low, stunned. "As in Federal Bureau of Investigation?"

"The very same."

"How do you know?"

"It was written all over him." He flicked a glance at her again. "His boots were new."

Alanna couldn't help looking down at his own boots. They were scuffed and supple, and well-worn. The heel was ground down on one side. What a thing to observe. What kind of background did he have that he would look for those things as a matter of course? "So what do we do now?"

"Run."

The man was a splendid conversationalist. A fount of anecdotes and intriguing facts. They *were* running or rather, driving away. She sighed. "Could you tell me where we're going? Just a teensy-weensy clue," she went on snidely when he didn't answer. "After all, I am involved in this mess."

"The airport."

"For what?"

"So you can board the next plane out of here."

"Oh," she murmured. Her mind raced as she watched the landscape whiz by. "Where would I go?"

"Anywhere. Just go. Take the first flight out of Denver. Get back to wherever you came from and dye your hair brown."

Dye it? Simple for him to say. "I know you think I don't know anything," she said, struggling to control her anger, "but may I remind you that I came here for a reason? I have business in Denver."

When he flicked his gaze over her a third time, she felt as though he considered her an amoeba, who'd lost a few brain cells. "And may I remind you that this isn't some game, lady. I told you yesterday that you've stumbled into something dangerous. You better get the hell out of here while the getting's good."

"I can't just leave," she continued to object. "My clothes are at the hotel. I have—"

"I'm not going to argue with you," he cut in, his voice rumbling in that low sexy way. "And I'm sure as hell not about to rescue you again. All I can tell you is that if you have any desire at all to stay alive, you'd better get your butt on a plane and go."

The airport had come into view. He started the circle around the terminal, screeching to a halt in front of a pair of electronic doors. People were unloading luggage, signaling for skycaps, and kissing and hugging their loved ones. Apparently she was supposed to get out.

She turned to him, for some strange reason wanting to help him. After all, he *had* saved her life that morning. Didn't she owe him something? He seemed so desperate, and it was obvious he was into something terribly risky. Something dreadful. What could possibly be so important that it would drive a person to risk his life for a briefcase full of papers?

"Look," she said, "my father is a doctor, and my mother is a lawyer. I even have an uncle who is a United States senator. If you tell me what's going on, I could ask them to help you."

She might have announced that she was tainted, or that she had grown tentacles or something equally awful. Slowly he turned his head to stare at her in astonishment. Then he repeated, "Your uncle is a senator?"

Stunned, she nodded.

"A United States senator?"

"Yes." She frowned. "I don't know what kind of trouble you're in, but he might be able to help you."

He kept staring at her. "What committee does he serve on?"

"My uncle?" she asked, unable to understand his line of questioning. "Foreign relations."

"I'll be damned," he muttered. "I'll be goddamned. Foreign relations. And I've been driving you around Denver. This is too good to be true."

Before she realized that he had shifted the Jeep into gear, he gunned the motor and swerved the vehicle back into traffic. For the second time that day she clutched the seat to keep from falling out.

"My God, what are you doing?" she shouted over the squeal of tires as he just barely missed sideswiping a car. "Where are you going?"

The other driver, clearly irate, held up one hand in an obscene gesture and shouted, "What the hell's the matter with you, buddy? Get a license!"

"Get lost," he barked back.

Alanna closed her eyes and clutched the roll bar again. He was driving so crazily they were both going to die. Obviously the emotion she should have felt when he swooped her from the street a half hour ago was fear. Out and out terror. Why hadn't she put the seat belt on? But he slowed the car as soon as they reached the highway. Or rather, he started driving with some semblance of sanity. Glancing behind them, she realized that the airport had disappeared from view so rapidly it was like looking through the wrong end of a telescope.

"Excuse me," Alanna said when her heartbeat had slowed. "I know I asked before, but you were busy dodging cars. Now that we've left the airport, do you suppose you could tell me where we're going?"

"To make a phone call."

He was succinct all right, too succinct. "A phone call," she repeated. "I thought you wanted me to leave town."

"I did."

"What happened?"

"I changed my mind."

"Great." She fluttered her hands in the air and nestled them in her lap.

"Sorry, but you're not going anywhere," he said, turning off the highway onto a peripheral road. He kept looking in the rearview mirror, as though expecting someone to find them at any moment. "Except with me."

Except with him... interesting. He changed his mind rather quickly. "Let me get this straight," she said. "Two seconds ago you wanted me to leave town. You wanted me to get on the first plane out of Denver. You told me I was in danger. Now we're going to go make a phone call?"

"Right."

"That's all?" she asked, annoyed to the boiling point. "That's all you can say? Right?"

He frowned at her. "Lady, you talk a lot."

"Mister, you don't talk at all," she shot back. She'd had just about enough of his flippant attitude and curt remarks. No, she'd had just about enough of everyone she'd encountered in this godforsaken state. Since the moment she'd arrived she'd suffered one abuse after another. "I want to know what's going on."

He sighed. "Sure. We're going to make a phone call."

"And?"

"What the hell more do you want me to say?"

"Why!" she pointed out. "You could tell me *why* we're going to make a phone call."

"I'm going to tell my friends about you."

For some reason she didn't think he was really talking about his bosom buddies. For some reason she thought he meant enemies rather than friends. "Tell them what?"

"Who you are."

"In other words, you're kidnapping me," she said quietly. "You're abducting me."

"I guess you could call it that," he said in that low, rumbling voice that made her shiver involuntarily.

"What else would you call it?"

"Using your name."

"Oh," Alanna muttered. "Of course. I should have guessed. My name. May I ask for what purpose?"

"Blackmail."

The word had a nice ring to it. Nice and criminal. "Wonderful." She nodded. "Just wonderful. I'm sure blackmail is infinitely better than kidnapping. Now, since we're on a roll, do you suppose you could fill me in on the details?"

"What details?"

"For starters, why did you change your mind about what to do with me?"

"Your uncle."

Oh, yes. The senator. She'd made the mistake of revealing her relationship to a prominent citizen, and now she was paying for her snobbery. "Score one. Okay. Who are you blackmailing, and why?"

"No one you'd know."

"Try me," she said. "I may surprise you."

He glanced at her again. "You already surprise me, lady. And you don't need to know anything more."

So they were back to square one. "For my own protection," she supplied, expecting the curt reply. She got it.

"Yes," he said.

Sighing, she shook her head. She could tell he was growing weary of answering her questions. But he was no more weary of her than she was of him and his macho attitude. Still she persisted. She was, after all, involved in the situation. "You are aware that both kidnapping and blackmail are illegal?"

"Yes."

"You can go to jail."

"Yes."

He didn't seem concerned. "You know, you can't keep me against my will."

"How's that?"

"Just what I said," she went on. "You can't keep me against my will. I won't let you."

That seemed to amuse him. He turned to her again, glancing at her as the wind tumbled through his dark hair.

The edges of his mouth were turned up in what might have passed for a smile. "What are you going to do about it?"

"Leave."

He laughed outright then. "You're a scrappy dame, aren't you?"

For the life of her, Alanna couldn't say why she found his remark offensive. She'd been called worse than a dame. Vastly worse. "I fail to see what that has to do with anything," she said angrily.

"It was just an observation," he admitted. "You've got a temper, too."

"So?"

"Tell you what, lady—"

"Please don't call me that."

He frowned at her again, this time looking at her as though he thought she'd lost her marbles. "What?"

"Lady. It scares me," she explained, and for a moment she also wondered if she wasn't losing it, telling him he scared her. In the game of life, the kidnappee didn't admit to the kidnapper that he was frightening. But she wasn't crazy. The situation was. And her fear was a normal reaction to an abnormal situation. If only she could get a grip on herself, calm down. "I—I don't like to be scared."

"I don't know many people that do," he said. "All right," he went on, after pausing a long moment. "Your name's Alanna, isn't it?"

"Allie for short."

"Right," he said in confirmation, his eyes on the speedometer. They were going seventy miles an hour. "Tell me, Allie," he went on, picking up the thread of the conversation where they had left off, "how are you going to leave? Are you going to jump out of the Jeep?"

She glanced to the door, watching the ground whiz by. The small tufts of green growing alongside the road blurred into a straight line. An occasional tree broke up the rocky landscape. A fence. She hadn't thought about how she would leave. Now she was forced to. "You have to stop sometimes."

"I wouldn't get out then, either."

"Why?" she asked, unable to prevent the note of triumph in her voice. He couldn't keep her, and they both knew it. She would run the moment he stopped. There would be people around, people who would help her. She could get away.

"Because I need you," he answered. "And I don't have any scruples at all. You ought to have figured that out by now."

"Scruples?" She frowned. "What do you mean?"

"I mean you won't get away."

"How are you going to stop me? You can't stop me."

"No?"

"No," she said, but her moment of triumph faded as he leaned over and pulled the gun from his boot. He placed the weapon on the seat between them. It was dark and ugly, like she'd remembered, gleaming and scary looking. Though she'd been wrong in her previous estimate. It would blow a hole in someone's head the size of the Grand Canyon.

"I've got a little news flash for you, Allie," he said, placing his hand back on the wheel and calling her by name. "If you make one move without my telling you to, I'll make you regret it. *Lady.*"

She stared at him. The way he delivered the words, so casually, so blasé, as if human life meant nothing to him, gave her the shivers. He'd do it, too. He'd shoot her. Of that she had no doubt. This man had killed before. Without compunction. What was she entangled in?

"Understand?" he asked after a few moments had passed.

She nodded. How could she help but understand? He'd been quite explicit. He'd been graphic. "Yes, I understand."

"Good," he said as he pulled off the road and parked beside a phone booth. The sun was a hot ball in the midmorning sky, beating down on them mercilessly, like his gaze on her. "I wouldn't go for the gun, either. In case you've forgotten, I'm faster than you are. You haven't forgotten?" he said when she didn't answer.

"No."

"Well—" he kept glaring at her with the macho stare that told her he had the upper hand "—now that we've reached an understanding, have you got some change? Like I mentioned before, I need to make a phone call."

As it had many times in the past, Alanna's temper overrode her common sense, and she felt herself start to burn with fury. How dare he ask her for money for a phone call! She smirked at him. "Why don't you call collect?"

"What?" He frowned at her, obviously not expecting her to defy him.

"Look, mister," she said angrily, "you may have me at a disadvantage, but you don't have the upper hand yet, and I wouldn't give you a quarter if we were all alone in this universe and you were calling God."

Surprisingly he laughed, long and hard. When he at last stopped, he looked at her and said, "You're sure a spunky broad, aren't you? But look, I don't think God answers long-distance."

As the man scooped the gun from the seat and got out of the car, Alanna simmered hotter than the sun. She turned her head away, refusing to rise to the bait. How dare he laugh at her and poke fun at her predicament! She'd meant every word.

He paused at the door of the phone booth. "Coming?"

"No," she said stubbornly. "I'll wait here."

"You won't leave?"

He knew she couldn't. "No."

"Good."

Right then a car pulled around the corner. Alanna turned to glance at the boxy-looking brown sedan. Along with an official seal, the words, *The United States Government* were emblazoned along the side. Two men sat inside, the wide brims of their six-gallon hats nearly touching in the small confines of the car. Cowboys? The FBI?

"Damn!" the man who had kidnapped Alanna swore.

In nearly one motion, he covered the ground from the phone booth to the Jeep. He leaped in, started the engine, shoved a hat low on his head, and pulled her next to him so quickly she wished that God did answer long-distance.

"Lean your head on my shoulder," he said as he slid the Jeep in gear and started to drive slowly away, "and if you want to live until lunch, don't look up."

Chapter Four

The brown sedan turned into the gravel lot beside them. Allie could hear the tires crunch on stone. Though soft, the sound seemed loud, magnified, like death groaning toward her. Or salvation. They could help her! She started to sit up and call out to the two men when the man beside her pushed her back into the seat.

"I don't usually repeat myself," he said in a low, ominous tone. "I told you to move closer and not look up."

Allie swallowed hard. God, he petrified her. He was so big and tough. Savage.

"Now," he commanded, and she scooted closer, placing her head on his shoulder.

What would happen if the two men recognized him? He had just admitted that the other agents had shot at him earlier, and not at her. Did they want him dead? Would they start shooting again, even with her at his side, clinging to him? Her presence hadn't deterred the men this morning. And if she had to weigh which she feared more, she would choose her kidnapper. The image of the Indian lance on his belt seared into her head. She could feel the press of his hard, muscled chest against her cheek, and could see out of the corner of her eye, the large hand that dangled off her shoulder. Added to that was the harsh glare of his cold blue gaze, and she huddled against him, praying for anonymity.

As though totally indifferent to the danger he was in, the dark stranger slowly shifted the Jeep from one gear into another, driving right past the brown car. Allie could feel his muscles move, bunch, flex, extend as his arm brushed against her breast. She gasped, surprised at the electric contact, slight though it was, and hunched back, not wanting him to touch her again. Why did it send a charge that pulsed to her very core?

"Don't move." Whether it was her action or the fact that he could sense the tension building in her, ready to spiral out of control, he added gruffly, "We'll be fine. Smile. And sit closer. Run your hand over my chest."

"No." She couldn't touch him.

"Do it, Allie," he commanded in no uncertain terms. "Pick up your hand and put it on my chest."

How had she gotten into this mess? All she'd wanted to do was come West and sell women's lingerie. Taking a deep breath, she lifted her hand to his chest, laying it flat on the dark matting of hair that sprouted from his open shirt. The silky cushion prickled her palm sensuously as she slid her hand back and forth over it. His skin felt surprisingly soft, yet hot and hard, burning her, and she could feel his heart thudding rhythmically.

"Now smile."

She twisted her lips into a grimace. "Anything else you want me to do?" she whispered. "How about if I stand on my head or do a jig? I'm also good at juggling."

She could almost feel the rumble of laughter in his chest. He thought the oddest things were funny. "You're doing fine," he answered. "Just keep your head down and keep smiling."

Allie was too afraid not to do his bidding. Molding her lips in a thin line across her teeth so tight they hurt, she kept smiling and rubbing her hand over his chest. His shirt felt soft, too, the fabric smooth and velvety, so supple that she could feel the outline of a scar on his chest. Long and jagged, it had to be a knife wound. She wondered how many

fights he'd been in. How many battles. She could almost see
him out riding in the wilderness, chest bare, war lance in
hand, the feathers floating on the wind, with his powerful
thighs astride a great white stallion, full mane, hooves rear-
ing magnificently into the air.

"Something wrong?"

Everything was wrong.

"No," she said quickly, not wanting him to know she had
been daydreaming. How could she have been thinking such
silliness in the face of danger? With a kidnapper at that. *Her*
kidnapper.

Pulling onto the highway, he shifted the gears again,
rubbing against her. Involuntarily she drew her breasts
away. "There's six layers of clothes between us, Allie," he
said. "Sit still."

There were four layers of clothes between them. His shirt,
her bra, camisole and dress, but she didn't correct him.
"Where are they?"

"Behind us."

"Are they following?"

"No."

"Can I get up?"

"No. Sit tight."

"I don't want to touch you anymore."

Apparently he was as tense as she was, and her statement
seemed to exasperate him. "Lady, you don't seem to realize you don't have any choice," he started angrily, glancing
in the rearview mirror. Then he drew a deep breath and
shook his head as though to clear it. "Take your hand away,
then. Just keep your head on my shoulder."

She kept her head on his shoulder but stopped circling her
hand on his chest, letting it lie there. It was incredible, stupid, idiotic and unbelievable, yet the thud of his heart beating so calmly and forcefully soothed her nerves. "Where are
we going?"

"To find another telephone."

"And then?"

"Arizona."

Allie blinked her confusion. He decided things so fast, and reached such drastic solutions. She wasn't too good at geography, but Arizona had to be at least seven hundred miles away. "Now?"

He stared down at her as though he wondered if she were functioning on all cylinders. "I suppose we could lollygag around Denver a while if you'd like. Maybe we could even take in a few museums, check out the artwork."

Allie couldn't explain why his sarcasm should cut so deeply; normally she would've ignored his remarks. Perhaps it was everything she had been through. She didn't need someone treating her as though she were stupid. She felt tears spring to her eyes, tears of hurt. "You don't have to berate me," she said defensively. "I know we're in danger. I was just surprised. I hadn't expected you to go that far."

He didn't say anything for a moment. Then he glanced down at her again. "For all your bluster you don't hold up very well under pressure, do you?"

"Why do you say that?"

"You're crying."

Allie sat up and used her jacket sleeve to soak up the tears. It didn't matter what he thought of her! So what if he knew she was a coward. "I'm not crying."

"All right. If you say so." Despite his solicitude of moments ago, he turned chilly again. "You'd better get your seat belt on before we get into any more trouble."

"Are they gone?" She'd forgotten about the men following them, and she glanced over her shoulder. Several cars followed in a line behind the Jeep, but none of them was a brown sedan. It was a good thing, since she'd already sat up.

"I think they stayed at the phone booth," he said.

Hong Kong, or the phone booth, she didn't care as long as they weren't nearby. Yet Allie knew she certainly wasn't out of danger. She stole a glance at the man beside her. The set of his jaw was stern, hard. She had to get away. Just his presence petrified her. They weren't going fast now. Maybe she could jump out. She glanced toward the door.

"It's a hell of a way to die," he said as though he could read her mind.

She glanced back at him. His eyes were still glued to the road.

"Sometimes you don't even die. You just lie in bed all broken up, maybe paralyzed."

"You don't have to scare me."

"I'm not trying to scare you. I'm just pointing out how foolish it would be to jump out of a moving vehicle. How about putting your seat belt on?"

Although she hated to obey his orders again, Allie reached for her seat belt and snapped the pieces together. Defiance was one thing; stupidity quite another. Given his history, any second now he might go careening down the road. If she was going to die—and considering her status at the moment, she wasn't at all certain about her life expectancy—it wasn't going to be by falling out of a car.

Or by ants. Like in the movie she'd seen.

She would get away! She had a show to put on—a show that was vital to her career. She needed to find her designs and attend the presentation. But how? Eventually she would escape him, she vowed. If it took the rest of her life.

Allie didn't acknowledge the inconsistency of that particular thought. She just stared straight ahead, her mind whirling with ideas—each one discarded as soon as it was formulated. Turning the Jeep back onto the highway, the man merged with traffic. The landscape started to whiz by. Had it been just yesterday that she had ridden on this very road into Denver? And this morning ridden out again?

"Since you've kidnapped me and won't let me go, can you tell me where we're going in Arizona?" she asked, several miles later when he turned off onto another major route going south.

"The desert."

The desert? Her stomach lurched. It was blazing hot in the desert. And God, she hated heat. "Don't you have to cross the Rockies?"

"Yes, but I prefer the southern route," he answered. "I know the roads better."

"You expect me to wade through desert heat?"

He nodded, his eyes on the road ahead. "Sorry."

She knew he wasn't really sorry, just as she wasn't really expecting him to let her go. She'd had to ask, though. No way could she tolerate a day spent on sand that didn't hug a major body of water like the Atlantic. He had to stop sometime. She would get away then. But somehow she felt defeated, as if she would never escape. Defeated, and she'd hardly fought at all. Closing her eyes to keep from crying again, she leaned her head back on the seat and tried to tell herself that everything would work out fine. Normally she was optimistic, and any moment now she would open her eyes and be back in her apartment with the air-conditioning going full blast and the radio playing soft music.

Wishful thinking.

Ironically he turned on the radio to an easy-listening station. Sighing, Allie sat back up. Unfortunately dreams didn't always come true. Lord, her head hurt. "Do you have any aspirin?"

"Headache?" he inquired, though she doubted he cared, particularly since he kept his gaze fixed on the road. Surprisingly it was flat and the countryside surrounding them nearly barren. To her right the mountains loomed above, high and mighty.

"Yes," she said in response to his question, hiding the fact she also ached with heartache and fear.

"Is the cut still bleeding?" His eyes swung to her, and the glint in their icy-blue depths made an unwanted thrill pulse through her.

"I think the bleeding has stopped," she said as levelly as possible.

"You'd better clean it when we stop for gas."

She nodded. "I will. Do you have any aspirin?"

"No."

She sighed again.

"Don't think about it."

Easier said than done. He wouldn't think about it, she mused. A little head injury wouldn't bother him one bit. He'd jump on his horse and ride into the sunset even if the blood poured profusely from his head. An image of him straddling his great white horse with his head bleeding wavered before her, and she shook her own to clear it of the vision.

"Is anyone following us?" she asked. She'd noticed that his glances into the rearview mirror had increased, and his brow had pleated.

"No. But that doesn't mean they're not there."

Somehow that seemed more chilling than if they could actually spot someone. And she had to remember that he was the dangerous party. "I've never been to the desert," she said, for some crazy reason riddled with an urge to talk, even if to a dangerous desperado.

He glanced briefly from the road to her. She couldn't read his expression, but he seemed serious. "It's hot."

She already knew that. "Do you know somebody there?"

"Yes."

By now she knew him well enough not to prod for more information than he was willing to give her. It only riled him. "How long will it take us?"

"It's a long trip."

And she could tell it would be tortuous. They would have to go over the mountains. How she hated the mountains. They were designed for skiing, not for traversing. She felt sick. The heat and the mountains. They'd be her undoing. "Who are you?" she asked abruptly, needing to know urgently. "What do you do?"

"Why?"

"You seem—" She shrugged. "You remind me of a mercenary."

He glared at her. "What do you know about mercenaries?"

"Nothing," she admitted. "Once I happened to pick up a copy of *Soldier of Fortune* magazine, and you just seem like a...like an adventurer."

"I've done that, too. I take it you're not much of an adventurer."

She shook her head. "I live in Chicago."

"Which has to be an adventure in itself."

"It's a nice city."

"Safe?"

"I've never been kidnapped there." She paused, wondering why she was talking to him like this. And why he was answering her questions. "Do you work for the FBI?"

"No."

"Can you tell me your name?"

"I suppose it doesn't matter," he answered. "My name is Reeve."

Just like Superman, only that was Christopher Reeve. Funny, this man reminded her of someone like that, a man who was larger than life. Big and strong and determined.

"Reeve Chandler," he supplied.

"Are you a drug runner?"

"What?" He glanced at her again, frowning.

"I thought maybe you were involved with drugs," she explained. "The way you're running and looking for people. Or a hired assassin."

There was a brief pause, as he measured whether he could trust her. Then he said, "I wish it were that simple. The whole damned mess is so complicated I'm not sure I can explain it, but reducing it to its lowest common denominator, my brother is a CIA agent accused of spying. He's in jail in East Germany, and I'm trying to get him out."

That seemed a sympathetic mission. "Why do you need me?"

"I've been dealing with a man named Paul Sammison."

Allie nodded. "You mentioned him before."

"He's a CIA agent as well; he's Curt's boss, and he's promised me some papers with the names of some German double agents on it. I can trade the list for my brother."

"And he's reneged on his promise?" she guessed.

"Yes." Reeve nodded. "Several times. Now I have you, and he won't dare cross me."

"I don't understand. What do I have to do with the CIA?"

"Didn't you say your uncle is a senator on the foreign relations committee?"

"Yes."

"The CIA is under the auspices of that committee."

"Oh," Allie said, staring outside for a moment. Never in her wildest dreams would she have thought that her uncle's position would lead to her getting kidnapped, particularly by someone trying to thwart the CIA. "I have to try to get away," she said at last. She needed to find her designs. This was her career at stake. And she didn't like the idea that her flesh and blood would be used for some man's personal mission, the full nature of which still needed to be revealed.

"It would be easier on both of us if you'd cooperate," he answered at last.

"I have to try."

"I guess I understand that," he said after a long moment, "but you have to understand my position. I want to get my brother out of jail."

That was understandable, too, only Allie wasn't certain she believed him. His story, or the part he was willing to reveal to her, was as wild as the one she had told to the police. Since when did East German spies lurk in Denver, Colorado? Yet there had been those two men. They'd knocked her over the head to get her briefcase. Were they spies? What was there in Denver to spy on to begin with? Gold mines? The mountains? "What do you suppose they did with my briefcase?"

"The Germans? Probably tossed it in the trash."

She groaned. All her work, down the drain. Or covered by garbage somewhere, the black-and-red lace garter belts ruined, the fasteners dipping into greasy gravy. Tom Biner would be furious. He would pull himself to his full five-foot-two-inch frame and glare at her. "You lost your designs? Pray tell, how did you do that, Allie? A man? A man took you captive? What kind of man, Allie?" Mable Hill would snicker behind her glasses. They would have a lovely time making fun of her.

Allie lapsed into a silence. Reeve didn't say anything, either. The tires hummed on the pavement, bringing them ever closer to the New Mexico border. Allie kept hoping for a miracle, an answer to her dream—to be suddenly transported to her apartment. Occasionally she would steal a glance at the man beside her. Reeve. An odd name. She'd wanted to ask so many questions, how he'd gotten it, where he was from, the ants, but he hadn't seemed exactly the type for casual chitchat. Nor did the situation seem appropriate for casual chitchat.

She sighed and shifted position. The day was hot, and the farther south they went, the hotter it got, with the sun beating down on their exposed heads. Despite the wind roaring through the vehicle and the lack of humidity, sweat pooled down her back and made her clothes sticky. Road grit had collected in her mouth and on her teeth. Weren't they ever going to stop? They had passed Colorado Springs and a town called Pueblo long ago. Surely they needed gas. She could then towel herself down.

Allie wiped at her forehead. "Can you turn on the air-conditioning?"

For the first time in several hours Reeve glanced at her. It was almost as if he had forgotten her presence, except, of course he hadn't. Now he stared at her, his expression one of puzzlement. "This is a Jeep."

"So?"

He gestured to the sky, to the hot sun glaring down on them. "It's open."

"I know that," she said. His patronizing manner was beginning to irritate her. He acted as if she didn't have a thought in her head. "I'm hot. The air-conditioning would help. At least there would be cool air coming out."

"I don't have air-conditioning."

"Then could you turn on the fan?"

"There's wind coming in," he pointed out. "Sit forward."

"It doesn't help."

He grimaced, repressing a spasm of pain. Then he sighed, in surrender. "We'll stop soon. You're probably tired."

"I'm hot," she said. "And I have a headache, and I feel sick. And I didn't have any lunch."

He stared at her as though assessing her sanity. "Anything else?"

"No." What else could there be? Aside from being held captive, that is, and menaced at every turn. And infuriated that her important fashion line had been stolen.

"Why don't you take off your jacket?"

"I can't."

"Why not?"

She glanced down at the white bolero jacket. Underneath the sleeve of her dress was ripped. She could feel the wide rent in the fabric. "It goes with my dress."

"Really?" he said. "Too bad." And he flicked his gaze back to the road.

She had sounded like a city slicker again. "I didn't mean it that way," she said.

"Oh? How did you mean it?"

"My dress is ripped. The jacket covers it."

"I won't tell if you won't."

Alanna wasn't up to this. Nothing in life had prepared her for being abducted, and certainly not by a curt, arrogant man like this one. Didn't he understand that her slip would show? She didn't normally expose herself to strange men. Yet they were hardly strangers, he'd already seen her slip once. Not that it mattered. He hadn't been in the least bit interested.

Slowly she peeled off her jacket, and folded it into her lap.

Although she continued to shift position, dying of heat, it was three more hours before Reeve stopped for gas. He had turned off the interstate highway just before a town called Walsenburg. Then, turning again onto a dirt road, he drove to a gas station several miles away. Had he chosen it purposely? The place was so remote that the only people around were two old toddling men. Reeve waved off one of them, probably the proprietor, who had made motions to turn on the gas pump, and Reeve started to fill the tank himself. The other man was clad in overalls and dusty shoes, and carried a mining pick. He was leading a donkey to the air pumps. Why, Allie didn't know, but she suspected he wanted to tether the animal up awhile so he could relax. She wondered if he mined for gold. The whole scene was bizarre, as if sliced directly from the movies. Allie hadn't realized there were still people like them left in the world. She felt as though they'd gotten off a super highway and had entered another era.

"Do you want to go to the washroom?" Reeve asked after he'd set the gas pump back in place.

"Yes." Allie stepped down from the vehicle.

He jerked his head toward the two men. "I know you want to get away, but don't try anything here. They're nice old guys. I'd hate to see anything happen to them."

Allie nodded, knowing it was futile at the moment to try to escape. Where would she go? Down the steep road they'd just traversed to the highway? He'd gone in so many directions that she didn't even know which way they were traveling. South, she supposed, and west to Arizona. What the hell was in Arizona anyway besides scrub grass and sand?

"Fix your head, and I'll get some aspirin," he said.

It surprised her that he'd remembered her headache. "Fine."

"Wash out the cut well. It's important to get out the dirt. I'll try to buy us something to eat," he went on. "It looks like there are some snacks inside. Oh, you might be more comfortable if you'd rip out your sleeves. Keep your jacket handy, though. We're going to go through the mountains later. It gets cold at night."

"All right," she said, too exhausted to rebel.

When he turned away, she walked to the washroom. As she circled around to the back of the building, she noted that the gas station was typical. An old cola machine stood out front along with a rack of tires, both new and used, and an air hose lay across the cracked cement, coiled like a snake, waiting for someone to trip over it. Oil cans, along with various snacks and every brand of cigarette imaginable lined the shelves inside. The attendant that she had assumed was the proprietor sat out front in a straight-back chair, tilting it precariously against the wall. He had grease on his hands and clothes, as though he'd been busy. Yet there wasn't a car in sight, except for a shiny blue Lincoln Continental parked near the garage. It couldn't be his. Not unless he was related to the miner and had a gold vein tucked away somewhere.

Maybe she could steal the car, Allie thought, and get away. She glanced back at Reeve; he stood watching her, his gaze a warning.

She kept walking.

Once inside, Allie surmised that the washroom was more remote than anything else on the lot. It possibly hadn't seen a broom or mop in centuries. The floor was covered with dust. Rust stained the sink in a path that ran from the water spout. Spiderwebs and wasp nests decorated the ceiling. How could insects survive at this elevation? Denver was known as the Mile-High City, and since Reeve had turned off the interstate, he had driven even higher into the mountains. Surely the bugs had to have mutated to become so fit and hearty. The air was so damned thin it hardly allowed a person to breathe, let alone creepy-crawlies to crawl. Perhaps she ought to imitate their survival techniques, Allie thought. She sure as hell needed to become stronger.

In spite of the dirty surroundings, Allie washed her face and hands and rinsed the grit from her mouth. Taking a wet paper towel, she touched it to her head gingerly. As the day had worn on, her wound had started to throb more and more. Now that she could feel and see the edges, the cut itself seemed tiny. But the flesh around it was swollen; a large lump had formed and throbbed, probably the reason she had a headache.

There were worse things, Allie reminded herself. She could have a worse wound, or be lying dead on the street in front of the hotel. At least she was alive. That was one consolation. She stuck out her tongue at her mirrored image. She was thankful the surface was old and dirty, and she couldn't see clearly how awful she looked, but she knew it was certainly a far cry from this morning, when she'd walked pressed and freshened into the dazzling sunshine.

She almost laughed at the thought of how she'd primped and strutted around the hotel room this morning. She'd worried her hat into a daunting angle on her head. It was probably lying in the street now, flung into the gutter, crushed by countless cars, the white wool destroyed, like the garter belts in the garbage. She didn't even have a comb now. With a lamentful sigh, Allie started to rip out the sleeves of her dress as Reeve had suggested, but stopped. If she had to be here that was one thing, but she would not cooperate. She still had her pride, and she was making things much too easy for this man. She *would* get away!

Buoyed by defiance, she slipped her jacket back on, her sleeves intact. She opened the door to the bathroom and marched toward the Jeep. She had rounded the building when the old man in the greasy clothes spoke to her. The other old man with the donkey had disappeared from view.

"Want something cold to drink, lady? I got an extra soda."

He seemed a friendly sort. His face was brown and leathery, his brow wrinkled from shading his piercing green eyes from the sun. Was this her opportunity to get away? Allie paused, glancing at Reeve. The hood was up on the Jeep, and he was pouring water into the radiator.

"Your gent's busy," the old man went on. "He's still gotta check the oil."

Allie took the soda. "Thank you."

"Welcome. Where you headed?" he asked with interest.

"Arizona."

"Hot there."

Hot there? she mused. It was plenty hot here. She tipped the soda and swallowed. It was cold and wet, and it felt wonderful going down her parched throat.

"Don't have to sweat, though. Ain't no humidity."

"That's what I hear. You don't sweat here, either, do you?"

"Nope."

Why had she been perspiring in the car then?

"Have some trouble?" The old man gestured toward her nylon stockings. She'd forgotten that they were torn. "Figured you must have fell down."

Maybe she ought to blurt out the truth, tell him that she'd been kidnapped for ransom. But she hated to jeopardize the old man's safety. She didn't know Reeve Chandler very well, but she didn't doubt for a moment that he had meant every word of his warning. *They're nice old men. I'd hate to see them get hurt.* She glanced back at Reeve. The hood was down, and he stood beside the car, watching her. To a casual observer he seemed relaxed and at ease, waiting for her. Was he that confident she wouldn't say or do anything to give him away? Or was he just waiting for her to try? Earlier he'd threatened her with the gun. She'd never forget the look of it. Cold and blue. Like his eyes. Nor would she forget the way he'd tossed her around in that motel yesterday.

"No, I didn't fall down," she said at last. "I caught my stockings on the door of the Jeep."

"Rip your dress there, too?"

"Yes," she said, amazed at his perception.

"Looks pretty, all them polka dots, but ain't it kinda out of place for traveling?"

"It is uncomfortable."

"So's them shoes, I'll bet."

She nodded. Her feet had swollen, and the narrow toes had started to pinch her. "Very."

"Well, can't win 'em all. My wife used to wear shoes like that."

"She doesn't anymore?"

"She's dead."

"Oh," Allie said, embarrassed by her faux pas. Sympathy for this old man poured through her.

But he didn't seem to notice. "Killed by a drifter. Wrung her damned neck. Ain't nowhere safe no more."

"No," she agreed, now shocked.

"Nice vehicle," he went on, nodding toward the Jeep. "Good for these roads."

She nodded. "Yes. I'd better go now," Allie said, handing him the empty can and feeling overwhelmed. "Thanks again for the soda."

"Welcome," he repeated. "Looks like your gent's waiting for you."

She nodded. "He's a little impatient."

"Pretty girl like you, he oughta be. Especially considering those fellas looking for you."

Allie froze in midstep. "Fellas? What fellas?"

He tilted his head as though gesturing down the road. "Couple men dressed in suits. They were here not more'n ten minutes ago. They were looking for a big dark-haired guy and a gal in a red-and-white polka-dot dress. Guess that's you."

It didn't describe too many other people. "Were they German?" she asked anxiously. How had they found her?

"Nope. American. Figured they were the government. Looked like it. Said they were looking for you and that they were covering all towns and stations in the area. One of them gave me a hundred dollars to let them know if I saw you. Said just to call."

Allie's hopes soared. The government would help her. After all, her uncle *was* a senator. "Do you have the number?" she asked breathlessly. "Are you going to call them?"

"Nope."

She stared at him. "But they gave you money."

"Yup, they did, but your gent gave me two hundred dollars not to call."

What an old conniver! she thought. Playing both ends against the middle. "You told Reeve about the men?" she asked, glancing toward him, and seeing he was gone from the Jeep. They'd certainly had a long conversation while she was in the washroom.

"Shame about his brother," the old man said, shaking his head sadly. "Just like the government to ignore a fella down on his luck. Once they made me pay a bundle of taxes. Didn't have any money to pay it with, neither. Had to sell my interest in the gold mine. Paid out, too, the darned thing, the very next week. Lost my shorts." Allie glanced toward the old man's Lincoln parked not far away. He saw her and said, "The wife left me a little cash."

He'd probably killed her himself, Allie thought. Wrung her damned neck. Swallowing down her distaste, she tried to remain calm. "I see."

"Me and Patsy, we're in partnership now," he said. "Been panning a couple years up in the mountains in a little creek."

Patsy had to be the other old man. Allie stepped closer to him. It was a chance, but a chance she had to take. "Look, sir. I wondered if you might—"

"Ready, Allie?" Reeve interrupted, grasping her by the elbow from nowhere. "We better get going."

When had he sneaked up on her? And how much had he overheard? Of course, it didn't really matter. Obviously the old guy had already regaled him with the entire story.

"You gonna cross the mountains at night?" the elderly man asked him now.

"I figure we'll try."

"Gotta be careful."

Reeve nodded. "We will."

"Stop back sometime."

"Will do."

With his hand resting at the small of her back, Reeve walked her toward the Jeep. Allie's heart pounded in her throat as she felt his anger darken the air. What would he do to her now? Would he be upset that she had talked to the old man? He helped her up the steep step, into the vehicle. "Buckle up."

Not bothering to defy him, she reached for her seat belt.

"Are you angry with me?" No sense pretending.

"No," he said flatly. Had she not looked so panic-stricken when he'd touched her elbow, Reeve might have lashed out. He knew from her expression that she'd been about to enlist the old man's aid, but he'd throttled that at the start with cold, hard cash and a quick intrusion. He couldn't blame her attempts. He actually admired them. But he had other things to worry about—things like Paul Sammison. Things like his brother.

"Do you know the men who are looking for us? Do you think they're the FBI?"

"No," Reeve said. "They're the Mob."

He said it so blithely, so matter-of-factly, as though he expected them. How many people were chasing them? "The Mob? As in organized crime?"

"Yes."

"What do they want with us?" She didn't stumble over the term *us*. She didn't have time to wonder that she was suffering from one of those kidnap-victim syndromes.

He started the engine and shifted gears, pulling out on the road. As they went by the station, he waved to the old man, who waved back. "They want me, but I'm not sure why. They've been following me for quite a while."

Allie didn't know what to think. "What will they do to you when they find you?"

"Probably kill me."

Another matter-of-fact statement, as if he didn't care. "What did you do?"

"Nothing."

God, since when did people kill people for nothing? "And me?" she asked. "What will they do with me?"

"Probably kill you. Hang on, the road curves a bit."

Allie took a deep breath as he shifted the Jeep and headed up a steep incline. They had reached the mountains, the dreaded mountains, and the danger just kept increasing.

Chapter Five

Reeve had vastly underestimated the road. It didn't just curve a bit. It was downright tortuous, careening through rough, mountainous terrain, curving, dropping away, winding. The engine whined as they climbed upward. The tires hummed on the asphalt as they sped down and around. Despite the seat belt, still fearful of the open doors of the Jeep, Allie clung to the roll bar as he traversed the peaks and valleys.

After they'd topped several mountains, Reeve handed her a chocolate bar he took from his pocket. "There's some sodas in the back. In a cooler. Why don't you pop open a couple?"

Why argue? A soda sounded good. Actually, so did candy at this point. Allie was starved. She hadn't eaten lunch. She hadn't eaten breakfast, either. She let go of the roll bar long enough to twist around in her seat and open the small blue-and-white Styrofoam cooler. "Did you buy this from the old man at the gas station?"

"Yes," he said.

"How much did you pay him for it?"

"Fifty dollars."

She shook her head, repelled. "Nice racket he has."

"Last-chance service stations do well."

That one seemed to do particularly well, she mused. She wouldn't have been surprised if both men played road scams on innocent vacationers, traveling by car with their families. It would be just like the old man to pretend to be sick and rob them or something.

But at the moment she had worse problems. "Aren't you concerned about the Mob looking for us?" she asked a few minutes later. So far Reeve hadn't even mentioned the danger they were in.

"No."

"Why not? According to that old man, they're scouting all over, in search of us. They were at the same gas station we stopped at. That seems a strange coincidence. I don't know much about clandestine activities, or even about running from people, but I would certainly be concerned. In fact, I'd take another road."

"There isn't another road, not for hundreds of miles," he answered. "Besides, this is rough country. They could drive off the road somewhere, disappear. I'm not concerned. And if I were concerned, there's nothing I could do about it, anyhow, except get where I'm going as fast as I can."

She supposed that did make sense. "Did you make your phone call?" she asked, though she wondered why she cared. She didn't care; she was just curious. She had noticed a pay phone at the gas station, and him heading for it.

He nodded. "The meeting's set up."

"Were—did you tell Sammison about me?"

"Yes."

"Was he upset?"

"No."

How deflating. She glanced at Reeve. He was always in such control. He even handled the Jeep with ease—the big Jeep. In spite of his casual air, there seemed to be an energy about him, an aura of command. Odd, how electricity seemed to hover between them. "Did you tell him about my uncle?"

"Yes."

Reeve had told Sammison a lot of things, namely that he wasn't going to tolerate any more foul-ups. He wanted the

names of the German double agents, and he wanted them
now. The agent had been surprised about Allie, and agreeable. The problem was, the man had been too agreeable.

"And?"

"And Sammison is meeting me."

"That's all? You did tell him you're holding me captive?"

"Yes."

It was nice to know she was missed. Feeling suddenly despondent, she sighed and glanced down at her chocolate bar.
In the general scheme of things she knew she wasn't really
all that important. She hadn't expected the people he was
dealing with to mobilize the National Guard or call the
White House, but at least the man called Sammison could
have had a reaction. Anger, perhaps. A warning to Reeve.
An inquiry as to her well-being. Did her family know where
she was yet? Her uncle?

"Aren't you hungry?" Reeve asked.

The chocolate was white in spots, faded. "It's old," Allie said, turning it over to look at it. "There's probably mold
on it."

"I ate mine, and I haven't died."

She didn't remark. But her first thought was that he
could've eaten salmonella, and not died. He was entirely too
healthy. "Do you have anything else?"

"All they had was the candy."

Handing it back, Alanna took a sip from her soda. She'd
lost her appetite anyhow.

"Not hungry?"

She shook her head. "No."

"It's going to be a long time before we stop for dinner."

She shrugged. "I'll survive."

"Okay." He shrugged his shoulders, as well. "Suit yourself. But if you're going to get away from me you're going
to need some energy."

She shot him a disdainful glare. "Please don't make fun
of me."

He turned back to her with a surprised expression. "I wasn't making fun of you. I was just pointing out a tactical problem."

"It's *my* tactical problem, not yours," she said, not wanting to discuss her lack of appetite, not wanting to discuss anything with him.

Yet hardly moments later she sighed and gave in. If she waited for him to talk she would wait forever. "Where are we?" she asked as he shifted gears again, to climb another mountain. An occasional car passed them, cars loaded with families and camping gear.

"Somewhere near the San Isabel National Forest."

"Do we have far to go?"

"Yes."

Still brief, succinct. Didn't the man ever use more than a single syllable?

Far was something he didn't underestimate. Allie thought they were going to *drive* forever, too. They finally stopped for dinner very late that night in a small town deep in the San Juan Mountains, in southwest Colorado. They'd come up on the place from out of nowhere, rounding a steep incline and going down the other side. It was situated at a bend in the road, and a gas station, drugstore and a small diner blared their neon signs. Several cars were parked in the lot to one side, and a row of semitrailers hugged the other. Apparently in this part of the country, this was the big time. Over the mountains and through the woods to Dale's Diner.

By now Allie was so hungry she could have eaten six of the candy bars, mold and all. Her stomach rumbled and groaned, and she felt sick from the sweet soda she had consumed. She wanted a big, juicy hamburger so badly she could taste it. And she was cold, freezing to death. For the past fifty miles all she'd done was shiver. Her only thought was to get inside and get warm. When had it gotten so cold?

"Maybe you ought to take your stockings off before we go inside," Reeve told her. "They're all torn. People might wonder what happened to you."

Why was he worried about her stockings? Her dress was a more obvious flag that would cause attention. The red-and-white polka-dot creation would stand out among the jeans and warm jackets of the patrons sitting inside the café like a firecracker at Christmas.

"I suppose they're nice folks, too," she answered. "And you don't want to see them hurt."

"Something like that."

He sat beside her, waiting. She fidgeted a moment. "Look, I promise not to say anything."

"So?"

"So I won't say anything to anyone. I'd like to keep on my stockings."

"I'm running out of patience, Allie."

She sighed, knowing she wasn't going to get out of doing as he'd told her. But how was she going to take off her panty hose with him looking on? His gaze already sent bolts through her. How was she going to lift up her dress? "Close your eyes."

"What?"

"Close your eyes," she said louder.

"God, I don't believe you," he muttered.

"I have to lift up my dress."

He nodded. "I know, but if you don't do it now, we'll drive on."

It was useless fighting him. Allie knew that, but she kept remembering the motel, where he'd teased her unmercifully about the garter belt and called her sexy lady. She recalled the blue depths of his measuring gaze when he bothered to look at her. She gulped down her fear. Trying to muster as much dignity as she could, considering the circumstances, she wiggled her hosiery from her hips. Reeve didn't turn away. She could feel his gaze burn into her.

He couldn't help but stare as she pulled her stockings down her legs. Damn, but she was sexy. Long legged and gorgeous. Even disheveled. In spite of himself he felt a rush of desire tighten at his crotch. This was one hell of a time to be looking at a woman. His brother was in an East German prison camp, and everybody from the CIA to the Mob was chasing him. And her. Yet he didn't turn away.

Since she didn't have any other shoes, Allie slipped her high heels back on. Between the swelling, lack of stockings and the way her teeth chattered, she had a hard time getting them on her feet.

"Ready?" He was sure ready.

"Yes." She shivered again. "I'm cold."

"It's warm inside." He wished he could reach across and gather her into the warmth of his arms. But he fought back the impulse, angered with himself as he stepped from the Jeep.

Allie was oblivious to his condition. "Do you think those men from the Mob are here?" she said as they walked toward the diner.

He shook his head without even looking around. "No."

"Did you check the cars?"

"Why?"

She shrugged. "I noticed a Cadillac in the lot."

"You think members of the Mob drive luxury cars?"

She shrugged again. On *Miami Vice* and *Hunter* they did, or else they had limousines with chauffeurs.

"Relax," he told her, placing his hand at the small of her back and guiding her inside. "No one's here."

Reeve didn't remind her not to speak to anyone as they entered the building; he didn't have to. They'd already discussed that option, and his expression told it all as he held open the door for her: one word from her, and she was dead. She couldn't help looking around, though, and trying to pick out anyone who might be part of the Mob, anyone who might be looking for them.

The café was full of diners, some she concluded were town residents, others travelers through the mountain pass. No one had on a suit.

"All clear?" Reeve asked her a few minutes later.

She glanced at him. He was making fun of her again. "I was just looking. It doesn't hurt to look, does it?"

"No, I guess it doesn't."

For all his nonchalance, she knew he'd looked around, too. Naturally wary, he'd asked for a booth in back, and sat with his back to the wall. He could see every person in the café, as well as anyone coming in. Not taking any chances, instead of letting her sit across from him, he'd steered her to the place beside him in the booth, hemming her in.

He did allow her to visit the washroom, warning her again with his gaze not to try anything. She couldn't have enlisted help if she wanted to. Only a little girl was there, trying to wash her hands in the sink that was too tall. Allie lifted the child up and then practically took a bath herself. Using paper towels, she washed her face and hands and legs, rinsing liberally. But the water was as cold as the outside. Shivering, she ran her fingers through her hair, feeling refreshed.

When she came back, Reeve steered her into the booth, beside him again. Apparently he'd washed, too. His hair was wet and he smelled of soap. "Did you speak to anyone."

"No."

"Good girl."

High praise. He took up most of the booth, and consequently their thighs touched. Allie ignored it. She also ignored the shivers that wisped up her spine whenever his arm brushed against hers, telling herself she was just cold. After all it was freezing outside, and she had taken a bath in cold water.

Reeve must have noticed the cold, too. Or else he was just crowded. He had moved away. Still she could feel the heat from his body. She glanced outside, but all she could see was their reflection in the window. A dangerous man and a frightened woman, two strangers thrust together because of circumstance.

Feeling tiny and insignificant, and very, very vulnerable, Allie edged closer to the wall, delighting in the electric heater blasting warm air below the table. When the waitress came, she ordered a hamburger, and ate it later with relish. Amazing how a person didn't value heat or food until it was denied.

Or safety.

Once she'd gotten warm and had something in her stomach, she looked around the café again. Surprisingly no one had noticed them when they'd come in. Perhaps all the patrons were also cold, and busy concentrating on their own problems. Travelers were an odd lot, she thought as she glanced at a man and woman several booths away. They were hunched over their coffee, talking seriously. The woman looked up and smiled.

Allie smiled back. Maybe they considered her just as odd. Here she was going through the mountains decked out in a crazy red-and-white polka-dot dress, sitting next to a tall, dark man who was the image of a cold-blooded killer. Yet the waitress had seemed interested in Reeve, she thought. And so had the woman over at the counter. They'd both given him looks. Looks that said, *I'm yours, honey, just say the word*.

"What do you suppose women see in you?" she blurted.

He glanced at her. "That's a weird question, considering the circumstances."

"I've thought a lot of things were weird today," she answered, "including the circumstances."

He shrugged. "Finish up your meal, Allie. We have to go."

She took a sip of milk, but studied him. She supposed he *was* handsome in a rugged sort of way. And tall. He moved with a grace uncommon to most big men. Silent. Maybe they liked his hair. Most women were attracted to that thick, longish mane, and hadn't she already noticed it was as dark as the midnight? Truthfully she admitted, cold-blooded killer or not, he practically reeked of that irresistible combination of danger and seething sensuality that drove women wild. They probably dropped at his feet, eager for the chance to spend the night with him. And he would be good, too, in bed; he'd make a woman feel like a woman.

If she lived through the night.

"Something wrong?"

He always caught her staring at him. Quickly she shook her head. "No."

"Ready? We should get moving. We still have a long way to go."

Allie sighed and scooted from the booth. Although a bell above the door tinkled whenever anyone entered, she hadn't noticed the man in the dark suit come into the café. Or his partner. Not until Reeve was nearly at the cash register, and the partner entered, too. This one was tall and sleazy looking, dark haired and dark skinned, with a mustache that gave him an air of meanness. A thin scar ran from his eye to his ear, and he carried himself stiffly erect, daring anyone to defy him.

Her heart hit the floor, and she stopped dead in her tracks. "Reeve, is that them?"

Apparently Reeve had noticed the men, both of them; he'd elected to leave while a bunch of people were clustered around the doors. "No."

"Are you sure?"

"Just keep walking, Allie," he said, pushing her in front of him. "Don't stop. Get in the Jeep while I pay the bill. And for God's sake, don't panic."

But she had already panicked. Her breath came in short gasps, and she felt her heart start to flutter in fear.

"*Go,*" he commanded softly.

She swallowed hard and went out the door, shivering as the chill air and the dark night enveloped her. But she didn't have time to worry about the cold or the darkness. It didn't occur to her to defy Reeve. Or to run from him. Not now. Not with the ugly-looking man in the café close on their trail. Just one glance and she knew he would be a far worse captor than Reeve was, because he wouldn't stoop to torture; he would outright kill, and enjoy the act. While she didn't want to be held captive by Reeve Chandler, she realized rather quickly that he was vastly preferable to the two men inside the café.

Allie wasn't ready for a wild ride through the mountains, particularly in the pitch-dark night, but she knew it was coming. Jumping into the Jeep, she clamped on her seat belt and held on tight. She didn't have to wait long. Reeve rushed from the café, jumped into the vehicle, turned the ignition and peeled out of the parking lot in one quick motion.

She glanced back, expecting the two men to follow. Instead, a big, burly man in uniform ran out of the café and jumped into a squad car, activating his lights and siren.

"That's a policeman," she said. "Where did he come from?"

"The café. He's the local sheriff."

Strange, she hadn't noticed. But she'd been busy watching the women watch Reeve. Actually she'd been busy watching Reeve herself. "Who told him about us?"

"Probably a news bulletin. Or an APB. I imagine the cops have gotten something out on us by now."

"Us?"

"Me," he corrected as he careened around a curve. "And you as my hostage." The tires squealed, and the Jeep skidded across the road, narrowly missing going over the cliff on the other side. They stayed upright just by his sheer skill at driving.

"Where are the mobsters?" she asked breathlessly.

"They're not stupid, Allie. They can see the sheriff, too."

She noticed he didn't deny the identity of the men as he had inside the café. They skidded around another curve, and she murmured. "Oh, God, we're going to die."

"Just hang on. I've got an idea."

Whatever it was, she hoped he acted soon. She couldn't take much more of this. Considering the way he was driving, subjecting herself to torture or even outright murder would be smarter than sitting here clinging to the roll bar. She held on to the metal so tightly it was a wonder she didn't leave dents. She had just concluded that he was manufacturing his idea when he crossed the road and careened around the guardrail on the other side, barreling straight down the side of the mountain. Allie wanted to scream, but the sound stuck in her throat as the Jeep bumped and lurched across the rocky terrain.

Battling the wheel, Reeve made his way to a thick copse of trees, nestling the vehicle inside at the same moment he clicked off the lights and shut down the engine.

Allie glanced behind them. No one in his right mind would have driven off that road. No one except a desperate man. But then she had already concluded that Reeve was desperate. "Won't the sheriff see our tracks?"

"It's too dark."

"He has a spotlight. I saw it on his car."

"I'm counting on him driving right on by without realizing we've left the road."

"What if he isn't fooled?"

"Then we try again."

Doing what? Allie looked down the mountain. Four-wheeling through the Rockies wasn't exactly her idea of fun. How she prayed the sheriff was either stupid or tired or both. She'd never wanted to fool anyone so badly.

Tension filled the next few moments as they waited for the squad car to either drive by or find them. Allie had trouble breathing. She would take a breath in and forget to breathe out, or she would breathe out and forget to take a breath in. She sat frozen, afraid to move. Then the squad car rounded the curve and drove by. The sheriff was going fast, but the moment was so slow that she was sure she saw her life flash in front of her eyes. When she regained her composure, she thought about calling out to the sheriff. But knowing that Reeve would just take off with her again made her realize her folly.

Not one to waste time, as soon as the squad car was out of sight, Reeve restarted the engine and backed out of the trees, heading back up the incline.

"Aren't you going to wait until he's gone?" Alanna asked.

"He is gone."

"I mean far away."

"No."

What did she have to do to get him to utter more than a single syllable? "What about the mobsters?"

"They're probably behind us."

Accelerating the engine, Reeve bumped them back onto the road. Just then headlights appeared from around the curve. Ominous-looking headlights. "Is that them?" she asked.

"I don't know."

She was growing upset. Fear always made her excitable, and she couldn't remember ever being so frightened, not even yesterday, when he'd held a gun to her head. "Can't you tell from the shape of the lights?"

Reeve shook his head. "I'm not a car buff, Allie. And if I were, I don't even know what kind of car the two men are driving."

"Do you think the sheriff has stopped?"

"I think he's still ahead of us."

"Driving?"

He sighed, obviously growing equally exasperated. "Yes, driving. Look, Allie, don't worry about it. Okay?"

"I have to worry about it," she snapped, starting to lose control. "Somebody does if you aren't."

"Yes, I am," he answered quietly. "I just worry differently than you do. Now hang on. We've got to get off this road."

Alanna didn't get to continue their argument. If she thought he had driven recklessly before, it was nothing compared to what he did now. As they rounded a curve, they came to a rare crossroads, an old dirt road cutting through the mountains, and he pirouetted the Jeep onto it so fast she thought surely they had entered a time warp. Adding to the danger, he had shut off his headlights so that no one could see them. Unfortunately he couldn't see, either. The night was inky black; not even the moon illuminated the sky. All she could make out was a few feet in front of her, the outline of a mountain straight ahead, and the slope of a steep cliff on the other side. One slip and they would crash into rock or go over a sheer drop into nothingness.

Reeve drove several yards and then stopped, glancing back. The car lights that had been following behind them flashed by. Now, in the silence of the dark night, Allie could hear the siren in the distance.

"We've lost them," she said. "Both of them."

"Hopefully."

"What are we going to do?"

"Go on," he said in that low, rumbling voice. Shifting the Jeep back in gear, he started forward, bumping along the ruts. It took a few minutes for her to realize that they were on an old mining road.

"Do you know where we are?"

"Yes."

"Are we still going to Arizona?"

"Yes."

"Do you know the way from here?"

"Yes."

The hell with trying to get him to talk. Not saying anything more, Allie sank into the car seat shivering. Now that the danger had passed, she was cold again, freezing.

"Why don't you go to sleep?" Reeve suggested.

She was amazed that he had spoken to her without her prodding. "I can't. I'm cold." Only this afternoon she'd been dying of heat.

"Think about something warm."

She did—a nice, hot cup of coffee, steam clouding the air, which made her even colder. "I guess I'm not into meditating."

"Close your eyes and try it."

He wasn't even shivering. "Aren't you cold?"

"No."

What kind of a man was he? He wasn't cold, and he wasn't scared. Yet he was desperate. "Is your brother guilty of spying?" she asked abruptly.

"That's what he's been accused of."

"Was he on a mission?"

"The government calls it covert action."

"Why did the government deny knowing him?"

"Because they seldom admit to spying or to knowing spies," he said.

She felt jarred, and reflected that sometimes life seemed unfair. She'd heard her uncle talk about spies once. But then he'd heralded them as heroes. "So you decided to save him?"

Even in the dark she could sense that Reeve had turned to look at her. She could sense his energy, his anger. "Yes," he said. "And if it's the last thing I do, I'll get him out of jail."

She didn't doubt him for a moment. Yet it all seemed so incredible. Such a convenient story. While Allie was certain that his brother was in trouble and that Reeve was trying to help him, she wasn't at all sure he was telling the truth about the situation. Why would the man called Sammison try to double-cross Reeve? CIA agents didn't do things like that. They had to report to their superiors like any other employee. Also, why would the government deny someone's existence? It just didn't make sense. And if his brother was in such a predicament, why wasn't Reeve there, in East Germany, instead of here? Then there was the FBI and the Mob. How and why were they involved? So many questions and not enough answers.

Leaning her head back against the seat, Allie stared up at the sky for a long moment. "Is it cold in East Berlin?"

"I think their weather is similar to ours. Why?"

"I just wondered if your brother was cold."

Reeve didn't answer, and Allie kept staring at the dark sky. Finally huddling down in the seat, she closed her eyes and imagined the sun beating down on her skin, fiery hot, heat waves radiating from the liquid ball of fire. It surrounded her, enveloped her in its warmth, soothing and comforting her.

When she woke up they were out of the mountains. It was close to dawn. The dark sky had turned to gray, and the landscape on either side of the road had changed from steep cliffs and inclines to something that looked like it came from out of a science fiction movie. Red soil and rocky sand stretched on as far as the eye could see. Here and there buttes rose into the air, stark in their nakedness. Trees were few and far between. Once in a while a tuft of scrub grass or sagebrush poked up from the ground.

They'd reached the desert.

Allie yawned, just then realizing that she had slept against Reeve's shoulder and that he'd tossed a jacket over her. His jacket? It was thick and warm, made from buckskin and lined with fuzzy sheepskin. Strangely comforting. Almost as comforting as being snuggled next to him. She bolted upright. How could she have consorted with the enemy? The question shot through her like a bullet.

"Something wrong?"

Every time I touch you, I feel weird, she wanted to say. Every time I look at you, I shiver. "No," she said, simply.

"Sleep well?" he asked as she rubbed her neck. She was already hot.

"My neck hurts."

"How's your head?"

"Awful." She looked around again. "Where are we?"

"Close to the Navaho Indian reservation."

Automatically she glanced back, behind them. No one followed. It was as if they were alone in the universe. An alien universe. "Can we stop soon?"

"In a few minutes, so we can get some supplies."

Where? Anything resembling civilization was not anywhere in view.

"I know a family that lives nearby," he said, apparently guessing her concern. "They run a trading post."

"Won't they report you to the authorities?"

"No."

An hour later Allie could see why. He didn't just know the family. They appeared to be either close friends or relatives, she couldn't tell which. The store had appeared suddenly, like a mirage on the horizon, smack-dab in the middle of the rocky, red sand. It was hardly an oasis, though. It sprouted out of the scrub grass and soil, so dusty and worn, it looked practically a part of the landscape. Off to one side several sunbaked mud homes faced east. On one of them a television antenna rose from the roof, an odd mix of old world and new technology.

"Do people live in those houses?" Allie asked.

"Some. They're called hogans. Though most Navaho live in wood houses now." He gestured to the clustered buildings. "This is the trading post, but it's really a minitown. Families come to shop, visit or sell crafts to the tourists."

Now Allie could see that there were several long buildings connected to one another: a hotel, a store and a post office. The only thing that hinted of green was the tiny garden that bordered the store. Stalks of scraggly corn growing in clumps rose into the air along with a few wilted tomato plants growing in between. How hard it must have been to till the soil, and raise the crops. The people had to be a hardy lot to survive in these elements.

Reeve pulled next to the gas pumps and filled the Jeep before heading around front toward the store. It was still early, and no one seemed to be up and about.

"Don't they lock the gas pumps?" Allie asked, following beside him.

"No. The people are honest."

What about strangers? she wanted to ask but instead focused on deciphering what he meant by 'the people.' "By 'the people' you mean the Indians?"

"Yes."

When they got to the porch, she noticed the shades were drawn. Notes were tacked to the door, little hand-printed flyers advertising everything from open hours and the cost of a soda to a flock of sheep for sale. "Are you sure someone lives here? The place looks deserted."

"They're asleep. Besides, the hotel's full."

"How do you know?"

"Window shades."

She glanced at the windows on the neighboring building. "Where are the cars?"

All that sat out front was a pickup truck. Once, on a television show, she'd heard it referred to as the Navaho convertible.

"Parked around the side."

"Do your friends run the hotel?"

"Yes. But it's just for tourists." Reeve knocked softly on the door and waited. After a few moments he knocked again.

"They'll never hear you," Allie said.

"They're Indian," he answered as if that negated her statement. Sure enough, a few moments later, someone lifted aside the curtains and glanced outside. The motion was so stealthy that Allie nearly missed it, except that Reeve had smiled, acknowledging the flicker of movement.

"You're loosing your touch, Jean," he said softly when a woman stood framed in the doorway. "I had to knock twice."

"Reeve!" Considering his previous statement, Allie was surprised to see that the woman was white, or at least mostly white. She was tall and plump, and her face seemed kind and understanding. In fact she looked like the quintessential mother. Allie wanted to fall into her arms and be comforted.

"Oh, Reeve!" the woman exclaimed again with a broad, pleased smile. "Come in." She hauled him inside the door, Allie following. "And who is this?" She didn't wait for an introduction. "You've been holding out on us, Reeve. Shame on you, all these years telling us you were a confirmed bachelor." She took Allie's hands. "My, look at you." Glancing back to Reeve. "She's very pretty."

"Thanks."

Allie glanced from the woman to him, wondering why he was allowing her to think they were an item, but he was busy talking. And now the woman was fussing over him. "How are you?" she went on, touching his cheek fondly, patting his growth of beard. "What are you doing here?" She looked around as though expecting someone else. "Where's Curt?"

"I'm still trying to get Curt out of jail," Reeve answered as an old man shuffled into the room, his face lighting up with pleasure. Only he was Indian, and he called Reeve by another name.

"Wòòdii," he said, embracing Reeve. He was squat, and he had true Native American features: a broad forehead, high cheekbones. His jet-black hair was longish and streaked with gray. "It is good to see you, son."

"It is good to see you, Danhi. I'm sorry to disturb you, but I need some supplies."

The old Indian swept his arm around the store. "Help yourself. Whatever I have is yours."

Allie stood to one side, watching. Obviously the three people shared great affection for one another. It was also obvious that Reeve was part Indian. They knew his brother. Yet who were they? The old man had called him 'son.'

"I'll just take a few things," Reeve answered. "I'll only be gone a couple days."

"I'll get a pack ready." The woman had already started around the store, picking up things and piling them on the counter.

The inside of the store was just as rustic as the outside, Allie noticed. Colorful hand-loomed rugs decorated the wood walls. Everything from baskets to vases made from sand, lined the shelves. In addition to food, little cloth dolls and turquoise jewelry littered the tables set up in the aisles.

A pop machine stood near the back and a pay telephone hung on the wall beside her.

A *telephone*.

Slowly Allie turned her head to stare at it. All she had to do was dial the operator and give her location. Which was? She could tell them she was in Arizona, near the Navaho reservation. There had to be police nearby. They would come and help her. Reeve was busy talking. And she had to get away. Didn't she?

Surreptitiously, watching him the entire time, she lifted the receiver and started to dial the number.

"Are you having trouble with the phone, dear?" the woman asked, coming up beside her. "I'm sorry, but Reeve didn't introduce us. What's your name?"

"Alanna Martin."

"Why, that's very pretty. Did you have a hard trip, Alanna?"

"Yes," Allie answered, realizing that the woman had noticed her dress, which was dirty and wrinkled.

"The hardest part is ahead of you. I'll make sure you've got plenty of supplies. Go ahead and make your call now," she went on, "but don't worry if you have trouble. That phone doesn't always work well. It's connected to the Navaho system. Just be patient and stay on the line. The operator will eventually answer."

When Reeve turned around to glance at her, Allie regretted even thinking of making a call. "Alanna must have knocked the receiver off the hook by mistake, Jean," he said. "She doesn't want to make a call."

"Really?" The woman frowned. "I would have sworn she was making a call."

"I was just waiting for Reeve, and I backed too close to the phone." Replacing the receiver, Allie moistened her lips nervously, waiting for him to turn back to the old man. Maybe she could appeal to the woman for help.

"Well, now, if you wait for Reeve you could wait forever," the old woman chatted away. "Many women have. Say, do you like smoked beef? I have some in back."

"Beef would be fine," Allie answered, but as soon as Reeve turned from her, she clutched at the woman's arm. "Ma'am? Please, ma'am," she whispered. "Can you help me? I'm in trouble."

The woman was instantly sympathetic. She frowned. "Why, what's the problem, dear?"

"Reeve—" Allie cleared her throat and glanced at him. "Reeve has kidnapped me, and he's taking me to the desert. Can you help me get away?"

The sympathetic expression remained, but the woman's voice was firm. She pursed her lips. "Reeve Chandler doesn't have to kidnap his women, Miss Martin," she said quietly. "They flock to him. But if he has kidnapped you, then he had good reason. I'm sorry. I can't help you."

Allie must have looked as surprised as she felt. Kidnapping was a federal offense. Surely aiding and abetting a kidnapper was a crime, too. Would no one help her?

"I'm sorry," the woman said again, shaking her head. "I'm so sorry."

Not knowing what else to do, Allie glanced around, but before she could think of another question, Reeve came and took her arm, leading her back outside. "We better go. The tourists will be up soon."

"Do you want some smoked beef, Reeve?" the woman asked him. "I can get it from the back."

"Don't worry about it, Jean. We'll be fine. I'll catch some game or make some fry cakes. You could put Allie in some clothes—a pair of jeans if you have them."

"No, thank you," Allie cut in. "I'll wear what I have on."

He glanced at her. "You're going to be uncomfortable."

"I'll survive."

Didn't he realize that taking the clothes would be like admitting defeat, admitting that she would never get away? As long as she kept on her clothes there was hope. But he just shrugged and steered her toward the door.

The old Indian man followed them to the Jeep. Reeve helped Allie in on her side and then went around and hopped in behind the wheel. Starting the engine, he paused. "By the way, Danhi, there are some people following me," he said.

"The police?"

Reeve nodded. "The police, too, but they'll probably show up later."

"This is the reservation. They do not have jurisdiction here."

"They'll still have questions. Though it's the other men I'm worried about," Reeve explained. "Don't put yourself in danger. Tell anyone who comes where I've gone."

The old Indian tossed his head toward Allie, his expression a question.

"Her uncle is a United States senator," Reeve said.

"You're taking her to the desert?"

Reeve nodded.

Talk about insults. His manner indicated he thought she was weak.

"And you?" the old Indian asked.

"I'll be fine," Reeve answered.

The man Reeve had called Danhi frowned. "I know you'll be fine in body. In spirit I am not so certain. Be careful, Wóódii."

Reeve laughed. "I think you'd like to see me shanghaied, old man. Don't worry. She's not my type."

Though his statement was certainly true, for some reason Allie felt as though he'd insulted her again. Reeve even felt a twinge of conscience. He'd been damned attracted to her.

The old man wasn't fooled. "I'm not worried as much as I am wary," he said. "She is stronger than you think. Take care."

"Take care of yourself," Reeve answered, nodding. Then he drove away.

"What was that all about?" Allie asked when he'd pulled onto the highway going south. By now the sun was beginning its westward trek in the sky, and the day was growing hot.

"Danhi thinks you have put a curse on me."

"A curse?"

"The Navaho are superstitious. Danhi thinks that because I have captured you, that you can now capture my heart."

She hadn't thought he had a heart. And if he did, surely no woman would ever be able to capture it. Maybe want it, but they'd find he was as elusive as she'd found him to be. "Are you part Indian?"

"My great-grandmother was Navaho."

So her image of him on a great white stallion carrying his war lance hadn't been all fantasy. "Do you live on the reservation?"

"No, I have a ranch over near Flagstaff, in the San Francisco Mountains. But I used to live here, and I'm familiar with the area."

"Is that why you're meeting Sammison here?"

"Yes. The area is mostly desolate. I don't want to endanger more people than I have to."

"What about your friends?"

"Danhi and Jean will be fine."

"Are they husband and wife?"

"Yes."

That was all he had to say? "Reeve?"

"Yes?"

"Thank you for the jacket last night."

"You're welcome. I'd forgotten it was in back."

She sighed. "What are we going to do now?" She supposed she had accepted her lot. Like it not, she was still with him.

"I have to meet Sammison in the morning," he said. "For now, we're going to lose ourselves in the desert."

As she had several times that morning, Allie glanced back behind them. Still no one followed.

"They're there," Reeve said.

"The police?"

"No. Sammison. The Mob."

"How do you know?"

"I can feel it."

Strangely, so could Allie. She glanced to the scenery on both sides of the road. It hadn't changed a bit, except perhaps to grow more barren and desolate. She knew the danger that lurked behind them, but what was out there, in the desert?

She hated to admit it, but Reeve was right: she wasn't very strong.

Chapter Six

The desert was all that Alanna had thought it would be: hot, tiring, desolate. Reeve had told her that this area wasn't really considered the desert; the real desert was south of here. But to her, the landscape seemed so barren it could have been the Sahara. He had turned off the road a few yards from the trading post, headed toward the buttes and cliffs in the distance. For the next several hours the only landscape she could see was rocky soil and miles and miles of sagebrush-tufted sand. So when he topped a hill and came to a clump of trees, she was really surprised.

The small grove of green looked out of place in the sun-baked, red-hued atmosphere. Considering what they had driven through all morning, it was almost lush. Cottonwood and box elder trees and even a few clumps of grass clung to the barren soil.

"There's a river here," she said, noticing the small stream meandering through the grove of green.

"It's really a wash," Reeve answered, parking the Jeep deep in the trees and getting out, "for when the rains come. We're lucky there's some water. This time of year there's not usually much left."

"It rains here?" Getting out behind him, Allie glanced around, unwilling to believe that the terrain surrounding the tiny oasis had seen water for centuries.

"July and August are considered the monsoon season. It rains almost every day." Kneeling on the bank, he splashed water over his face. Now she could see that the stream was shallow and narrow. "The rains can be fairly devastating, too," he went on, moistening a large handkerchief and tying it around his forehead, Apache style. Now he looked even more Indian. "There are flash floods and homes washed away. Campers killed. Don't drink the water."

She nodded, kneeling also to wash her face. If that was what happened, she was thankful it was only June. But then again it was just past noon, and the sun was so intense she felt her skin sizzle. The shade of the trees was a welcome respite. But some raindrops would have been welcome.

"Do you have a kerchief?" Reeve asked.

"No."

Going to the Jeep, he rummaged around in the pack and found a length of cloth. "Wet this and wrap it around your head."

Realizing the folly of objecting, Alanna dipped the cloth into the stream and tied it around her head. It felt cool against her scalded skin.

"Come on," he said, shouldering the pack and starting to walk away. "We've still got several miles ahead of us. I want to get there before dark."

Allie knelt by the wash, staring at him. "Come on? Where are we going?"

"To meet Sammison."

Reeve hadn't waited for her. He'd just tossed the words over his shoulder as he plowed through the light underbrush. "Wait a minute," she called. "I thought you were meeting Sammison in the morning."

"I am."

"Where, for God's sake?" And where in the world was he going now?

"South of here."

"South of here, how far?" she shouted, knowing what was coming, but denying it. He had left the Jeep and was walking out into the desert—into the hot, desolate sand. "Reeve, what about the car?"

"It's a Jeep. I'm leaving it here."

Scrambling to her feet, she tried to catch up to him. But her high heels kept sinking into the sand. "Reeve, wait," she called. "I don't understand. Why are you leaving the car—the Jeep?" she corrected. "How far is it to where you're meeting this man?"

He turned to her. "I'm leaving the Jeep because I don't want anyone to see me approach in the morning. On these dusty roads, driving a vehicle is like handing out a calling card, and I need the element of surprise. Since this is one of the few areas in the desert in which to hide anything big, it happens to be the best place to leave the Jeep."

At last he'd spoken to her in more than monosyllables. But what a speech. She'd caught up to him and she stood staring at him incredulously. "You're going to *walk* to where you're meeting Sammison?"

"Yes."

"And you expect me to go with you?"

"You are my hostage."

She kept staring at him. Finally she shook her head. "I'm not going."

He shrugged and turned away, starting to walk again. "Suit yourself."

What a strange attitude. He was letting her stay? That surprised her as much as anything else. She'd thought he needed her. "Reeve, I can't walk in that sand," she said, trying to explain. "I have heels on."

"Take them off."

"I don't have any other shoes."

He shrugged again. "Break off the heel."

She was horrified at his suggestion. "These shoes cost a fortune."

He paused and turned to her, patiently. "For all that they cost, they're not doing you much good now. You've taken off your jacket even though it goes with your dress. What's the big deal about fixing your shoes so you can walk?''

He still thought she was a stupid woman, and treated her as such. He didn't understand that it wasn't fashion that kept her from doing all those things—it was principle. She dug in her heels. "Look, Reeve, you've kidnapped me, and you've bossed me around and dragged me to this godless state. I understand that you're desperate, but I'm telling you, no matter what you do to me now, or how you threaten me, I am not going to walk in that desert.''

''I suppose you'd rather die when Sammison sees us approaching tomorrow.''

That did sound silly. "No, but if I walk in that desert I'll sweat to death. It's hot.''

''There's no humidity, Allie,'' he reminded her.

''It's still hot.''

''I gave you a headband. Do you want a hat?''

''I want to go home,'' she said.

''Sorry.''

''I'm not going,'' she repeated, but he had fixed the pack again and turned away, walking from her. ''Reeve!'' she shouted, stamping her foot angrily. ''I'm not going.''

He flicked his gaze back at her. ''Fine. See you tomorrow.''

He was just going to leave her?

''Oh.'' He turned back to her. ''By the way, watch out for the snakes.''

Damn! Damn the man! Involuntarily she glanced at the ground. ''There are snakes here?''

''Rattlers. Sometimes they nest in groups. There are scorpions, too. If they get on your body at night you have to flick them off carefully. They'll sting you if they feel threatened.''

''Oh, God.'' She hated reptiles and insects, and shuddered to think how she'd survive a night alone. ''Darn it!'' She kicked the sand.

Reeve paused just over a hill, leaning on a tall rock and waiting, as if he had known all along that she would come running. At least he didn't lord it over her. When she reached his side, he said, "Do you want me to fix your shoes so you can walk?"

Allie had a real stubborn streak. Sometimes it overrode her common sense, and it surged to the fore now. So he thought she wasn't very strong, did he? Well, he'd see just how strong she could be.

"No," she said angrily, swishing out into the desert in front of him. With each step she sank into the sand. "I'll wear them just like they are."

"Fine."

She could hear the laughter bubbling up in him, but ignored it, just like she tried to ignore him. She found it more difficult to ignore the heat and the sand. The farther she walked—or rather, struggled—the hotter it got, and the harder it became to put one foot in front of the other. The sun beat down on them relentlessly. Allie's lips were dry and parched, and her legs felt as though they were going to collapse under her. Her back ached from walking at an angle. She thought surely it would break and fold her in two. Still she wouldn't admit that he was right and give him her shoes. She knew her behavior went beyond stubborn, but it was the only thing that kept her plodding through the god-awful sand.

Reeve didn't seem the least bothered by the strenuous activity or by the heat. He wasn't even puffing. Between her back and her legs, Allie wasn't certain which hurt the most. And her mouth was drier than the desert itself. She kept in front of him by sheer willpower alone.

Just when she thought she could not possibly take another step, Reeve stopped. "Hold up, Allie," he said. "Don't you think you're being silly? You're ready to drop." When she paused and turned around, he held out the canteen. "Here. Drink some water."

She might have taken the water had he not called her silly. Or ordered her. She was sick and tired of his orders. No matter how he made her feel in more serene moments. Allie shook her head stubbornly. "No, thank you."

"Aren't you thirsty?"

"No."

"I see."

But from the way he was looking at her he didn't see. "I'm fine," she insisted.

"All right, you're fine," he agreed. "Here." He picked up a small pebble and handed it to her. "If you won't drink, at least put this under your tongue. It'll stimulate your salivary glands and keep your mouth wet."

Just like a dog. She lifted her chin angrily. "I don't need my salivary glands stimulated. I told you I'm fine. And my mouth is perfectly fine, too."

"Right." He raked his gaze over her, taking in her dirty dress, bare legs, straggly hair. "I hate to tell you, but you sure look fine."

Why was he provoking her this way? "Have you ever glanced in a mirror?" she returned smartly. "You don't look so great yourself."

"This isn't a contest, Allie."

"No," she agreed. "It's some kind of vendetta."

He sighed. "Why the hell are you being so stubborn?"

"Because I *like* to be stubborn," she retorted. "No man tells me what to do. Including you. I won't have any water, and you can't make me drink."

He swore. His eyes, driven by their own power, roved over her curvaceous if tattered form, and against his better judgment, he caved into his admiration. The tension ripened between them, and he imagined what it would be like to crumple her into his arms, and smother those sweet lips with his own.

Allie had frozen, soaking in the charged air. The thrust of her jaw had softened, she seemed to lean toward him.

Suddenly he swore crudely again. He turned and stalked away. Next thing he knew he'd be raping her. It was bad enough he had hauled her into the desert, used her as a hostage, made her life miserable. She was such an innocent. Besides, he didn't have time for a relationship, not now, not ever. An involvement with Allie would be consuming. She wasn't your ordinary one-night stand. Unlike the women he knew. She was something special, something to treasure. And he had his brother, Curt, to think of. Curt who was in that lousy jail, his time rapidly running out. If Reeve didn't get him released soon, the Germans would begin the next phase. And then all the world couldn't save his brother.

A few minutes later Reeve returned, handing her the canteen. He didn't seem angry anymore, but his jaw was set in a hard line. "Here."

Allie had dropped to the ground, shaken by their encounter. She hadn't had much experience with sex, but she could tell when a man wanted her. The swift, hard reaction of Reeve's body to hers had frightened her more than the danger they were in. And she had responded to him. She had wanted him, too, in that flash of an instant. What in the world had gotten into her? She had to remember that he was a dangerous man. A maverick, a rogue, a man who was all heartache.

Subdued now, ready to cooperate, she took the container from him and swallowed greedily. Though it was warm, the water was wet. It tasted cool and refreshing. Why on earth had she refused it?

"Don't drink too much."

Nodding, she handed the canteen back to him. "Thanks."

Reeve didn't remark. Recapping the water, he tossed the container aside. "Give me your shoes."

Silently she pulled them off her feet and handed them to him. "They do this in the movies," he said charmingly, then he ripped off the heels in one swift jerk. He handed them back. "It should work." Then he picked up the pack. "Now. Let's go."

Allie just sat there. "I can't wear them," she said quietly.

"Why?" He turned back to her, his expression still hard and set.

"It's more difficult to walk in them this way."

"You can't go barefoot. Your feet will bleed."

She got up from the ground and brushed off her dress. "It appears I don't have much choice."

"Fine," he said. "Go barefoot. Maybe it'll do you good to suffer. Put a pebble in your mouth and find something to cover your head. The cloth tied around your head isn't enough. You're starting to burn."

He was just now noticing? They'd been in the desert for two days. "What should I use?"

"I don't know." He gestured to her outfit. "Your sleeves are still around. Or use that fancy underwear."

What was it with people out West and her underwear? Hadn't anyone this way seen red lace before? "My underwear is taffeta," she said.

"Is something wrong with taffeta?" he asked.

She wasn't being stubborn now, just practical. "It's hot. It doesn't breathe."

"I see," he said again. "God knows I wouldn't want you to be hot."

"What?" she asked, squinting at him, ready to spar with him again.

"Never mind." He whipped the handkerchief from around his forehead and tied it over her head, covering most of her hair and the cloth he knotted on earlier. His movements were jerky and hurried, and his expression was so rigid his face might have cracked.

Knowing she'd pushed him beyond his limits, was in fact still pushing him, Allie wanted to say something to diffuse the situation. "Thank you for the water, Reeve," she murmured as he fiddled with her hair.

"Sure."

She drew in a sigh. Couldn't she ever please him? He couldn't even accept an apology from her. "Why are you so nasty to me?"

"I'm not nasty to you."

"Yes, you are. You're either nasty to me, or you ignore me, or you speak to me in one-syllable sentences. I still don't know what's going on, why you're doing this." She gestured around the desert.

"I told you my brother is in jail in East Germany."

"You think I'm stupid, too."

Now he sighed. "I'm not a patient man, Allie, and for some reason you try what little patience I do have."

"I don't mean to," she said. "I just want to understand, and it's so hot," she concluded lamely.

"I know."

She glanced at the trail ahead of them, at the miles and miles of sand stretching beyond the horizon. It wasn't really sand, but rocky soil that had eroded over thousands of years from wind and weather. "Did you know I've never seen sand before except in a play lot?"

"Haven't you ever been to the beach?"

She shook her head. "I was a privileged suburban kid. We had heated pools. Sand is too messy. Even now I live in an apartment with a pool."

They stood in the middle of the wilderness, talking quietly. "Didn't you ever go on vacation? To Florida or California?"

"No." She gave a light laugh. "My parents are doctors and lawyers. We went to New York City on vacation or on shopping excursions. Occasionally we visited my grandparents in New Jersey. I've never been anywhere except a big city."

"You're doing all right, Allie."

"Am I?" She laughed again, only now it was a mocking sound. "You know, it upset me that you told that old Indian man that I wasn't very strong."

"I could be wrong."

She shook her head. "I doubt it. I would have made a great Southern belle. I would have been perfectly content to wile away my days on the front porch of a plantation, fanning myself and sipping a mint julep. I guess I'm not accustomed to any hardship."

She wasn't accustomed to the sun, either. Unconsciously she rubbed her arms. Now that she had stopped to think about it, they tingled and burned.

Perhaps it was her despondency. Perhaps just plain old human kindness. Allie wasn't sure of the reason, but Reeve knelt on the ground and poured out some water from the canteen, stirring it to make mud.

"Here." He rubbed it on her face and arms. It stung where the sandy soil dug into her tender skin, yet his fingers were gentle. Tender. "This should help."

"Thank you," she said softly, unable to move away. She felt mesmerized by his touch.

He nodded. "Let me know if it starts to hurt again. I'll put some more on. Ready?"

She had to think a moment, to shake off the feel of his hands on her. Then she nodded. "Yes."

As the day wore on, and they walked further into the desert, Allie almost wished she had her temper to sustain her. Since she wasn't wearing shoes, her back felt better, but in addition to her legs aching, her feet had developed a mass of blisters. She couldn't have put her shoes on if she'd wanted to.

"Reeve?" she called after a long while.

"Yes?"

"When are we going to stop?"

"Soon."

"I'm tired." She was growing irritable again.

"Don't think about it."

That's all he ever said, don't think about it. Didn't he ever thing about anything? "What are we going to eat?"

"I'll catch something."

"Reeve, I'm tired," she said again.

"Just a few more miles, Allie."

"My feet hurt," she complained.

If he reacted to her remark, he didn't show it. He just kept walking. She sighed. "After all this, I sure hope we manage to sneak up on him."

"Sammison?"

"No. Goliath."

"You've got a bad temper, Allie," Reeve said, stopping.

Since she was plodding forward, looking at the ground, and not at him, she ran into him. Nearly falling, she glanced up. Reaching out, Reeve caught her and helped her to sit on the ground. It felt so good to be off her feet. Actually it felt good to be in his arms. Comforting. "You all right?"

She nodded. "I gather I'm going to survive." She wasn't sure if her feet were going to make it, though.

He let the pack down beside her. "Who do you take after, Allie? Your mother or your father?"

"My mother has the temper," she answered, knowing what he was getting at, "but my father is stubborn."

"Hold still." Kneeling beside her, he opened the canteen again and poured water over her bare feet. It felt heavenly, cool and soothing. "Better?"

"Mmm," she moaned. "God, that's wonderful."

He laughed. After dabbing her feet dry, he took a first aid kit from the pack and treated her blisters. One by one, he padded them with soft gauze. "There," he said when he was done. "That should help."

Odd, how he could be testy with her at one moment and kind to her the next. Before, when he'd put mud on her face, and now when he treated her feet, he was gentle. Her aches and pains today, she had to admit, had been brought on mostly by herself. "Thanks."

"I'll make you some moccasins after dinner. I noticed Jean put some leather in the pack."

"Are we stopping?"

He nodded. "We'll have to move under that cliff—" he gestured to a butte a few yards away "—so they don't see us if they come tonight."

"Are we that close?"

He gestured again in the distance, only the other way. "The place where I'm meeting Sammison is just over that hill, right off the road. We'll go in around dawn."

She'd heard him tell the old Indian that it was an abandoned gas station. "Then what?"

"After Sammison gives me the papers I need, I'll take you back to the trading post. Jean and Danhi will make sure you get home."

She nodded agreement. It would be wonderful to be home. She would languish in air-conditioned comfort, savor the poolside patio, stroll down cement-lined avenues. Her air conditioner would not be too cool. A perfect seventy-two degrees. And she would never, ever look at a picture of a desert. "And if Sammison doesn't give you the papers?"

"I don't think he'll cross me this time. Your uncle is too influential."

Not influential enough to help her so far, though, she couldn't help thinking. "Do you suppose Sammison ever notified my uncle?"

"If he didn't, the news media has," Reeve answered.

"Do you think my family knows I've been abducted?" When she returned, and if they knew, her father would want two hundred blood tests; and her mother would want to file suit.

"I'd count on it." Reeve held out his hand. "Think you can make it to the butte?"

"I'll try."

Now that she had stopped, it was even harder to walk again. Leaning against him, Allie hobbled over the ground, wincing in pain.

"This is stupid." Suddenly Reeve scooped her into his arms, cradling her against his chest.

"What are you doing?" she asked, startled.

"If you stay off your feet tonight," he said gruffly, start-ing to cart her across the terrain, "maybe you'll be able to walk tomorrow."

Strangely Allie didn't argue. At first she didn't know what to do. She felt confused, bouncing around in his arms with nowhere to put her arms except around his neck. Finally she gave up, clasping her arms around him and resting her head on his shoulder. It felt as comforting as before, when she had slept next to him and had leaned on him. She could hear his heart beat rhythmically.

"Reeve?"

"Yes?"

"I'm sorry I'm such a bother. I should have tried to wear the shoes."

"Might have been a good idea."

"I thought I'd tilt the wrong way."

"Right."

Wasn't he even affected by their closeness? Allie cer-tainly felt something strange happening to her. But the way he dumped her on the ground underneath the cliff and wheeled abruptly away from her, she doubted that he felt anything except impatience. She stared at him. Just when she'd thought they were getting along, he turned into a bear.

The cliff was tall enough for a man to stand under, and when he came back with the pack he towered over her. "Reeve?" she called again, still uncomfortable with the schism she sensed developing between them. "Are you an-gry at me?"

"No."

"Yes, you are."

"No, I'm not, Allie," he said. The less she knew about how she stirred him, the better.

"I'm really sorry I'm such a pain," she went on. "This has been difficult for you, too, hasn't it?"

"No."

"Please talk to me," she said.

He had been going about his business, unzipping the pack, pulling out utensils, gathering tumbleweed, piling it together for a fire. He paused and stared at her for a long moment. "What do you want to talk about?"

She didn't know where to begin.

"I don't mean to be so stubborn. I just can't help it."

"It's all right, Allie."

"No, it isn't."

He stared at her again. "Shall we argue about it?"

Why couldn't she say the right things to him? She shook her head. "No. I don't want to argue."

"Neither do I." Now he nodded. "How are your feet?"

"Better."

"Good, we'll have dinner soon."

"Aren't you hot? Tired?"

"Not really. I like the desert."

He would. He was the type of man who could fight the elements and win. She could see him now, on his horse, war lance in hand, challenging the sun and the stars and the moon, pulling them from the sky.

My, she was getting poetic. She must have had too much sun.

"Want to wash off the dirt?" Reeve asked. He tossed her the canteen and a washcloth.

She caught them both. "Thanks."

"Just try to conserve the water. It's all we have, and we need it for drinking and cooking."

"Okay." The peace between them felt so pleasant. She just hoped it lasted. Although she didn't use much water, it felt wonderfully soothing. She dabbed the wetted cloth across the parts of her body she could reach. She wasn't about to undress in front of Reeve, and wash full-fledged. He must have felt the same. When she was done, he took a clean cloth and washed, too. She watched him, the supple movements of his body. He even moved like an Indian, she thought, smooth, lithe, no wasted motions.

"Do you want to change into those jeans now? I think Jean packed them."

"No." She shook her head, still unwilling to admit defeat. If she wore her dress, then she was preserving her dignity, her self-respect, her identity. But then again, the dress had become so tattered, maybe those qualities would be better served in fresh clothes. Refusing for the moment to change, she studied Reeve. Whether or not he understood her motives, he didn't say. Stalwart as ever. He was pulling several brownish discs from the pack, placing them in the fire. The odor was strong, slightly rancid. "What is that round stuff?" she asked, pointing.

"Sheep chips," he said. "Dried droppings. We use them for fire. Wood's hard to find in this climate."

That was certainly true. Aside from the grove this morning, trees were few and far between. Allie watched him fiddle with dinner. Although she knew the sheep droppings were dried and they were mostly digested grass, the thought of burning them disgusted her. "What are you making?"

"Fry cakes. They're a Navaho staple."

After mixing cornmeal, he placed spoonfuls of the gruel-looking mixture into hot oil to cook. "I thought you might make rattlesnake stew," she said.

"Why?"

"To prove that there are snakes here," she said. "I think you were fooling me. We've walked all day, and I haven't seen a single snake."

He just glanced at her. "They're here. Snakes sleep during the day. It's too hot for them in the sun."

"And the scorpions?"

"They're around, too." Handing her a plate of food, he sat down across from her. It was growing dark, but she could see his features flicker in the light from the fire.

She'd been lying before. He didn't look a bit bedraggled from what they'd been through. He seemed to fit into the harsh environment as though he'd been born into it. In a way he had. Though he was only part Indian, his heritage had to have prepared him for survival. It had given his skin a coppery cast that glistened in the light. His hair, so dark and thick.

She glanced away when he looked up. "Aren't you hungry?" he asked.

She picked up a fork. "Very."

Surprisingly the fry cakes tasted excellent. Then again, she was so starved that just about anything would taste good. "What are they made from?"

"Blue corn."

"That stuff I saw growing in the back of the trading post?"

He nodded. "It looks scraggly, but it bears well."

It had to. Perhaps everything here adapted to the harsh environment. If she stayed long enough she might even get acclimated.

At that, Allie almost laughed.

After dinner Reeve cleared their dishes, swishing them out with sand, and packing them away. Then he retrieved a piece of leather, and started to cut it with a knife he pulled from his boot. It was long and thin and razor-sharp. The blade glinted in the firelight.

"Toss me your shoes," he said. "I'll use them to measure the moccasins for size."

"What are you going to sew them with?"

"I'll punch holes with the knife and make strips from the leather. You just weave it in and out tightly."

She watched, fascinated as he deftly stitched up the moccasins. Suddenly he stopped, turning slightly to stare at the ground beyond the cliff. Allie couldn't see a thing in the inky darkness, but apparently Reeve could.

"Don't move," he said.

With a flick of his wrist, he tossed the knife over near the edge of the rock. It thudded hard into the ground, quivering, as it struck a rattlesnake, slicing off the head.

Going over, Reeve picked up the snake by the tail and held it in the air. "Still want some stew?"

Allie stared at the reptile and shuddered. It was at least four feet long, huge and fat, and it had an entire row of rattles. God, how she hated snakes. "No, thanks."

He tossed it into the desert. "It was attracted by the fire."

"I thought they didn't like heat."

"It's night. It's getting cool now," he said, handing her the moccasins. "Try them on. I think they'll fit."

She slipped them on her feet. They were perfect, soft and supple. They didn't even rub her blisters. She smiled and wiggled her toes, locking eyes with him. "Thank you. These are great. They feel wonderful. Do you think they'll hold up?"

"Indians have used them for centuries. If I'd known they'd make you so happy, I would have made them two days ago."

She laughed. "Am I that irritating?"

"Lady," he said softly, "you drive me nuts." In more ways than one, he mused, though he kept the remark to himself.

She didn't apologize, for she didn't know exactly what he meant. A long, lonely howl broke the silence. She glanced out at the dark night.

"Relax," Reeve told her. "It's just a coyote. They howl mostly at dusk."

"There are so many creatures out here," she said.

"It is a wilderness, Allie."

"It just seemed so quiet today. So desolate."

"The desert is desolate during the day. The animals sleep, avoiding the hot sun. At night they forage for food."

And each other. She could hear them now, hunting, stalking, issuing tiny cries into the night. A hiss sounded beyond the barrier of rocks, followed by a pebble rolling down an incline. Sharp nails scrambling across rock.

Rising, Reeve banked the fire. "Tomorrow morning's going to come early," he said, tossing her a blanket. "We better get some rest."

How were they going to do that? Between him and the snake and the coyote howling, and all the other animals pattering past, killing each other, she would never sleep. She watched as he stretched out his blanket beside her. "Are you going to lay here?"

"Yes."

"Next to me?"

"I'm three feet away."

"I can't sleep with you next to me."

"Sure you can," he said, lying down and covering himself. "Just close your eyes. I told you, I have other concerns. I'm not interested in sex."

"Neither am I."

"Good, then what's the problem?"

"Nothing."

Allie tried to relax. She really did. She took deep breaths, but she kept thinking of the snake. What if there were more of them? He'd mentioned that they nested in groups. What about the scorpions? And where the hell was the coyote? She'd seen pictures of them, and they had ferocious-looking teeth.

"Reeve?"

"What?"

She hated to admit it. "I'm scared."

Silence. "Just go to sleep, Allie."

"I can't."

He sighed. "What do you want me to do about it?"

"Can you build up the fire?"

"We don't have enough fuel. We need to save the chips for cooking. Besides, they won't burn very high."

She breathed in. Any moment now she was going to embarrass herself and cry. Damn, why wasn't she stronger? "Reeve, I can't sleep."

"Look, I'll sit up and keep watch," he said. "Okay?"

He hadn't been close to her at all, considering the actual physical distance between them but when he moved away she felt cold, and more vulnerable than ever. She lay there for a moment. "Do you think you could talk to me again?"

He sighed. If he didn't lull her to sleep, she'd toss and turn all night. He couldn't jeopardize tomorrow. "What do you want to talk about?"

"I don't know. Tell me about your ranch."

There was a pause. "It's a ranch."

"Do you have horses?"

"Yes. Horses, Allie."

"I hate it when you talk in monosyllables and sentence fragments," she said.

Reeve sighed and flopped back down next to her, scooping her into his arms and pulling her against his body. "Lord, lady, you are a trial. I suppose you're cold, too."

"Yes."

"I'll keep you warm. Now close your eyes and go to sleep."

Being near him was even worse than listening to the night creatures. They fit together perfectly, too perfectly, and she felt comfortable in his arms, very comfortable.

Allie started to move, but he just gripped her tighter. "I said, close your eyes, Allie. *Now.*"

Yet he was intimidating. By this time she knew better than to defy him. She would never sleep, but she clamped her eyes shut anyway. It was just one night, she told herself. So what if he had taken her captive? He hadn't hurt her. And it wasn't as if there was anything sexual between them. There was some underlying tension, but they had both practically signed a pact against sex. So why couldn't they come together for warmth and comfort? In just one day she would be back home, and the danger would be over.

Wouldn't it?

Chapter Seven

It was still dark when Reeve woke Allie, shaking her gently. "Allie, it's late," he whispered as though someone might overhear. "We've got to get going. I want to get to the gas station well before dawn."

Allie sat up and pushed her hair back from her face. She combed back the tangled mess into some semblance of order and tried to ignore the ache that throbbed in her head. Along with every bone in her body. She felt as if she'd been hit by a Mack truck. Perhaps it was from lying on the ground. Sleeping in her clothes for the second night in a row hadn't done her dress much good. Between the dirt, wrinkles and rips, it had aged irreparably. Her belt had come off sometime during the night and lay abandoned nearby. She'd leave it behind. Anticipating the heat of the day, she removed her jacket. What must she look like?

Reeve didn't give her time to ponder her appearance. Rushing her along, he took her blanket and folded it, shoving it into the pack. He handed her one of the leftover fry cakes that had dried and hardened. "Here, better have something to eat."

"Do you have any coffee?" she asked. Along with everything else, she was physically exhausted. Although she had slept in his arms all night, her head cradled on his shoulder, she felt dead tired, as though she hadn't so much as closed her eyes. Yet she knew she'd slept like a corpse. She hadn't even turned over.

"Sorry. I didn't want to build a fire. We're close enough to the road that someone might see the smoke. How about some water instead?"

Nodding understanding, Allie drank from the canteen he handed her and bit into the flat corn cake, telling herself that in just a few hours she could have all the coffee she wanted. And a comb. As soon as she was rescued she would take a long, luxurious bath, and do her nails, and brush her hair until it shone—after she took some aspirin. God, her head hurt.

"Do you want to wash up?"

She glanced at him. Odd that he'd offered. "Won't you need the water for later? For drinking."

"I could probably use it."

She kept looking at him, trying to figure out the puzzle. What was this man really involved in? Whatever it was, it was complicated. "Reeve, where are you going after you meet Sammison today?"

"Back to Denver."

"What about your brother?"

"That's why I'm going to Denver." He turned to her. "I plan to meet the FBI and trade the names for Curt's release."

"The names of the East German spies?"

"Yes."

"I thought the FBI didn't want their names released."

"They don't. They don't have a choice. I intend to release them anyhow."

"Reeve?" she said abruptly. "What exactly did your brother do?"

"I told you he was accused of spying."

"And?"

He paused. "What do you mean?"

"I hate to sound so callous about this," she said softly, "I understand that you care for your brother deeply, but if he's a spy, doesn't he deserve to be in jail? Spying *is* illegal."

"He's a CIA agent, Allie. There's a difference. When you're doing something illegal in the name of your government, it gets all mixed up with patriotism."

She wasn't certain about whether that made sense. "What do those East Germans do here?"

"They spy, too."

"No. I mean, what do they do in Denver that they have the opportunity to spy?" she asked.

"They work in the plutonium plant."

She frowned. That meant the East Germans were very close to this country's source of nuclear fuel. And nuclear weaponry. She vaguely recalled some articles she'd read. "People used to demonstrate there?"

"I believe they still do."

She nodded, comprehending. "Then the East German spies give the East German government our secrets."

"Right, but they're double agents."

"They're spying for their government, but they're really working for the United States government," she clarified.

He nodded. "They tell the East Germans what we tell them to say. They give our supposed secrets."

"Why?"

He shrugged. "Life, liberty, the pursuit of happiness. This is the land of opportunity, Allie." He had packed their belongings, and he sat on a rock beside her, biting into his own corn cake. "I'm sure they want to live here as much as anyone else."

"But they're betraying their government."

"True."

"And if you trade for them, they'll die," she said. "Their government will kill them."

"Probably."

That he took it so lightly surprised her. "How can you—isn't that murder?"

"Maybe. In the strict sense of the word, maybe it is. I don't know anymore." He stared at her as though judging how much he could tell her, how much she would believe. "Allie, the last time I heard from my brother was a week ago. He was in a hospital, and he got a message out with a visiting doctor."

"Was he sick?"

"No, not really sick. He'd been bitten by a rat. It was only on his toe, and nothing was really wrong with it, but the East Germans swore that it had turned to gangrene."

"How awful," she said, her heart pounding.

"It's worse than that. They're preparing a history, in case the government comes looking for my brother. You see, when prisoners don't respond, and the U.S. government doesn't come after a time, the captors turn to more drastic measures."

Allie shook her head. "I don't understand. They have him in a hospital, and they're treating him for gangrene."

Reeve's eyes darkened, his body sagged. "No, Allie, they're getting ready to torture him. Everyone in the field knows how. First it's a toe, then it's the foot, then it's—"

Allie cupped her ears. "All right, all right, Reeve," she said, feeling her stomach lurch. "They can't do that."

"Tell them," he said.

She wished she could. She wished, even more, she could comfort Reeve. Though he had dragged her into the desert, and was using her as a hostage, she wanted to take him into her arms and soothe the hurt, the pain he had suffered. It was obvious that he had suffered right along with his brother. How unfair life could be. "What about our government? Can't they do something?"

"They've denied his existence, remember?"

"But if they know about what the East Germans are capable of, won't they do something? He's an American. And he's a CIA agent."

Reeve laughed, that low, rumbling sound that even now sounded sexy, only it was laced with bitterness. "Allie, the

United States government isn't going to help my brother. Not unless I force them into it.''

Allie sighed.

"I don't even know if he's dead or alive," Reeve went on, "As I said, that was a week ago. But I have to keep trying to help him, prevent the worst from happening. I have to get him out of there.''

Tears sprang to her eyes. She fought them down. She may not agree with his philosophy, but she could certainly understand his goal. "Reeve, why did your brother join the CIA?''

He glanced at her sharply. "It doesn't really matter, does it?''

She shook her head. "No. I suppose not. How—how old is he?'' she asked, for another crazy reason not wanting to break the tenuous bond they had managed to form.

"Twenty-five. He's just a kid. Funny thing," Reeve continued, his expression one of regret, "had he just talked, he wouldn't be in the hospital. All he had to do was tell them what he knew.''

Allie didn't have any problems understanding that, either, not if Reeve's brother was anything like the man with whom she'd spent the past few days. "You wouldn't have talked, would you?'' she asked softly.

"I guess not,'' he admitted.

"Patriotism?''

His laugh was still bitter. "No. Hell, no. God, it's crazy, isn't it? Curt wouldn't talk, and I wouldn't have talked, and every damned time somebody suffers. And all because of some damned warped sense of being a man.''

He would pride himself on being strong, invulnerable. "What about the East German authorities? How do you know they'll release your brother?''

"I don't. But it's another chance I have to take. Actually it's my only chance. I figure I won't give them the names until Curt's been released to another country.'' He glanced at the lightening sky. "Look, Allie, I know you'd love to talk, but we have to hurry. Get your stuff together."

How he confused her. One moment he was so kind, the next, cold and abrupt. Somehow he seemed different this morning. Hard again. Tough. His height and size, threatening. What had happened to the man who had embraced her all night to keep her from being afraid? The man who had shown such compassion on the trail? Made her moccasins?

Perhaps it was the gun he had pulled from his boot that made her remember the danger they were in. She'd forgotten about the weapon. It looked so deadly as he flipped open the chamber and checked the bullets. "Things could get sticky this morning, couldn't they?" she asked softly.

"A bit," he answered without turning to her. "If you do what I say, everything will go fine."

Curiosity, more than any sense of moral judgment, made her ask. "Reeve? Is it difficult to kill people? What's it like to take a life?"

He stopped in the midst of checking his gun and stared at her. "Why?"

"I just wondered."

In one quick motion, he flipped the chamber back in place and shoved the weapon back down in his boot. "I play this little game, Allie. It's called survival, and sometimes people get hurt. It's unfortunate, but that's life. Have you got your moccasins?"

"Yes."

"Be sure and shake them out before you put them on. Out here you need to look out for scorpions. They can get inside your shoes. Do you want any more fry bread?"

"No."

He hoisted the pack onto his shoulders. "Then let's go."

Just like that?

But Allie didn't know what else to say. What had she expected. A ceremony? Goodbyes? She didn't even know him. Yet she felt like she'd known him forever.

Without further discussion, she stood and walked in front of him. Reeve carried their things. When they topped the hill, he swung the heavy pack off his back and carried it in his hand, as though ready to let go at any moment and draw his weapon.

No cars were at the station. It was old and run-down, long abandoned. The roof was caved in in places, and the sides had huge holes. Several boards hung at right angles to the ground. Even from a distance, the gasoline pumps looked rusty and out of place. Tumbleweed had caught in the hoses coiling around the ancient pumps, and wind had piled sand in tiny drifts at their bases. A gentle wind fluttered a stray piece of paper up against an old tire rack. Someone's garbage. It fluttered up and down. Up and down, the soft sound was loud in the still air.

Ominous.

"Hold up a minute," Reeve said from behind her when they had gotten close. "Better let me go in front. Crouch down and stay behind me."

"There's no one here."

"Never trust appearances, Allie. You get hurt that way—or worse."

Though she was going home, her heart had already started to thud with dread and the anticipation of danger. At his statement, the dread soared. "Would they hurt us?"

"Just stay behind me."

But no one was at the station yet. After Reeve had examined every inch of the building, he propped the pack against a rickety wall. "Looks like we're the first to arrive," he said. He motioned her down and handed her the canteen. "Here. Have a sip. Relax for now."

Sure. As if she could relax. By now she was so keyed up, worried about what would happen, that the blood roared in her ears, and her pulse pounded frantically. Anything could go wrong. "What time are they supposed to be here?"

"Dawn."

It was already dawn. The curtain of dark had lifted quickly, turning the sky to the leaden gray that always heralded the sun's arrival. The moment hovered between night and day. "Do you think—maybe they might not come?"

"Sammison will be here."

"Where do you think he is?" she whispered. More than anything, the wait was making her nervous.

"On his way." Reeve was typically short.

ADRENALINE SURGED THROUGH Paul Sammison's veins, making his heart beat faster than normal. But it beat with anticipation. Along with his driver, he'd been riding for hours, all the way from Kansas City, where he'd flown yesterday. It was worth the sacrifice, though. What was fatigue? Any moment now he would arrive at the rendezvous point, the old abandoned gas station where he planned to usher Reeve Chandler home. To his maker.

The portly man with him spoke up. "Do you think I should slow down?"

They were traveling fast on the dirty road, and a ball of dust blew around them. "No. Chandler knows we're coming."

"We're early. I figured we'd beat him there."

Paul Sammison shook his head and smiled. They'd never beat Chandler. Not at the espionage game. They had to outwit him, without his knowing he was being outwitted. "If you think you're going to surprise Reeve, forget it. He's already there."

"How do you know?"

"Because I know Chandler. Besides," he added, his heart beating faster, "I can feel it."

"What about the girl? Can her uncle give us any trouble?"

"If she gets hurt, maybe. But she could have an accident," Sammison suggested. He tsked. "Terrible tragedy."

"Good idea." The portly man smiled.

"We'll make sure it looks like Chandler did it. She probably already knows too much, anyway. No loss. The advantage is on our side there," Sammison went on. "Chandler won't want her hurt. We just have to be careful to play the game on our terms."

"Which are?"

"We have the upper hand. If this works our way, we're both going to get a promotion."

"And if it doesn't?"

Sammison stared at the man driving. "You know, Dirk, you ask all the wrong questions."

Dirk just shook his head. "I'm a realist. You know as well as I do that anything could go wrong. Maybe you should have called Denny to meet us. I like the way he handles things. Nice and easy. No mess."

"What? And let the agency know I'm involved with the Mob?" They had a helicopter trailing behind them, ready to gun Chandler down the minute the girl was safely inside the car. "I'm not that stupid. Besides, Denny's people have been chasing Chandler for days. They haven't managed to catch up to him yet."

"The man eludes the Mob, he eludes the agency, he eludes the Germans, he eludes the police. Sounds like a slippery devil. He could elude us."

"He won't." Of that Sammison was certain. He was going to blow Reeve Chandler sky-high. But if he did not succeed, German agents waited in Vegas. "Don't worry, I have an alternate plan."

"Always thinking, aren't you?" Dirk smiled. "You know, one of these days Chandler is going to figure we're on our own and go over your head."

"He already knows I'm acting on my own," Sammison answered, "but don't worry, he won't notify anyone. Not as long as I've got the names he needs." Anxious now for action, he pulled a gun from an ankle holster and twirled the chamber. "Why don't you step on the gas, Dirk?" he said. "It's time to get this little chore over with."

ALLIE AND REEVE WAITED by the old abandoned building. Time ticked by slowly. The sun rose in the sky, casting a red hue over the desert.

Red like blood.

Suddenly Allie noticed a cloud of dust gathering in the distance. A calling card. She glanced at Reeve, her heart pounding with a combination of anticipation and dread. "Is that them?"

"I imagine so." Taking the canteen from her, Reeve helped her to her feet. "Look, they want you alive, Allie. Remember that."

Gosh. Suddenly she knew it was going to be even worse than she had thought. "Why?"

"Because you're an innocent pawn in all this," he said. Then he winked at her, like he had that day back at the motel. He handed her the unspiked shoes from the pack, along with her belt and jacket. "Take care, pretty lady. I hope you get your designs back. And don't make any detours, like last time."

For once Allie didn't care about her designs. And his calling her *lady* didn't frighten her at all. She clutched the shoes in her hands. "Reeve, what will they do to me?"

"Don't panic, Allie," he answered. "They'll just question you."

"Debriefing?"

He frowned. "Yes, why? Where'd you hear that term?"

"Television." Along with cop shows, she watched spy programs occasionally. *Equalizer*, *Magnum P.I.* Her heart thudded erratically as the ball of dust grew larger and closer. Just what did debriefing entail? Would they let her take aspirin? This was the Central Intelligence Agency she would be dealing with. The same Central Intelligence Agency Reeve had been dealing with. Would they torture her? Oddly the thought of what was about to transpire made her heart start to hammer in fear. Once on *Miami Vice* the good guys were so bad they made the criminals look downright virtuous.

"I'll bet you watch cop shows," Reeve said.

"Miami Vice," she murmured, feeling more and more anxious as he led the way around to the front of the building. What a crazy thing, to be afraid of her rescuers. Only three days ago this man had scared her. He still scared her. His size, his physical prowess, his desperation. The feelings he gave her scared her, too. The wisps of awareness up her spine. The lurch of her heart when she looked at him. The breathless anticipation at the thought of his touch.

He laughed. "Figures."

She had turned to him to see what he meant, when the black sedan shot out of the dust ball and skidded to a stop just yards away from them. Sand sprayed up around the tires.

"Stay right in back of me," Reeve said, shoving her behind his body as he stepped forward and cocked the gun. "And remember, unless I tell you otherwise, as soon as they give me the briefcase, run like hell."

Allie's panic grew. "Run?"

"Yes."

"Why?"

"Because they're probably going to shoot."

"I thought they wanted me alive."

"They do, but they want me dead."

Apparently the once-shiny black car was fully air-conditioned; the windows were closed and darkened.

Heaven.

Or impending hell, depending on your point of view and what was going to happen.

Allie didn't know what to think. She watched as a short balding man wearing sunglasses got out of the driver's side and closed the door. A tall blond man carrying a briefcase stepped from the passenger side. Sammison, she presumed.

"Chandler?" he called, closing the door, too, and leaning against it. The gray three-piece pinstripe suit he wore looked out of place in the red landscape. He shaded his eyes. "Where's Miss Martin?"

"Right here," Reeve answered. "Behind me."

"Is she hurt?"

"She's fine."

"You're in a world of crap, Chandler. Her uncle's madder than a wet hornet."

Reeve didn't remark one way or the other. "Do you have the names this time?"

"With a trump card like her? Of course." Sammison slid the briefcase he was carrying along the ground. It skidded to a stop in front of Reeve's boots. "Send Miss Martin over, and we'll call it a deal."

So her uncle had made a difference. In a way, Allie was pleased. In another, she was just frightened. She started forward, like Reeve had told her, but he pulled her back. "No. Stay here." He turned to the tall blond man. "Just like the deals we've made in the past? Open the envelope you've got tucked in your suit jacket and pull out the papers. Toss them over here so I can read them."

"You don't miss a thing, do you?" Sammison said.

"I've been around the block once or twice," Reeve answered. "What's in the briefcase? A bomb?"

"I'm not stupid, Chandler."

"Neither am I. You could be more original, you know. Toss over the papers."

"How about if I hand them to you? You can't read them if they're on the ground."

"I'll try hard. Just slide them over." Reeve cocked his gun to one side slightly, a warning. "*Out* of the envelope and right side up."

When Sammison complied, Reeve didn't reach for either the briefcase or the papers, though he did glance briefly at the typewritten pages spilling out of the envelope. He gestured again with his gun. "Okay, now step away from the car."

"Sure thing." Sammison smiled. "Why don't you send Miss Martin over? You've got what you want."

"Where's your gun?"

"You wouldn't disarm a man, would you?" He gestured around. "Not in this terrain."

"I like staying alive."

"Too bad your brother wasn't as careful as you are," Sammison remarked. "He'd be alive today."

"He'd better be alive," Reeve warned, "or you can count on sharing his fate."

Sammison just shrugged. Without being told, he pulled a pistol from a shoulder holster inside his suit jacket and skidded the weapon across the ground. It landed beside the briefcase.

Reeve gestured to the other man. "Now your partner."

"I'm unarmed."

The other man was wearing sunglasses, and it bothered Reeve that he couldn't see his eyes. Most of the time, when a man was going to make a move, his eyes gave him away. Reeve would have to use some body language of his own. He tipped the gun higher, right in line with the man's forehead. If he fired, the bullet would land smack-dab between his eyes. "And I'm Minnie Mouse."

Noticing the aim, the other man glanced at Sammison and shrugged. Then he scooted over a similar-looking weapon, taking it from a shoulder holster.

"Okay, Chandler," Sammison said, "we've played your game. Now get Miss Martin walking."

"Who's in the back seat?"

"No one."

"Open the doors and let me see."

With a smug smile the tall blond man jerked open the back door to the sedan. They had a clear view inside. It was empty. "Would I lie?"

Reeve just arched an eyebrow. "Okay, Allie," he said to her. "Listen carefully. Walk slowly to the car. Be ready to step aside, and hit the ground if there's any shooting."

"Oh, God," she murmured.

"Go," he said firmly, pulling her out from behind him. "And for God's sake, don't freeze up."

Why was he always so impatient with her? She hadn't even done anything. "I won't," she said, barely above a whisper.

Still clutching the clothes he had handed her, Allie stepped away from Reeve, walking in front of him to the car. Each step seemed like a mile. Ten miles. Twenty. It took an eternity. Any second she expected to be gunned down. All she could think of was bullets flying in every direction.

"Everything's fine, Miss Martin," Sammison said to her when she hesitated. He moved to hold open the car door for her. "You're doing great. Come on, get in."

Allie stepped forward again.

"Come on," he repeated, gesturing to her. "Try to move a little faster."

She wasn't sure what made her glance over the buildings behind them. Perhaps it was her time spent with Reeve, and having to keep an eye fixed over her shoulder. More likely it was the inflection in the man's tone, as though he wanted her in the car and out of harm's way. Quickly. Just as she was about to climb inside, she looked back and realized that the dark speck in the sky was a helicopter, and that it was growing larger. These men had double-crossed Reeve again. They were going to shoot him down from the air.

"Reeve!" she shouted, knowing she had to warn him. "Reeve, look out! There's a helicopter."

"Damn!" Sammison cursed, diving for her. "You dumb bitch! You're going to get us all killed."

But she jumped back, running around the side of the car to escape his lunging hands. "Reeve! Did you hear me? There's a helicopter."

"Get in the car, Allie!" Reeve shouted back. Taking advantage of the foray, he scooped up the guns and the papers, then ran toward her. "Hurry! Start the engine and go."

But the short heavyset man had started for her around the other side of the car. Swiftly, before he could reach her, she opened the door and slid inside. She wanted to huddle up in the seat with her clothes in her hand and fall apart, but she knew she had to do something to get away. Dropping the items, she locked the doors and climbed over to the front seat. The keys were in the ignition, and without even thinking about what she was doing, she turned them.

But her hands and feet were trembling so badly she couldn't get the car started. Pumping the gas pedal, she turned the ignition again. The engine made a grinding noise, then died.

"Start, dammit," she murmured. "Please catch."

Outside, Sammison was shooting at Reeve. Apparently he'd had another gun tucked away somewhere. The bullets rang out in the still air as the helicopter scudded low. The huge rotor blades whirred, stirring up dust and sand. The tufts of tumbleweed that had caught in the pumps skittered across the ground, and the sand swirled into the air. The terrain was torn asunder in a cloudy, red storm.

By then the heavyset man had reached the car door and was jerking on the handle, trying to force it open. Just as he started to smash his fist against the window, the engine caught, sputtering to life. She floored the pedal and shoved the transmission into gear. The car lurched forward, almost crushing the man's feet.

Skidding across the terrain, she narrowly missed Sammison too. She hadn't meant to hurt either agent; she was just nervous, and the car was unwieldy in her hands. And she wasn't even aware that she was helping Reeve. She braked to a halt beside him and leaned across the front seat, tossing open the door. "Get in!"

He jumped inside, not bothering to say thanks. He just held his leg and shouted, "Go! Get the hell out of here!"

Allie didn't need to be told twice. She floored the pedal. The car shot forward like a bullet.

"Wait!" Suddenly, Reeve shouted to her. "Allie, stop! The pack. We're going to need the pack."

"For what?"

"Just pull up over there," he told her. "Try to shield me with the car."

She braked to another skidding halt. Dust swirled around them, but it wasn't enough of a camouflage. As he ran, bullets rained around him, sparking little tufts of sand into the air. Sammison ran toward them, firing rapidly. The other man had moved up, too, closing in. It wasn't until Reeve limped back in the midst of the barrage of gunfire that Allie realized that he was already wounded. Why on earth had he rescued the pack?

"You're hurt," she said when he jumped back in the car. "They've shot you."

He didn't seem concerned. "It's just a flesh wound. Don't worry about it. Go."

"But you're hurt."

"For Chrissake, Allie, will you drive the damned car?"

Sammison and his partner were closing in, running toward the car. "Reeve—"

"I'm going to be more than wounded if we don't get the hell out of here," he cut in. "I'm going to be dead. And you're going to die with me."

"They can't shoot at me," she said, "my uncle is a senator."

Reeve laughed. "Remember my brother?"

When the side window shattered, pierced by a bullet, Allie realized that Sammison and his partner weren't aiming. They were more concerned with capturing Reeve than in saving her. Now they crouched near the ground, just a few feet away, firing one bullet after another. They crawled closer. Where had they gotten the weapons? Apparently they'd had more guns than one each. Overhead, someone in the helicopter was firing a weapon. She'd watched enough cop shows to know that they would aim for the tires.

"Allie!" Reeve shouted. "Will you please go? Drive the damned car."

"Hang on," she answered, coming back to life and flooring the gas pedal. Thinking she was going to hit the building, she swung the car around and headed between the gas pumps. The car bounced to one side, metal grinding as she grazed one of the ancient tanks, but she clung to the steering wheel, tugging it back and forth to maintain control.

"Christ, you're going to get us killed," Reeve muttered as she careened around the other pump, hitting the tire rack now. As she headed toward them, both Sammison and the heavyset man straightened, then turned on their heels. They ran and at the last minute dove to the ground out of her way.

"I'm sorry," she answered back. "Now you know how I felt when you drove."

"But I knew how to drive."

She didn't have a ready comeback for that. He was right. She'd never been a very skillful driver. The first day she'd gotten her driver's license she'd slammed her father's Mercedes into the garage wall. And now, living in the city, she took buses to work. "Where should I go?"

"Straight," he said as an explosion rent the air.

Allie glanced back. The gas pumps had blown up, probably from the force of the collision—or from a stray bullet. Then she realized she'd run over the briefcase.

"What do I do now?" she asked nervously.

"Just keep going."

She kept the foot pedal to the floor. But at the road she didn't know what to do. "Now where?"

"Who the hell cares?" Reeve muttered, then shook off his despondency. "Left," he called out. "Turn left. We've got to lose the chopper."

A difficult task to accomplish. Just as she turned onto the road, the helicopter came through the smoke and flames like a giant mosquito, right on their tail.

"Are you sure it's the government?" Allie asked, trying to look in the rearview mirror at the men hovering above them. One of them leaned out, rifle in hand, firing. She flinched and skidded the car across the road as the shot hit the hood ornament, knocking it off with a thud. One moment it was there, the next it was gone.

Reeve clutched the dashboard with one hand. "Who else would it be?"

"I thought maybe it was the Mob." They were still shouting at each other, the excitement pumping up their adrenaline. "What do you think happened to the Mob?"

Reeve shook his head. "Damned if I know. But this is hardly the time to figure it out."

The helicopter was gaining. Allie glanced around, not knowing what to do again. "Do you have any ideas, Reeve? Where do you want me to go?"

"Up ahead make a hard right."

"Beyond that cliff?"

"Yes."

"It's not a road."

"Oh, hell," he answered. "Now you're going to argue with me? Turn the car, will you, Allie?"

She glanced at him as she pressed on the brake and whipped the steering wheel to the right. The car bumped and lurched over the rugged terrain, but she was more concerned about him. Beads of sweat had broken out on his forehead, and his leg was bleeding. He still held on to the dashboard, but he pressed his other hand around the wound. Blood seeped through his fingers. "Does it hurt badly?"

"No, it tickles. Just watch where you're going, Allie. I'll be fine."

She glanced in the rearview mirror. "We didn't lose them."

"Make a U-turn."

"This isn't a Jeep, you know," she said. The car was hard to handle. "I can't turn on a dime."

"Try a wheel. Now!" he called out suddenly. "Turn right."

The helicopter had kept up with her. And she was headed straight at a cliff. She started to skid to a halt. Panic lanced through her. "Which way, Reeve?"

"Keep going," he said. "Hurry up. Speed."

What was his problem? "We'll hit the cliff!"

"At the last minute, veer to one side."

"You watch wild television programs, too. He's not stupid, Reeve," she shouted above the helicopter's roar. "He's not going to crash into the cliff. I'm sure he can see it as clearly as I can."

"Yes, but he's flying low. Maybe he'll hit the wires when he makes the turn."

"What wires?" Allie hadn't noticed the high-tension wires strung along the road. Where in the world had they come from? Apparently neither had the helicopter pilot. Right then, turning with her, one of the helicopter blades hit something. There was a split-second pause of dead silence. Then a zapping noise like something was being fried, and the chopper exploded in the air.

"Good God," she murmured.

"Get back on the road," Reeve told her. "Quickly. Get the hell out of the way and keep driving."

Allie was too upset not to obey. Whipping the car back onto the road, she pressed on the gas pedal, wanting to flee from the awful scene on the ground as quickly as possible. The helicopter had fallen straight from the sky in the exact position where it had exploded, a fiery ball searing the sand and scrub grass for yards around it. There was no doubt that no one on board had survived.

"Do you think we should stop?" Allie asked.

"For what?"

She shrugged. "They were human beings."

"They were trying to kill us."

She had to agree. But she couldn't dampen her qualms. Her hands started to tremble, and she wanted to cry.

Reeve must have noticed. "Don't fall apart now, Allie," he said to her. "You've got to keep driving."

If only she was a more capable person. *Calm down*, she told herself. *Keep driving*. This was just a little excitement. A little excitement, like any other excitement. She could handle it.

"Where are we going?" It was odd to be on the same side as her kidnapper, cooperating with him. Moments ago she'd verged on getting rescued and going home.

"To get the Jeep."

"What about your leg?" She glanced at his wound. "Is it still bleeding?"

"Unfortunately."

"We should get you to a hospital."

He shook his head. "Just try to get to the trees where we left the Jeep. We'll figure out what to do from there."

"Do you think Sammison—where do you think he went?"

"After all the things he's done to my brother, I'd like to think he's out in the desert stranded with no food and no water and no sense of direction."

She'd heard it was easy to get lost in the desert, particularly when the sun was high in the sky. She was glad Reeve had known where he was going.

"But knowing Sammison," Reeve went on, "he's probably back at the gas station radioing for help."

"Did he have a radio?"

"More than likely. Or else the helicopter could have radioed for help before it crashed."

"Who will come?"

"More CIA agents."

She still felt awful thinking of the crash. "Reeve, what were those wires?"

"Electricity."

"I realize that," she said. "Where did they come from? They seemed so out of place in the middle of the wilderness."

"There are few true wilderness left in the world, Allie. The twentieth century has arrived. Do you remember the hogans we saw at the trading post?"

"Yes."

"How do you think the televisions were plugged in?" He jerked his head back. "That was an old, abandoned gas station, but at one time it had electric lights."

Sad a way of life had gone, but then those wires had saved their lives. She shook her head. "What are we going to do with this car?"

"Ditch it."

"Are you going to try to contact Sammison again?"

"I don't know. I have to think through my options. I'll figure something out." As he talked, his low, rumbling voice grew weaker and raspier. The wound kept bleeding. His jean leg was soaked.

She frowned at him. "Do you think it hit an artery?"

"The bullet?" He shook his head. "No. It's just a flesh wound." Yet he could hardly speak.

"Reeve, I can't do this alone."

"What do you mean?"

"I mean, don't faint on me."

He laughed. "Me? Faint?" But he flinched and licked at the sweat on his upper lip as he gestured to the left. "The Jeep's that way."

She had to veer off the road, and they started bumping out over the terrain again. The car was harder than ever to handle, and she had to wrestle with the steering wheel to maintain control. She felt like a tank driver. More than once the jolts reminded her the car was no Jeep. "Reeve, what if we stall?"

"We walk."

Right. With him bleeding and her panicking. He uttered things so nonchalantly, so crisply, as if danger were no major matter with him. "Do you think they'll be able to find us?"

"If we're not careful. Scared?"

She nodded. "Yes."

Reeve's lips formed a slow sensuous smile. "You did pretty good."

She laughed, recalling her near misses. "Oh, right."

"You saved my life."

She couldn't say anything to that.

"I appreciate it."

Startled, she wondered if that was a thank-you. Glancing at him, she admired the strong thrust of his chin and soaked in that his words were as close to applause as he'd get. A warm glow filled her. "You're welcome, Reeve."

Now he laughed, long and hard.

"What's so funny?" she asked.

"How's your head?"

She thought about the swelling that had ached so unbearably that morning. The bones in her body. "Okay."

"And your feet?"

Strange she hadn't noticed them, either. But then, she'd been busy trying to stay alive. "Blistered."

"What's so funny?" he echoed with a smile. "Your feet are blistered, you've got a headache, you can't drive worth a damn, and I've got a bullet in my thigh. We're quite a pair, aren't we?"

She flicked her glance to him again. Yes, they were quite a pair. And they were out here in this hot, barren desert dodging helicopters and driving around looking for a hidden Jeep. "We're alive."

Once more he laughed. "It sure as hell feels good."

The remark wasn't as odd as he made it seem, so high, so god-awful cheerful. Although she knew the adrenaline had to be pumping through him as it was through her, he was acting crazy. Too crazy. Things were bad enough with her having to drive the car. All she needed was for him to fall apart. Maybe he had lost a lot of blood. "Are you all right, Reeve?"

He leaned his head back on the seat and grinned. "Allie, I've never been better."

Chapter Eight

A little bit of green had never looked so good. Though she knew they were far from safe, to Allie, the small grove of trees where they had hidden the Jeep represented a haven, a welcome respite from their frantic flight across the desert. Reeve's mood continued high, even when she barreled the car alongside the Jeep and jammed on the brakes so hard, he lurched forward.

"Are you all right?" she asked, running around to open the door for him. She could tell that he was growing weaker. "Can you manage?"

"I'm fine," he answered, swinging his leg out stiffly. "Can you get the pack?"

She went to his injured side to help him up. "In a minute. Here, hold on to my shoulder."

"I'm too heavy for you."

For once she knew she had to take charge. "That may very well be true, but I sure don't want to try to pick you up off the ground when you fall."

He laughed. "Allie, I'm not going to fall."

"You're weak, Reeve."

"Maybe. Okay, I'm weak." Nodding agreement, he placed his arm around her shoulder. "Ready?"

She laughed, too, at the way he said it, as if they were going somewhere. In fact, since they'd been together, he was constantly asking her if she was ready. She never was. "Ready," she complied. "Where to?"

He jerked his head to one side. "Over there by that tree, I guess. Damn!" he swore as he shifted position, trying to bear his own weight. Allie forced him to lean on her. "Looks like a good place."

She helped him over. "What are you going to do then?"

"Look at my leg."

Then what? There wasn't much to see anyhow, except blood. And there was an awful lot of that. "Who do you think shot you? Sammison or his partner?"

"Sammison," Reeve answered, limping across the ground. "He had a derringer strapped to his ankle. I should have known he would carry an extra weapon."

She settled him by the tree. The pain had to be excruciating. Expelling a long, agonizing breath, he held on to the wound as he dropped to the ground. For a moment he blanched. Allie thought for sure he was going to pass out, but he clenched his jaw and positioned his leg for comfort. Blood seeped through his clamped fingers.

"You should elevate it," Allie said.

Reeve nodded. "I will. Where's the pack?" he asked, leaning his head back against the tree trunk. "We're going to need it. There's a first-aid kit inside."

"I'll get it." She rushed to the car. So far she had stood helplessly by, watching him. Now she would help alleviate his pain; nurse his wound.

"Bring the entire pack."

"Okay," she called.

The pack was heavy, but she managed to drag it across the ground. Dropping it beside him, she knelt to rummage through the contents, but Reeve sat forward and whipped open a side flap. Only he didn't pull out a first-aid kit. Instead he produced a bottle of tequila. It was at least a quart.

Pausing, Allie stared at him. "Where did you get that from?"

"From the pack."

Obviously. She wondered when he had bought the quart and stowed it away. "Do you always carry liquor?"

"I like to be prepared."

"Is that why you went back for the pack?" she asked after a long moment. "Dodging all those bullets?"

"It's good tequila."

"You risked your life for a bottle of tequila?" She couldn't believe her ears. She was seeing and hearing it, but she couldn't believe it. How brazen of him to jeopardize their lives for a bottle of liquor.

"I was already shot."

She shook her head incredulously. "Reeve. Why in the world . . ."

But he wasn't listening. Holding the bottle in one hand, he pulled the cork out with his teeth and spit it on the ground. "Want some? It's good stuff. It'll put hair on your chest."

She straightened. "I don't need hair there."

His wayward eyes roved over her torso. "No, you don't, lady," he said. "But I do."

He upended the tapered bottle and took a few swigs.

Allie glanced at the bottle clasped in his hand. A worm curled in the bottom, magnified to the size of the snake he'd killed last night—or, almost. It looked unappetizing. "Surely you aren't going to drink the worm?" She sounded appalled.

"What?"

She gestured to the clear, liquid contents. "There's a worm floating in there."

Reeve's lips curled into a smile. In one deft motion he covered the opening with his thumb, tipped the bottle upside down, and when the alcohol-embalmed worm drifted to the neck, dropped it out on the ground, spilling only a few drops of liquor. Then he brought the bottle to his lips and took several long swallows. The liquid started disappearing like it was going down a fast-flowing drain. He coughed once and drank some more.

Allie was stunned. No one in their right mind would risk
his life for a bottle of liquor. And no sane person would endanger his life a second time by drinking it so fast. Then
again, she'd already learned that this man was different
from others—very different.

He wiped his mouth and took another long swig.

Her anxiety spilled over. "You're going to kill yourself,
Reeve," she chided. Living in a doctor's household, she was
well aware of the effects of alcohol. Taken in large quan-
tities or chugalugged it could cause cardiac arrhythmias, and
death. "Reeve," she repeated when he didn't answer.
"Reeve, stop it." She tried to take the bottle away from him,
but he pulled it back and swallowed more of the contents.
"You're drinking too fast," she told him. "You're going to
make yourself sick."

"No, I want to get drunk," he muttered at last, pausing
to speak.

She sat back, dreading what she knew was coming next.

"I don't want to feel any pain," he said. "You're going
to have to take out this bullet for me, Allie."

She almost laughed, except it wasn't funny. Somehow,
knowing his request was coming hadn't cushioned the
shock. Reeve didn't realize what a chicken she was. She was
a doctor's daughter, but a chicken when it came to paper
cuts and ingrown toenails. How could she carry through
what he requested?

She gazed into his smoldering, slightly hazed-over eyes.
"You're kidding."

"Unfortunately, no."

She shook her head. "I can't do that. I can't take out a
bullet. This is ridiculous."

"Sure you can. It's not very deep. Here." With only a
slight wince, he readjusted his body, reaching for the thin
leather pouch tucked into his boot and handing it to her.
"You'll need my knife. Be sure to sterilize it. I killed the
snake with it and didn't wash it. And be careful, it's sharp."

"You expect me to cut out a bullet with your knife?" She kept shaking her head back and forth as she tried to soak it in.

"As soon as I get drunk." He took another long swig of the tequila, sputtering again. Even from where Allie sat, the liquor looked hot, as though it scalded as it went down.

"This is stupid," she said, panicking. "Look, Reeve, why don't we got to a hospital? You need medical attention. I'll drive you. Come on, get in the car. Just tell me where to go. We can get there."

He laughed. "Sorry, Allie, I'd rather take my chances with a bullet than on a road with you."

"Don't be silly. You need professional medical help, Reeve."

"Can't," he said.

She was growing exasperated. She placed her hands on her hips and glared at him. "Why not?"

"Because there isn't a hospital for miles," he answered. "Besides, those were CIA agents that died in that helicopter crash," he reminded her. "As soon as the agency finds out about it they'll swarm over every medical facility from here to Japan."

"But I don't know how to do this, Reeve," she told him.

"Didn't you say your father was a doctor?"

Laughter bubbled to her lips. Hysterical laughter. "Yes, but I don't know anything about gunshot wounds. I inherited his nose, not his medical expertise."

Reeve just grinned and swigged some more tequila. Already his eyes were growing red rimmed and his speech was slurred. "You're a funny lady, Allie, do you know that?"

"What?" She leaned closer to hear him.

"You've got to know something about medicine. You lived with him all these years."

"All right. I do know something," she said. "I know how to cure athlete's foot, lance boils and bandage paper cuts."

He grinned again. "Don't have any of those things."

"Oh, God."

"You're a pretty lady," he went on, tracing a finger down her cheek and along her hairline. A thrill swept through her. "You know what? You're a pretty lady, and you wear the kinkiest, sexiest damned underwear I've ever seen."

She didn't move; she just stared at him in disbelief. This man lying below the tree simpering at her was not the same man she had dealt with over the past three days. This man was stark raving mad.

"God, you're already drunk," she summed up. And no wonder. All they'd had were the fry cakes that morning. The alcohol had to have hit him like a lead sinker. She grabbed the bottle from him, this time successfully. "If the bullet doesn't kill you, this will," she said. "It's got to be eighty proof."

And he'd consumed over three-quarters of it.

"Ninety," he corrected. "Lissen," he said, already slurring his words. "Do a good job—okay, pretty lady?"

Her frustration rose, and she found herself having to lash out. "Will you stop calling me pretty lady?"

"But you are," he said with a silly grin on his face.

"My looks hardly have any bearing on what's happening."

"Have you ever had a man, Allie?" he now asked, a devilish glint in his blue gaze.

"Of course I've had a man."

"How many?" he challenged.

Allie shook her head. This was preposterous. Why in the world was she discussing this with him? He was drunk. Rip-roaring drunk. And he was a comical drunk at that. Why couldn't he just sleep, like normal drunks?

"How many?" he repeated.

"A dozen."

He laughed. "And I'm Minnie . . . Minnie Mouz."

"Oh, Reeve," she moaned, shaking her head back and forth in confusion. He couldn't even formulate the word. She fumbled for his pulse, and felt it race. But it was at least regular.

"Allie?" he slurred, trying to focus on her face. "Take—take my knife."

"Reeve, I can't do this."

"Got to," he said, "Got to get it out. Jus-just don't slip."

She pounced on his words. "What if I hit an artery?" she pleaded. "Reeve, if I take out the bullet it's going to bleed."

"Already bleeding."

"It's going to bleed more."

"Shallow," he said. He was drifting off to sleep. "It's just a little bullet. It'll stop bleeding."

"How do you know?" She shook him. "How do you know it's shallow?"

"Had lots. Got to do it, Allie." With that, his head fell to the side, and he was out cold.

Allie sat staring at him. "Reeve!" She shook him again, but he just snored loudly. "Reeve, wake up."

She glanced around the trees frantically. What was she going to do now? He really expected her to remove a bullet? But how? God, she wasn't ready for this.

Neither was he. She glanced back at him. If she didn't do something soon he would bleed to death. Or die from an infection. Lead poisoning. Maybe she could get him to a hospital by herself. Sure. How was she going to wrestle him to the car? The man was drunk. He'd directed her to this grove. She didn't even know which way to go. It looked as if she didn't have much choice. She didn't know how to remove a bullet, but if she wanted to stay alive and get out of this desert, she'd have to *learn* how—pronto.

She got slowly to her feet. If she'd had long sleeves she would have rolled them up, but she still wore her dirty red-and-white polka-dot dress.

It was time for action. Trying to calm her trembling hands, she knelt down and tugged at the rent in his jeans, moving the fabric so that she could see the wound. The least she could do was examine it. He'd been hit high on the thigh, in the fleshy part of his leg. The bullet hole was small and round; blood pooled in the center. More blood had dried on the muscle and hair. Pressing gingerly on the bruised flesh around the bullet, she tried to gauge its depth. Fresh red blood oozed out around the edges, but she could feel the bullet wiggle back and forth. He was right: it was shallow.

Sitting back on her heels, she looked around the campsite again. First things first. She would need a fire and some water, and something with which to apply pressure. And she had to get his pants off.

She stood up.

Ten minutes later, everything was assembled, the first-aid kit at her side. Allie picked his knife from the water she'd boiled it in and held the blade over the camp fire. Reeve hadn't moved a muscle since he'd passed out, not even when she'd pushed and tugged at him, trying to peel off his jeans. He was practically comatose, rolling whichever way she shoved him. She only hoped he didn't move now. All she had to do was pry the bullet out, then clean the wound with lots of soap and water, and tape it up tight. No matter how she'd been hurt, all her life her father had told her to wash her scrapes well and apply pressure to stop the bleeding.

The knife blade was sharp. As Allie turned it she could see little stars glimmer in the firelight. This was it. She took a deep breath. Gritting her teeth, she pushed back her hair and leaned over his leg.

"Reeve, I'm sorry," she murmured.

Allie was amazed when the bullet came out. Although he had started bleeding heavily when she placed the knife into the wound, slipping it to one side, she had kept gently probing, working beneath the bullet, pulling, ignoring the nervous sweat that broke out on her forehead and along her back. Reeve had bucked once, muttering that crude word he used often. She'd sat on him to keep him quiet.

"No!" he shouted, but he mumbled and went back to sleep.

"Oh, God," she prayed. "Help me."

She went back and tugged on the bullet. It popped out suddenly, flipping into the air like a coin. She had been concentrating so hard she fell backward.

Righting herself, Allie tossed down the knife and grabbed a clean gauze pad. She dabbed at the blood that poured from the shallow wound. She had to stop the bleeding. She had to clean it, too. What if soap and water wasn't enough? Next he'd want her to do major surgery. Spying the bottle of tequila, she hesitated. Then she shrugged. Alcohol was alcohol. They used it in movies. Her father kept a supply— of the nondrinking sort—in his medicine cabinet.

After washing out the wound, Allie poured most of the remaining liquor over it, watching as Reeve's muscles twitched in response. It had to burn like hell. Figuring it couldn't do much more damage, she sprinkled some antibiotic powder she found in the first-aid kit into the wound. Whoever had packed the kit had shown foresight. They knew about liquor, too. She wondered if his friends, Jean and Danhi, had known that someone would get hurt. Apparently they had. With a heavy sigh, Allie took out a dressing and taped it firmly to his leg, wrapping everything tightly with a wide piece of gauze. Lastly she cleaned him and covered him with a blanket.

When she was finished, she stood up to survey her handiwork. Odd, she felt giddy, and she hadn't had a drink herself. She'd done it. She'd built a fire and removed a bullet, unaided. Now all she had to do was keep him alive. He looked okay, if a little worse for wear. He was pale, but he was breathing. Once in a while he snored or mumbled something aloud, still drunker than a skunk. The dressing looked good enough to be professional. The white gauze stood out against his tanned skin. He seemed hot, covered with the blanket. But she left it on, not knowing what else to cover him with. He was practically naked. All he had on was his shirt and his white jockey shorts.

At least her underwear was red. Kinky.

Sexy, too. Or at least he thought so.

She glanced at the bottle of tequila. Realizing consciously that her behavior was a result of reaction, and not caring, without a moment's hesitation she reached for it and walked to another tree to sit down. What the hell. She deserved it. He was going to sleep for a long time. Besides, she needed something to stop her hands from trembling. Leaning back, she took a long slug. The liquor burned like fire all the way down to her toes, but she coughed and took another sip. God, it was awful. Still she drank some more.

Had Allie known more about alcohol, she would have realized that, considering her size and weight, it would hit her harder than it had Reeve. And faster. She felt dizzy. And giddier than ever, but she took another drink, emptying the bottle. Right then Reeve snored aloud, sounding like a donkey braying. She glanced at him and giggled. Actually giggled.

Kinky, huh? He'd just see kinky.

Somehow knowing that she was growing just as inebriated as he had been, and once again not caring, she reached for his knife and lifted the hem of her dress. With another giggle, she slashed a long strip from her red taffeta slip and tied it around the white dressing, looping the ends into a giant bow. Pleased with herself, she staggered back to the tree, picked up the bottle of tequila and sank to the ground. Exhausted, as well as somewhat tipsy, she fell into a sweet oblivion and slept.

ALLIE WOKE A FEW HOURS later to the sun beating down on her face. But she was under a tree. When had the sun moved? Then, still slightly inebriated, she remembered that it made its westward trek in the sky every day. It was a law of physics or astronomy or something—she couldn't remember which.

Though they hurt, she opened her eyes. Reeve was still sleeping. She could see his chest moving up and down, but more than that, she could hear him still snoring. For her part, she felt even worse than she had that morning, if that was possible. Her head ached, and her back ached, and her feet were killing her, but her stomach was the worst. She felt nauseated, weak from the lack of food. The fire had gone out. She needed to get up and cook something to eat.

But first she had to get rid of the scorpion crawling on her hand. She became aware of it slowly, a light brushing feeling along her arm, and she tilted her head to look down at the small brown arthropod, its distinctive tail curled high in the air. What was she going to do now? They were poisonous, weren't they? And they liked to bite.

More nervous sweat popped out on her forehead, and she lay very still, waiting for the thing to leave. A chill went down her spine, this time a chill of fear. She had really gotten into a mess. People shooting at her, bugs crawling on her. And all because of a briefcase full of frilly underwear and a mess-up by a hotel clerk. Where was Tom Biner that morning? Working on a design? How about Mable Hill? Did they even care that she was missing? That she was about to be stung by a scorpion?

Allie tilted her head again to glance back at the creepy creature. It sat on her knuckles, flexing its tail, seemingly not at all anxious to leave. Damned bug. She wasn't going to lie here much longer. So what was she going to do? Staring at it the whole time and moving carefully so as not to jar her hand, she wiggled around and poised her other hand in readiness. In one quick motion she flicked the insect away. Then, jumping to her feet, she stomped on it with her moccasined foot, angrily squishing it into the hard ground.

Afterward she stared at it a long moment. Lord, she was getting to be brutal. But she hated bugs. And snakes. She glanced around fully expecting a rattler to strike out at her in retaliation. But nothing moved. She went to the fire, gathering tumbleweed and retrieving sheep droppings from the pack to get it restarted.

After she cooked something to eat, the next thing she was going to do was take a bath. The water in the wash might not be fit for drinking, but it would certainly do for washing. She supposed she ought to wash Reeve, too.

Strangely happy, humming a tune, Allie set about lighting the fire.

REEVE FELT AS IF HE'D BEEN run over by a steamroller and left to die. His head pounded, and his leg ached, and his throat felt parched and dry. It was all he could do to open his eyes. A canopy of black, punctuated by stars, greeted him. It was night. Or else he had more than a hangover. What the hell was he doing in the desert? He eyed the cliff in the distance confirming this was the desert. He'd been dreaming that he was in the middle of a cool mountain stream, the water pouring over him, bathing him in soothing luxury. Now his back itched, and he was hotter than the sun.

Tossing off the scratchy blanket, he looked down at his leg, propped high in the air, and graced with a huge red bow. Where the hell had that come from? Had Allie removed the bullet? Then he remembered: the shooting, the bumpy ride, the tequila, then blackness. No wonder he felt like hell.

"Allie?" he croaked.

She had built a fire. He could see her standing on the other side, washing out a pot. She'd taken off her polka-dot dress. She was wearing a pale blue shirt that struck her practically at her knees and a pair of jeans. His jeans? They were huge; she had them hitched up with a blue-speckled handkerchief, the same one he'd worn around his forehead just yesterday. She looked clean, as though she had bathed. Sensuous, vulnerable. Her hair was wet and pulled back in a leather thong. A piece of tumbleweed stuck at a jaunty angle from one side, like a decoration.

"Allie?" he said louder. His throat felt raw from formulating the single word.

She turned to him. "Hi. Are you awake?" Coming toward him, she smiled. "How do you feel?"

"Awful."

"You'll feel better soon."

"What the hell's on my leg?"

"A piece of my slip," she said with another grin. "It's colorful."

"Where are my clothes?" It had just occurred to Reeve that he was naked. Stark nude. Even his jockey shorts had been removed. He flung the blanket back on him.

She glanced up at a tree limb. "I washed everything. It should be dry soon." She gestured down at the clothes she was wearing. "I got these from the pack, but there wasn't anything left for you to wear."

Reeve wanted to choke when he saw his clothing hanging from the tree limb. She'd spread out his jeans, shirt and underwear right alongside her damned red dress and left him naked. A bright red lace brassiere fluttered in the breeze like a flag at full mast. "Did you take off my clothes?"

"Yes," she answered.

"All of them?"

"Every single stitch," she answered, smiling at him.

"And you washed me?"

"Yes." She nodded. "You really are full of scars, Reeve. You've had a lot of wounds. You mustn't have been a very good mercenary."

He frowned at her. She seemed less fearful, almost . . . whimsical. "What the hell's gotten into you, Allie? What's going on?"

She laughed, almost gaily. "Nothing special. I just feel good."

He glanced around the campsite. "Where's the rest of the tequila?"

"I drank it," she said, gaily. Then her brow pleated. "Why do they put a worm in it?" she asked as if the world spun on his response.

He groaned. He needed a drink. Blinking, he gazed at her through fog-hazed eyes. "It indicates it's genuine Mexican tequila. In Mexico, and some other places, it's macho to drink it. Here in this country, it's mostly proof of origin."

She'd been studying the upthrust of his jaw, the slant of his cheeks. She couldn't restrain a question surging in her all day. "How many women have you made love to, Reeve?"

He stared at her. "What?"

"How many women have you—"

"I heard you the first time," he cut in, struggling to sit up. Damn, his leg hurt. He throbbed all over.

"Better rest while you can," she said. "Here." She handed him a fry cake. It was soggy and half raw in the middle. "I think they turned out pretty well for my first batch. I've never been a very good cook. So how many?"

"How many what?"

"How many women have you made love to?"

As far as Reeve knew, tequila had never caused any strange side effects, but Miss Alanna Martin was certainly acting strange. "Look," he said, tossing the food aside. "I'm not up to discussing my sex life with you."

"You asked me how many men I'd had," she said in defense.

He frowned. He didn't remember that at all. "I was drunk," he snapped.

She ignored his response. "Aren't you hungry?"

"No."

She handed him another cake. "Eat anyhow. You need nourishment. I'm curious," she continued. "What do you say to them? Do you talk when you make love?"

"God," he muttered. Why was she pressing this, particularly now when he ached all over. "I whisper dirty nothings in their ear. Come on, Allie, cut the crap and help me up."

"Where are you going to go?"

"I don't know. For a walk. I want to try my leg."

She giggled. "Naked, and wrapped in a blanket?"

Reeve stared at her. "Dammit, Allie, you took my clothes away on purpose, didn't you?"

She smiled her answer. "You're certainly upset about a few little clothes."

"It's not just my clothes, Allie, it's my freedom to move around."

She arched an eyebrow at him. "Do you remember back at the motel when you thought I was a hooker. You even called me sexy. I threw a shoe at the door." She held up one of her high heels, the ones he'd broken. "You know, these cost me half a week's pay."

"What the—" he muttered. "Allie, I don't know what's gotten into you, but I wish you'd come to your senses and stop this nonsense."

"Why? I feel great. I'm having a good time. For once in my life, I feel like I've accomplished something." Tossing the shoe into the fire, she swung around and spread her arms out to the sky. "I even feel sexy," she said. "Look at me." Swinging back to him, she gestured to the baggy pants and shirt. "Do you really think I'm sexy, Reeve?"

"I think you've cracked up, Allie."

She laughed. Allie couldn't say, herself, why she was acting so silly. She just felt so free. Strong. "I killed a scorpion earlier. Did I tell you?"

He shook his head. "No."

"I squished it into the ground. It was on my arm. I was going to beat back some snakes, too. Oh—" she went to the fire and picked up the coffeepot "—I made coffee. Want some?"

"I'd like my pants," he said.

"And I've been waiting for a coyote," she went on as though he hadn't spoken. "Tonight I'm going to howl back. Now," she said, placing the coffeepot back on the fire. "How about if I take a look at your wound?"

Reeve frowned at her. "Dr. Martin, I presume?"

She laughed again. "At least I didn't cut off your leg."

"I suppose that's a consolation."

"You better believe that's a consolation. There was a point where I was worried. And I got out the bullet." She knelt down beside him and slid the blanket from his leg.

Then she took off the dressing, studying the wound as though she'd worked for years toward a medical degree.

"How does it look?"

"Frankly I don't know."

He laughed, but he hurt so badly it came out as a grimace. Lord, she was crazy. "It feels good, Allie. I'm sure it's going to be fine. There's no redness."

"Is that what you look for?"

"Usually."

"Do you heal fast?"

"Let's hope so. We need to get out of here before somebody remembers this grove of trees."

"Sammison?"

"He doesn't know about it, but he might find Danhi, who does. By the way, what'd you do with the bullet?"

"I saved it for you." She took it from her pocket and placed it in his hand. It was nearly perfect. "Reeve?" she said, and her voice was soft and husky, "Do you think we're going to be all right?"

What brought that on? "We're doing fine so far."

"Yes." She nodded. They *were* doing fine. "Could I ask you a serious question, Reeve?"

"Sure."

"How many women have you made love to?"

He studied her for a long moment. What an odd thing to want to know. Why would it mean so much to her to have the answer? Maybe she was still drunk, feeling the affects of the alcohol. She probably wasn't used to drinking much. She also seemed thrilled by her triumphs—killing a scorpion, digging out the bullet, starting the fire. It kind of amused him. "Not that many, Allie."

"Do you think I'm sexy?" For some reason she needed to know. She remembered the first time he'd called her sexy lady, back at the hotel room. "Really?"

Reeve frowned at her. She was kneeling there beside him with hands resting on her legs. And her expression was so serious. She leaned closer. "Reeve? Please answer me."

"Oh, hell," he said. "Allie—" And then he kissed her.

She knew he was going to kiss her. Had been wanting to for some time. As he placed his hand on the back of her head and pulled her slowly toward him, her breath caught in her throat, and her stomach felt like jelly, and her knees buckled. Thank goodness she was already kneeling beside him. She would have fallen.

His lips were all that she'd thought they would be; hot, hard, demanding. She wanted to swoon and press against him, but she knew he was hurt. She placed her hands on his chest, the broad, bare chest that she had washed. It had looked bronze in the firelight, strong. The hairs prickled her as they had once before, sensuously.

"Reeve," she moaned aloud when he moved his hands around to cup her breasts. She wasn't wearing a bra, and her flesh swelled in his hands.

As if her voice had penetrated some fog, suddenly he pulled away. "God, Allie," he said, blowing his breath out in a long, frustrated sigh. "Jesus, I'm sorry."

"Why?"

"Why?" He shook his head in disbelief. "Look where we are—" He circled the grove with an arm. He seemed angry with her. "Look. I'm still in charge here. Take a blanket, and go to the car."

"But—"

"Just do what I say, Allie," he snapped. "It's late. It's time for bed."

"But what if someone comes? Sammison?"

"Believe me, lady, there are more dangerous things than Paul Sammison. And I'm it. Get a blanket and go. Now."

Allie was puzzled by his words, but accustomed now to obeying him. She took a blanket and rose to her feet.

"And lock the doors," he said.

She stood for a few moments looking at him. What had she done to get him so upset? "Good night, Reeve."

"Good night, Allie," he growled.

"I'm sorry."

He nodded. "Yeah."

She walked to the car, and looked back once. "Will you be all right?"

"Yes. See you in the morning."

If there was a morning. "Be sure and eat something."

He nodded. "I will, Allie."

"I could get you some aspirin."

"What I'd like is some more tequila," he mumbled. "Look, Allie, I'll be fine. Do me a favor and go. Okay?"

"You won't be cold?"

He laughed. "No, I won't be cold. And I'll try not to be scared. Good night."

She didn't like his mocking words, but swallowed her anger down. He was injured, in pain, after all. Just before she turned away she said, "Have a good night, Reeve."

Taking her blanket, she marched to the car and crawled inside. At least there weren't any bugs here. Or snakes. Or arrogant men. Only on that note, she had some strange regrets. She closed her eyes and went to sleep.

Chapter Nine

Either the tequila or the antibiotic powder did the trick, for the next morning there were still no signs of infection in Reeve's wound. Ignoring his foul mood, Allie checked it as soon as she got up.

"How does it feel?" she asked, studying the rapidly healing tissue.

"Like a gunshot wound."

"Really?" She could be a snit, too. "Good. At least we're in the right ballpark. I'd hate for it to feel like a knife wound." Applying a clean bandage, she topped his leg off with the red bow again and went to start the fire. "What do you want for breakfast?"

Reeve followed her with his gaze. "We have a choice?"

"I guess not."

"Are you cooking?"

"You're certainly not up to it," she answered. "Or do you plan to hobble over here and mix the cornmeal?" He glared at her, but her attention was caught by the tree limb. "Oh, the laundry is dry. Do you want your clothes? I can get you a shirt and underwear—but no pants. I need your leg free so I can check up on it."

That didn't seem to sit well with him. He liked to be in control. He scowled. "Well, Dr. Martin, thank you very much."

"Sure." She went to gather his clothes. "I'll help you get them on."

"I can manage," he said.

She wasn't about to argue with him today. She dropped the things in his lap. "All right."

He arched an eyebrow at her. "Testy, aren't we?"

"Almost as testy as you."

"I'm sorry," he said. "My leg hurts."

She nodded. "I know. Do you want an aspirin?"

"Please."

"Is that the first time you've ever used that word?"

"What word?"

"Please."

He scowled again. "Just give me the damned aspirin, Allie."

Allie smiled smugly as she handed him the small tin. Everything seemed so peaceful. It wasn't even hot yet. A gentle breeze lifted the leaves on the trees, and water trickled softly through the wash. Yes, everything seemed peaceful—except the two of them. Almost as if by unspoken agreement, neither of them had mentioned the kiss, nor the electricity that always seemed to linger between them. Both were aware of a need to stay apart. In the cold light of day, free of her alcoholic haze, Allie saw that a romance with a man pursued by the law was doomed, no matter how attractive he was, or how much adventure he brought into her life. No matter how much stronger a person she had seemed to become....

"So," she said conversationally, "what are we going to do today?"

"I suppose we could go shopping."

He would take her wrong. She glanced around pointedly and sighed as if she were tremendously disappointed. "There aren't too many stores. I think we'd have a tad of trouble."

Sighing, he said, "I'm sorry, Allie. I didn't mean to snap at you. But I think we'd be better off staying put for right now. I'm not up to traveling."

That was surprising. It wasn't like Reeve to admit to a weakness. "What about Sammison?"

"We hope."

She supposed that was as good as any other plan. "Perchance is there anything I can find us to eat besides corn cakes?"

"Yucca plants. You could fry up a batch. Or a rabbit if you can shoot it."

She laughed. He was as stubborn as she was. "Would you give me your gun?"

"No."

"I could have taken it from you, you know."

"You didn't."

"It wasn't because I was afraid," she said. "I wasn't."

He stared at her. "You've done a good job, Allie," he answered almost grudgingly.

"Thank you. I have done a good job." She was proud of her accomplishments. Five days ago she wouldn't have been able to look at his bullet wound, let alone remove the slug. She stopped in the midst of mixing the gruel and smiled again, fondly. "My parents should see me now. They wouldn't believe it. I'm actually cooking. Kneeling down on the desert floor preparing a meal."

"Does that upset you?"

She glanced at him. "In a way. Do you have a family? Other than your brother?"

He shook his head. "It's just the two of us. Our parents were killed in a flash flood several years ago."

No wonder he'd mentioned the rains. "Did they live in Arizona?"

He nodded. "In the mountains. They were out hiking, when one of the storms kicked up. They tried to save some people who had camped in the wash."

Strange, how the elements could be so devastating. Looking at the barely gurgling stream just beyond camp, it was hard for Allie to imagine rain so hard that it would sweep a person away. Yet she'd heard about flash floods, torrential downpours. "I'm sorry."

"It was a long time ago, Allie."

"After that you grew close to Danhi and Jean?"

"I'd always been close to Danhi. He married Jean after his first wife died."

She dropped the corn mixture into the skillet and watched it flatten out to fry. "Have you ever been married?"

"No."

"Can't find anyone?"

"Never wanted to."

A question popped to mind, and she wondered if she dared ask it. But she needed to know. "Do you have a woman?"

"A what?"

"You know, a woman. As in female. Do you have a woman?"

"I told you I'm not married."

"But do you have a woman?"

His glance at her seemed to last forever. She was surprised to realize that she was holding her breath waiting for an answer. Why would this be so important to her? Why would she even care?

"No," he said at last. "I don't have a woman. Do you have a man?"

"No."

"Why not?"

"I never found one I wanted." Until now.

But that was ludicrous. She couldn't want Reeve. She had to stop thinking those things. This silliness had to be the effect of washing him, of seeing his body, feeling that they might not survive, and of course, the alcohol.

"Allie?" He was the first to break the silence. She thought he was going to ask something important, but all he said was, "Is breakfast almost ready? I smell something burning."

"Oh!" Quickly she turned back to the fry cakes, fishing the one she'd been cooking out of the skillet. It was very brown and hard, and could be considered well overdone. "I'm sorry. This doesn't look much better than the ones I made last night."

"I'm sure it will be fine." Reeve had begun to look tired; the lines around his eyes seemed drawn. But he ate breakfast and drank the little water Allie gave him.

"We're almost out," she told him.

He nodded. "I'll show you later how to distill some that we can drink. Just keep conserving."

Of course he would know how to make water; he knew how to do everything. And unbidden, she wondered how he would make love.

Quickly Allie pushed that thought from her mind. "Reeve, have you ever seen the Continental Divide?"

"Yes."

"Describe it to me."

"It's an imaginary line that divides the continent at the point where the rivers start flowing in opposite directions and empty into different oceans. Why?"

"Just curious." She hid the fact she needed to stop thinking about how it would feel in his arms, skin to skin.

"We crossed it back in the Rockies."

"Really?" She thought for a moment. "When I get back to Chicago I think I'll design a line of lingerie with that name."

There was another brief silence. She could feel his eyes on her, and she thought he was going to laugh. Then he asked, "Did you go to school to learn how to design clothes, or are you just naturally talented?"

For a man who was normally quiet he was certainly long-winded this morning. Maybe he was thinking of sex, too. "A combination of both, I guess. I studied design for four years at college."

"Why did you choose lingerie?"

"I don't know." She glanced at him and shrugged. "I guess to break into the business. Lingerie was a field most open to new talent. Now I like it very much, and I like making women feel good about themselves."

He didn't remark on her admission. "Will your boss be upset that you lost your samples?"

"Tom Biner gets upset about everything, but the designs weren't irreplaceable. I have other samples at the office as well as drawings of them."

"Do you mostly draw?"

"Yes. And use my imagination."

"What's Continental Divide going to look like?"

She laughed. "Black, maybe, with beige bows. Plunging. Why?"

"No reason."

"Designing underwear isn't all frivolous, you know," she said. "There are a lot of considerations. Different women have different shapes—"

"You don't have to defend your occupation to me, Allie."

No, she didn't. And that was an odd revelation. Reeve was the type of man who would accept a woman for what she was and not expect or demand anything else.

She started to clean up. When she was done, he told her how to dig a hole in the sand and stretch plastic across it. Soon water would condense on the inside. Since Jean had included an abundance of plastic, she dug several holes. She didn't think anything could squeeze moisture from this wasteland, but within hours she had water for cooking and for them to drink. The water in the wash was good only for bathing.

Reeve fell asleep. Coming back to camp, she watched him for a long moment, thinking about all the things they'd been through, what had happened between them last night. In this relaxed moment, she let her mind roam. What would it be like making love with him? Touching him other than to bathe him? Or to nurse him to health? The thought of his hands on her made her feel fluttery inside. With a sigh she sat on the ground under her tree and started scratching a design in the sand.

Allie made more fry cakes for dinner. They weren't burned, but they weren't good, either. Still Reeve didn't complain. She could feel his eyes on her, watching her, and she could feel his kiss.

"Do you want some more coffee?" she nearly shouted, jumping up to break the tension.

"No. I'm fine. I'd like to shave, though, if you could get some water from the wash and help me."

"Sure." Anything to move away from him, to keep from looking at him.

But in order to help him shave she had to touch him, she discovered moments later, which was worse, vastly worse. Their bodies were close enough that she could feel the heat emanating from him as she sat beside him to hold the mirror he found in the pack. Jean had included everything except the kitchen sink.

With long, firm strokes, he scraped the knife along his face. "Can you hold steady, Allie?"

Clearing her throat, she adjusted the mirror. He certainly had time to think of sex now. She felt chills, thinking about it herself.

"Something wrong?"

"No."

"You sound hoarse."

She just shook her head. "I'm fine. I'm tired." Night was approaching.

"So am I."

Actually he sounded a little hoarse, too. She glanced at him, but he kept his gaze fixed on the tiny mirror. "Hear the coyote?" he asked.

Allie stared out into the desert at the lonely sound. "What's he crying for?"

"His mate."

She was sorry she had asked. "Are you about finished?" she sighed.

"Yes." He swished the knife clean in the pan of water she'd placed at his side and turned up his jaw, soaping it again. "One more stroke."

Allie licked her lips. Clean shaven, he was even better looking than before. Suddenly she had an incredible urge to touch his face, to stroke her fingers along his smooth skin. But that was crazy. Ludicrous.

"All done," he said.

She jerked the water away. "Do you want anything else? I'm going to bed."

"I'm fine."

This was silly; she was running away from him. "I'm sorry, Reeve. I'm really tired."

"I understand, Allie."

"I'm going to sleep in the car again."

He nodded. "Don't worry about me. I'll be fine."

The only thing she was worried about was herself, changing her mind. She wanted to lie beside him in his arms like she had two nights ago. Hell, she wanted him to kiss her again. She picked up her blanket, exasperated and confused as ever. "Good night, Reeve."

"Good night, Allie. By the way," he added, "thanks for your help."

"You're welcome."

"Are you feeling all right, Allie?"

"I feel fine. Why?"

"This is a strange conversation."

"It's a strange night," she answered, trudging off to the car. Why was he being so nice to her? Thanking her suddenly. Then again, he'd never really been mean to her, she admitted. They'd had a few spats, but that was because they were both stubborn people and he'd dragged her out in this desert. Yet he'd had good reason. He'd put up with her when she'd been so scared. He'd held her.

And he'd been honest with her.

Last night he'd sent her to the car. Was that her problem? Was she so angry because he'd rejected her? Just then the coyote howled again, calling for his mate. Damn! That was all she needed, an animal calling to his mate. Allie turned over in the seat and held the blanket over her head. She'd fix him. She wouldn't listen.

THEY HAD MORE FRY CAKES for breakfast the next morning. And for dinner. By that time Reeve was up and hobbling around the campsite. Although he had tied the bright red bow outside, like a talisman, he'd taken his jeans and was in command again. They had argued most of the day. Allie couldn't say why she was so irritable. She just felt like being mean and rotten.

Apparently so did Reeve. Once dinner was cleaned up, she sat against a tree trunk watching him pace back and forth. From the way he was acting, she doubted if he'd ever stayed in one place for more than a minute. "You're going to break open your wound if you don't sit down and relax," she said to him.

He flicked her a brief glance. "I'll be fine."

"I'm sure you will. But it doesn't hurt to be careful."

"Fine, I'll be careful." He flopped down across from the camp fire. It was night, and the moon had come out, flooding the desert with pale light. She watched it play on the back of his hair, making it look even darker than the night.

"We're leaving in the morning, aren't we?" she asked.

"Yes. We need to get going."

"No one's found us so far."

Reeve stirred the embers of the fire. "We've been lucky. Actually I think Sammison must have gone. If he was still here, we'd be dodging helicopters."

"Why would he leave?"

"He knows I'll find him. Eventually."

"Where are we going?"

"Vegas."

His split-second decisions, uttered in no uncertain terms, never failed to amaze her. "Are you going to try to contact him again?"

"No."

She frowned, confused. "Then why Vegas?" She didn't think he wanted to gamble. Then again, he was so unpredictable.

"I have a friend who's a newspaper reporter," he said. "He lives there."

"You're going to the news media?"

He nodded. "I figure my friend can break the story."

Allie supposed that made sense. Bargaining with Sammison hadn't worked. "Why didn't you tell the press before?"

"Because this whole mess was a matter of national security. I didn't want to interfere in a veil—covert activity," he explained. The press was considered to be the Fourth Estate, the last court of reckoning. "But Sammison has blackmailed me once too often. I'm finished playing his games. I'm taking the story to the press."

"Reeve, do you think your brother is still alive?" Sammison had alluded to him being dead.

He shrugged. "I wish I knew. It would be fast, if that were true. According to my calculations, he has a few more days."

"Curt joined the CIA because you recommended him, didn't he?" Allie guessed.

There was a moment where she thought he wouldn't answer. He just stared at her. "Yes."

"Were you an agent?"

"Once."

She'd thought so. "What happened?"

He shrugged. "The usual. I became disenchanted, tired of looking over my shoulder, tired of traveling all over the world with no ties and every person I met trying to kill me. Trying to kill them."

"So you retired?"

"I figured I deserved some solitude, so I bought a ranch in the mountains."

"Do you do much ranching?"

"Not really. I raise some horses. I've got a few head of cattle. A nice house."

From the sound of his voice, Allie was willing to bet that loneliness had caused much of his problem. It had to be difficult to be away from your home and family for long periods of time. She certainly missed her parents. Even her brother. "I have a brother, too," she said. "Did I tell you that?"

"No," he said tersely, but she saw the flicker of warmth in his eyes.

"He's older than me. He used to tease me mercilessly." She smiled, remembering the times Geoff had let her take the rap, times he'd nagged her, chided her. "He hates my clothes. He used to tell me that even my socks had labels."

"Did they?"

"Yes." She glanced at Reeve and laughed. "They still do. I like nice things. Including your jeans."

"They're a little large for you."

It bothered her when he looked at her, and she jumped up. "They're not bad."

"Your nose is peeling."

Still nervous, she rubbed at it. "It got sunburned the other day when I fell asleep."

"After the tequila?"

"I'm not accustomed to drinking." She wasn't accustomed to *him*!

Reeve reached to stir the embers of the fire again. Usually he let it burn for so little time, but tonight it spread a red glow in the air, almost as if they were saying goodbye. The moon had gotten fuller in the sky. At that moment it burned bright over the landscape, turning the bushes and scrub grass and cliffs into long, eerie shapes.

"The desert seems so vast," she said.

"The reservation stretches for miles," he answered. "It's as big as Connecticut and Massachusetts combined."

"You know, it's odd," she went on. "I think I'm going to miss it. It's really beautiful at night."

"It's beautiful during the day, too," Reeve answered. He'd been looking at her, but now he turned away. "You just have to learn to appreciate it."

The way they were learning to appreciate each other? She admired his strength, his ability. Curling her arms around her knees, she glanced back at the shapes in the distance. "But the night is special. The way the light hits the canyons. It's so unusual."

"Ghosts."

"What?"

He glanced back to her. "Indians believe that the lights are ghosts who are searching for loved ones. Or for peace."

How chilling. "That sounds scary."

He nodded. "I suppose in a way it is frightening. Death is frightening. And mysterious. To explain it, or perhaps deal with it, the people believe that you see some kind of light wherever a person has died."

What an odd superstition. Yet she knew many cultures held similar beliefs. She'd read somewhere that Eastern Indians believed that the soul had some kind of karma. And didn't parapsychologists talk about auras?

"What's it like being an Indian today?" she asked. The culture was so foreign to her.

"About the same as it's been for the past several hundred years," he answered, studying her. "Why?"

"It just seems so—"

"Savage?" he cut in.

"No."

Suddenly he loomed over her, looking angry. "Sure? Most women find that very fascinating. I'm one-quarter savage, Allie. Want to see which part?"

Allie was stunned at his tone. Yet in a way she wasn't at all surprised. Considering their history, when it came to personal subjects, it amazed her that they'd had five full minutes of civil conversation. "Why do you keep doing this, Reeve? Why are you so nasty to me?"

Shoving his hands into his pockets, he whipped away and stared into the darkness. "Oh, hell, I don't know. I'm tired of being here, wounded."

"That's not the real reason, is it?"

"No," he said, turning back to her. "I've never met anybody quite like you, Allie."

"Stupid."

"No. Naive."

"Sometimes—sometimes you frighten me, Reeve."

There was a long silence. Finally he shook his head. "No, I don't. You frighten yourself, Allie."

Allie wished she hadn't known what he was talking about, but she knew exactly what he meant. They both knew. The tension they were feeling was wearing them both down. Quickly she picked up her blanket and went to the car. "Good night, Reeve."

"Good night, Allie," he answered, but his voice mocked her. She could almost hear the coyote.

ALLIE DIDN'T MENTION the incident the next morning, and neither did Reeve. Like the kiss, they acted as though it hadn't happened. When she got up, feeling sick in the hot sun that had beat down through the car windows, he was ready to leave.

They skipped breakfast, but that was hardly upsetting. Allie had eaten so many fry cakes that she didn't want to see corn ever again. Reeve promised they would stop for something else as soon as they got near a town. She noticed he didn't mention a restaurant. Though he thought Sammison was gone, was he afraid people were following, looking for them?

"Reeve? Why do you think Sammison keeps blackmailing you?" she asked, thinking about the situation. "Do you

think he's getting something out of this? He doesn't act like
my idea of how a normal agent should behave.''

"You're right," Reeve answered. "He doesn't act like a
normal agent. I'm sure he's operating on his own, but it
took a few years to figure it out. That's one of the reasons
I've decided to go to the news media."

"The other?"

"It's time to blow this thing wide open." He glanced at
her. "Do you want me to let you go? I could drop you at the
police station."

''Do you still need me?''

"It would help."

"I'll stay."

"Thank you, Allie." He paused. "Scared?"

Only of herself. She shook her head. "No." She'd done
so much, accomplished so much. And it was odd, they were
on the same side now. The full story, when he'd revealed it,
was staggering. Her sympathies were totally with him. She
started for the car.

"We'll take the Jeep," he called.

Pausing, Allie glanced at the four-wheel drive vehicle.
"The car's air-conditioned."

"It's also got government license plates."

Her gaze fell to the official square tags. Obviously they
didn't have much choice. Unless they wanted to advertise.
"Do you want me to drive?" she asked, gesturing pointedly at his leg. He was still injured, after all.

"You must harbor a death wish, Allie."

"My driving is not that bad, Reeve. I was just nervous the
other day."

"How are you going to handle a stick shift?"

She hadn't thought about that. She looked back at the
Jeep. "Does it have power steering?"

He laughed.

"It was just a thought." She was going to have to bluster
her way along. "So. How are you going to handle the stick
shift?"

"I'll be fine."

"Sure. You're invincible. You've got a bullet wound—"

"I can manage, Allie," he retorted sharply.

Though she should have been accustomed to his terseness, particularly after last night, Allie was taken aback again. They'd been getting along so well this morning, and she was just trying to help. "All right." She swung up on the seat and fastened her seat belt. "Ready? Let's go."

When they finally pulled out of the grove, though, Allie was driving. Reeve had gotten behind the wheel, but he couldn't work the clutch. After several tries he shut off the engine and turned to her. "Just don't strip the gears."

She smiled. She didn't say "I told you so" because she doubted she'd do much better. She just got out and went around to his side, letting him scoot across the seat. The first few minutes had to have been pure torture for Reeve. He turned his face away as she ground the gears, ripping the transmission from first to second to third and fourth and jerking along the terrain like a stuck jackrabbit.

"Should I head for the road?" she asked when she'd gotten acclimated to shifting. The Jeep still bounced and swayed all over. "Or are we going to make our own way across the state?"

"Take the road."

"This is fun," she said as the wind whipped through her hair.

"Jolly."

She laughed. "Oh, Reeve, don't worry about your Jeep."

"I'm not," he answered. "I'm worried about us."

"So am I." Briefly she glanced from the terrain to him. "Isn't the Mob in Vegas?"

"The Mob is all over. Why?"

"I just wondered what happened to them."

"Don't worry, Allie, if the Mob wants us, they'll find us. They always do."

"Do you think Sammison hired them to get you?"

Reeve nodded. "Sammison and the East Germans, and probably separately. Both are desperate."

That's what she was worried about.

It took Allie over eight hours to get to Las Vegas. They stopped for breakfast at a small grocery store and for a late lunch at a tiny café in an out-of-the-way town. Although her arms and legs ached from handling the Jeep, Allie was having a great time driving it. No wonder he liked the vehicle. She felt like the queen of the road, and drove like it, too. Reeve made so many gasping sounds as she dodged cars, she thought for sure he was having a stroke.

"Lord, Allie, will you slow down?" he said when they reached the main drag through Las Vegas. It was glittery and neon-lit, and truly the Emerald City. "We're trying to avoid the police, not get a ticket."

"Everyone else is driving fast. Vegas is exciting."

"It'll be real exciting in jail or in a hospital."

"Sorry." She pressed on the brake. "Where to?"

"Turn left, right up here."

His newspaper friend lived in a small subdivision on the outskirts of town. Surprisingly there was a park right across from his home. With trees and shrubs and a flower-lined fountain. If it hadn't been for the flashy buildings, most of the town would have been as barren as the desert they'd just left.

"Park by the trees," Reeve told her. "Let's keep the truck in the shadows."

"This is a nice place," Allie commented, pulling the Jeep next to a curb. "It's so peaceful, considering how loud it is in town."

"You sound as if you're beginning to appreciate the West," Reeve answered.

"I am." She'd even grown accustomed to the heat. The night was still warm, the ground radiating heat it had soaked up from the sun. She glanced back at the house. "It doesn't look like anyone's home."

"I'll go see."

Reeve started to get down from the Jeep, when Allie joined him. She'd exited ahead of him. "I'll go, too."

"Scared?"

"No." But this time she was lying. The place was too quiet; the house was as dark as the night. And she had a strange feeling of foreboding.

Reeve must have been just as concerned, the way he crept up on the place, hardly throwing a shadow or making a noise. Heart hammering in her throat, Allie followed close behind, telling herself he was just being cautious.

The back door was unlocked. Reeve opened it quietly, cautiously slipping inside and skulking along the wall. Allie held on to his hand as her stomach did flip-flops.

"Reeve, nobody's here," she told him again, whispering now. "Let's come back later."

He shook his head. "We're here now. If Frank isn't home, we'll wait."

He made his way into the living room easily, as though he was familiar with the layout. All the while he crouched down, looking around, ever on the alert. The house was as inky dark inside as out. The only thing that illuminated the rooms was the moon, and it ducked in and out of the clouds as though teasing them with its fickle light.

"I want to check the bedroom," he said.

"Okay." She took a deep breath and followed. It was a good thing, for she didn't breathe again for several long seconds. Just as they rounded the door to the bedroom they saw the body sprawled on the floor. It had to be Reeve's friend, Frank. He had been shot through the head with a single bullet, which had formed a neat, round hole in the middle of his forehead. Though red fluid haloed his head, staining the carpet, hardly any blood seeped from the wound. His eyes were still open, staring up at them in surprise.

"Well, here's where the Mob went," Reeve remarked quietly, kneeling down to close his friend's eyes. "Sorry,

Frank." Taking her hand again, he tugged her toward the door. "Let's go, Allie. Let's get out of here."

For a moment Allie couldn't move. She was paralyzed by terror. They were back to running, dodging death.

"Allie, let's go," Reeve said.

He heard the click before she did. A gun. The sound came from beside the bed. Someone was hiding in the dark bedroom. Someone dangerous. Suddenly Reeve pushed her to the floor. "Roll!"

For once she didn't argue. She rolled across the floor as several shots rang out.

"Stop, Chandler!" a heavy German-accented voice barked.

"Damn! The Germans," Reeve said, picking up on the man's accent. "Get up and run," he told her.

Not daring to think, just propelling herself forward, Allie crashed through the house, knocking down furniture and hitting walls. Reeve turned to fire back at their foreign assailant. He emptied the gun quickly, giving them a short head start. "Hurry," he said, pushing her along.

Allie didn't need more urging. Thrusting open the kitchen door, she ran for the Jeep with all her might, jumping into the driver's seat and reaching for the key. A shadow darted away into the bushes, before she could discern what it was.

"You're getting better at this," Reeve said lunging behind her. "I didn't even have to tell you to get in."

"God, Reeve, I'm so afraid," she murmured trying to calm her shaking hands.

Oddly he smiled. "Actually, so am I, Allie. Let's go."

She reached for the key.

"Wait!" he said, grabbing her hand. "Stop! Don't turn the key."

"Why?" she glanced at him. "I thought you wanted me to go?"

"They're not shooting. Quick." He pulled her across the seat. "Jump. The Jeep is wired."

Just as they fell to the ground, a rain of gunfire broke over their heads. From two directions. She lifted an inquisitive brow at Reeve. "The Mob's still here," he whispered hoarsely, using an arm to force her low. "This is going to be interesting. Fired on from two sides."

"But why are both of them here?"

Reeve grinned. "Because Sammison's hedging his bet. They use different methods, but get the same results. If one fails, the other succeeds."

She realized now that the shadow she'd seen leaping from the Jeep, had been an East German or a mobster, rigging up a bomb. She shuddered. But before she could collapse, Reeve shoved her behind the front of the Jeep.

"This is what I want you to do. Run and use anything for cover—trees, shrubbery," he whispered. "Go."

Just as she started to move, fire singed her arm. Hunching down, Allie grabbed for it.

"You're hurt," Reeve said, apparently noticing the blood streaking her arm.

"I'm fine. The bullet just grazed me."

But it burned like hell. How in the world were they going to get away? Now they were both injured. Bullets kept flying past from both sides of the truck.

"Look, we've got to get out of here," Reeve said. Pausing a moment, he reloaded his gun, taking several bullets from his pocket. Had they been there all along? "When I count to three, roll along the ground, and then get up and run. Head for the strip. We'll get lost in the crowd."

He started to count. Allie felt like a guerrilla soldier as she rolled and weaved and crawled. Staying behind her, Reeve fired another quick volley at their attackers. Then he grabbed her arm and pulled her alongside him. They ran down the street.

"God, Reeve, I'm exhausted," she gasped.

"You're alive."

That was some consolation. "How—how did you know the Jeep was wired?"

"I told you they had stopped shooting. They were waiting for us to start the engine."

Thank goodness he was on the alert. There wasn't time for more talk though as a car careened around the corner, following them. Between Reeve limping and Allie bleeding it was amazing that they stayed in front of their attackers who were bearing down on them, their guns blazing. Dodging bullets, Reeve wove Allie up one street, down another, across a lawn, into another fountain, finally right onto the brightly lit strip of hotels crowded with people and cars.

A thrill chased through her. There were laughing people, happy people, people dressed to kill. *Dressed to kill.* She wanted to laugh hysterically at her pun.

"Allie!" Reeve snapped, bringing her from her madness. "Duck inside the building."

Music blared outside, and so many bright lights advertised the glittery motel-casino that Allie's eyes hurt. And she was more than exhausted. Her lungs hurt so from running that she thought they would burst. "Did we lose them?"

"Not yet."

Right then someone screamed as the car barreled up on the sidewalk. There were three men in the car now. It was just a glimpse, but she recognized the man from the restaurant, the mobster with the scar. He was sitting in the back seat.

"Look out!" Reeve shoved Allie inside the entrance just as the tires squealed and the car crashed into the building behind them. It burst into flames. More screams rent the air. Allie paused, but Reeve pushed her ahead. "Go!"

"Is anyone hurt?"

"No," he shouted. "Just go."

Taking advantage of the confusion, Reeve wove her through the crowds of people rushing to view the horror to an opposite door, outside and onto a golf course. "Are the men dead?"

"I think so."

She looked around them.

"Why would they crash into a wall?"

"I don't think they meant to crash," he answered. "They were trying to run us down."

"Reeve, what if people got hurt?"

"It's not our fault, Allie."

"But we led the men there."

"I don't think anyone else is hurt," he reassured her. "Everyone jumped out of the way."

She sighed her relief. "God, what are we going to do now?"

"Like any good soldier, find a hotel and regroup," he answered, studying the area. "This way."

Although she followed him, she couldn't help looking back. She was so tired. She'd heard the police sirens. "Will the police be looking for us?"

"I doubt they ever stopped looking for us."

She paused to catch her breath. "Reeve, the mobster from the restaurant was in that car, along with the two East German agents we've spotted again and again."

"Yes, I know, Allie."

"I thought they didn't like each other."

"It's not that they don't like each other, Allie. They're aware of the other's presence. The East Germans want to stop me from blowing their cover, and the Mafia was hired by Sammison as backup. In case the East Germans fail."

"And they'll work together until they...get you, Reeve?"

He sighed. "I don't think they much care. It's first come, first serve; sharing the car tonight was only a convenience. Look, Allie. Things aren't going to get better in the next twenty-four hours. In fact, just the reverse. You should prepare yourself for it."

In spite of the heat, she shivered. "I was afraid you'd say that."

What was she going to do now?

Chapter Ten

Allie stayed close to Reeve as they made their way across the golf course, ducking behind trees and shrubbery along the way. The farther they walked, the more distant the sirens grew.

Yet she still whispered. "Reeve? Reeve, how did you know it was the Mob that killed your friend?"

"The hit was clean," he answered. His voice was thick. She identified it as pain. "That's the way they do things. They probably couldn't pry any information out of him, so they shot him."

"What about the Germans? What were they doing there? Did they know him?"

She could see him shake his head. "I doubt it. I think they were set up."

She frowned. "By who?"

"Paul Sammison. He was the only person who knew I was friends with Frank. Hurry up." Taking her hand, Reeve pulled her closer. "Sammison must have told them," he went on. "They came and found Frank just like we did."

"But they seemed to know that you were coming."

"Sammison must have guessed that would be my next move. You see, if I didn't show, the Germans would have taken the murder rap for Frank's death. Right now Sammison's desperate. He doesn't want to be linked to East Germany because the agency would learn he's gone solo.

The government can't admit knowing my brother, but they can punish an agent who has gone astray.''

"But wouldn't the East German agents balk? Why would they take the rap for Sammison?''

Reeve snorted cynically. "Allie, they'd be deported at the least, and imprisoned at the worst. The U.S. government can't afford to do more. And anyway, by the time the East Germans revealed anything, Sammison would have been long gone from the country.''

He pulled her along. "But Reeve—''

"Look, Allie, let's talk at the motel. Right now, I'd just like to concentrate on getting away.''

"Is that where we're going? A motel?''

"We're both dead tired, and we haven't had a decent bath in days. I think that would be our best move.'' He paused. "How's your arm?''

"It feels like the bleeding has stopped.'' At least blood wasn't streaming down her arm.

"Good, we'll take care of it at the motel. Sorry we can't get any clean clothes. I'd sure enjoy a change.''

Only now Allie realized that she had lost her red-and-white polka-dot dress. They'd left it in the pack in the Jeep. The only thing she had was the shirt and jeans she was wearing. Not that she needed the dress; it was just a symbol of an old way of life, possibly gone for good, gone the way the dress was gone.

Hitching her jeans up, she trudged along. The golf course was beautiful, green and manicured, an oasis in the midst of the desert. Strange how water could change any landscape.

A long while later they came to a low, one-story building near the airport. Allie couldn't hear any sirens, yet when she looked back, in the distance the lights on the strip still blazed and beckoned them. It was odd. Several people had died, and not a thing had changed. The city hummed on.

The motel Reeve had chosen was busy, too. People were milling about, playing slot machines, diving into the pool or dancing to music on an equally green, well-watered lawn.

"I'll be right back," Reeve said, heading for the office. "Stay in the shadows and wait for me."

Allie glanced at him. "What if someone comes?"

"I won't be long."

She stood under a small tree. The gunshot wound, though just a scrape, stung like the devil. How had he been able to tolerate a bullet in his leg? And having it removed? Just the thought of washing her wound was enough to make her flinch.

"Ready?" She looked up, surprised to see him already. "Our room's upstairs, on the second floor." Since they were standing in the light, he glanced at her arm. "We should have grabbed the first-aid kit."

"I'll just wash it with soap and water," she answered. "It'll be fine."

"Okay. Let's go." He took her hand. "If you see anyone along the way just smile and say hello."

"Why?" Wasn't he concerned about being recognized? Or about how dirty they were? The blood crusted on her arm?

"So they don't think we're weird," he said.

Without further explanation he started up the steps, leading her behind. They met several people. With each one he smiled and nodded. They smiled and nodded back. By the time he unlocked their room, Allie was certain at least ten people had recognized them. She glanced around nervously as he opened the door and flipped on the light. The room was nice, clean and well lit. The beds looked comfortable, the furniture sturdy and attractive. A far cry from the last motel she'd been in.

Sliding the chain lock in place, he gestured to another door. "I think the bathroom's through there."

"Why did you speak to those people?" she asked. "Aren't you afraid they'll report us?"

"I doubt they even remember what we look like. Do you remember what they looked like?"

She gestured to her clothes, which were covered with dirt and blood. "We do tend to stand out, Reeve."

"We look like we've been hiking in the desert, which is what some people do out here, in spite of all the gambling furor downstairs. They go the Painted desert or to Hoover Dam. Besides, it's been my experience that most people aren't very observant, Allie. They're here for vacation, and unless something affects them directly they don't bother with their fellow man, particularly not to help."

What an indictment of humanity. But true. Even for her, for she couldn't remember a single face they'd passed. Since he swung around to toss the key on a dresser, she went toward the bathroom. "I better wash my arm."

"Good idea," he said.

The moment Allie flipped on the light she was sorry she'd gone near the bathroom. One look in the huge, brightly lit mirror and she wanted to throw up.

"Oh, God," she said, but it hardly expressed her feelings.

Reeve appeared in the mirror behind her. "Does your arm hurt that bad?"

"It's my pride that's hurt," she said, staring at her reflection. She was so scraggly looking she could have been one of the cacti bordering the highway. Actually two or three of them, and they would have been more attractive. Wisps of hair had escaped from the leather thong and now hung around her face. Her face was red and peeling and scraped here and there. "I'm a mess."

"Just a tad," he answered, picking up a washcloth and dabbing it along her arm.

"Ouch, that stings." She tried to pull her arm away, but he held her tighter.

"It's supposed to sting. Hold still."

She sucked her breath in as he scraped the cloth across the raw area. "Ouch! Look, I didn't give you those platitudes when I fixed your leg."

"I was drunk."

Ignoring her objections, he soaped the rag and rubbed harder. Allie let him tend her wound. Odd, they had come this far. Five days ago he wouldn't have cared whether or not she was hurt. They were quite a pair.

"There," he said, giving the area a final dab with clear water. "It's clean. I'll find a drugstore later and get some alcohol and Band-Aids."

"You can skip the alcohol," she told him. "Unless it's the kind we can drink. Gosh, I could go for some of that tequila."

He laughed. "I think I've taught you some bad habits, Allie."

"I could even eat the worm tonight," she declared. They were still standing in the bathroom. The bright light played on his features, the dark hair, the whiskers that had grown heavy again. "You know, I should be angry at you."

"Why?"

"Why didn't you tell me how bad I looked? I can't bear to turn around and see myself."

He laughed again and pushed a wisp of hair from her face. "You don't look so bad. Everything combined, you'd just scare a man to death."

"Reeve!" What an insult. "Gee, thanks."

"You're welcome. Want to shower first, or shall I?"

She glanced at him. Suddenly he was so laissez-faire about everything. They'd been laughing, joking. Wasn't he worried about what was happening? The people who had died? The police? "If Paul Sammison set all that business up, he has to be heavily involved with the Mob, doesn't he?" she asked.

"Seems likely."

"A CIA agent. How could the government hire a man with that kind of history?"

"I doubt he was involved with the Mob when the government hired him, Allie."

"He turned bad?"

"Probably."

"But why?"

He shrugged. "Who knows? Who can say what motivates the best of us? Greed? Need for recognition? I've seen good, decent men do the craziest things. Sometimes it's just the way it goes."

Allie supposed that was true. "Do you really think the Jeep was rigged to explode?"

"Yes."

"Why didn't it?"

"You didn't turn the key."

She shuddered again, thinking of how close they had come to death. They were still courting it. "We should report the vehicle. The keys are still in the ignition. If someone comes along and happens to start the engine—a kid or something—it will explode."

"Thank goodness it's parked in an out-of-the-way spot." He reached for the phone on the wall in the bathroom. Allie had always wondered who used them. Now she knew. "Just in case, I'll call the police."

He made the call as an anonymous tipster, then recradled the phone. He padded into the bedroom, with Allie looking eagerly on. "Where do we go from here?" she asked.

"Back to Denver. I think I'd like to try to talk to the FBI agents there. They might be interested in a deal—trading what I know about Sammison, for pressuring the other agency, the CIA, into securing a release for Curt."

"Why would they do that?"

"Because the agencies sometimes compete for kudos. From congress, the president, the justice department...depends on who's handing them out this year. And a maverick agent, who's been identified, is a hot commodity."

Allie frowned. "But Reeve, how much time do you think you have to get your brother released?"

Pain lurked in the blue depths of his eyes. He shook his head. "If Sammison was only calling my bluff, to distract me, then I figure not much. We'll have to see, Allie."

She hurt for him, and decided to change the topic. "Are we going to leave tonight?"

"No, I think we'll rest tonight."

"Aren't you worried we'll be found? I'm sure the police will be searching the motels for us, once they figure out we're in town. They probably have the make on your Jeep, and the license number, and it won't be hard to connect your phone call with the abandoned Jeep. They'll also suspect we did Frank in when they find the vehicle parked in front of his home, and his body inside."

Reeve pressed his lips together, and she saw the glint of pain again. "They will, Allie. Kidnapping, murder. But I can't worry about that now. And as far as the motels go, there are a lot of them in Vegas. If they do search, it'll take them all night. More than likely they'll think we've gone."

She glanced out the bathroom door at the two beds. Sleep sounded pleasant, particularly on a mattress. When she glanced back to Reeve he was already unbuttoning his shirt. "What are you doing?"

"I told you I'm taking a shower. You can either stay here and join me, or take your own."

Join him? Why would he say that? But he didn't even glance her way, so she doubted he'd meant what she'd been thinking. He just kept stripping off his clothes. Though she'd seen him without them before, Allie found herself leaning against the sink staring at him. He'd turned around to take off his boots, and the muscles in his back rippled and flexed with the movement. Once again she wanted to touch him, to run her hand across those muscles. They were hard and sinewy. His skin would be hot to the touch. She could remember how it felt when she had bathed him, so smooth and yet so rough.

One boot clunked to the floor and then the other. He tossed them into a corner and hung up his shirt. Unsnapping his jeans, he turned back to her. The muscles in his chest and stomach were as taut as the muscles on his back. There wasn't an ounce of fat on him. Her gaze followed the line of dark hair arrowing into the waistband of his shorts.

"Allie?"

Startled, she jerked her gaze away from his body. "Oh," she said, standing up straight and walking into the bedroom. "I'm sorry. I was thinking about something."

"What?" he asked as though he was concerned.

"Nothing special." She had to stop dreaming about him—his body. The last few days in the desert had been torment; she'd been at war with herself, and she was losing the battle. "Are you hungry?" she asked, looking for an excuse to leave the room. "Did you want me to call room service?"

"Sure. Why don't you order us a couple of steaks?"

"If you don't mind, I think I'll get chicken," she said, to mock her occasional flashes of cowardice. Why didn't she just admit that she wanted him and get it over with?

Reeve passed her and went into the bathroom. He partially closed the door and finished undressing inside.

The entire time Reeve was in the shower Allie thought about nothing but what it would be like to join him. By the time he came out, dripping wet, a towel wrapped around his hips, she was pacing the room restlessly.

He glanced at her. "Something wrong?"

"No." She looked away. She pointed to the television. "Do you think anything's worth watching?"

"Why don't you turn it on. No room service yet?"

"I'm sure they'll be here soon." She whirled. This was silly. "I'm going to shower." Noticing his leg, she paused. "Reeve, your wound—"

"Is fine."

"But we don't have any more bandages."

"It's healing well, Allie. I'll be fine. The air will do it good. Why don't you go ahead? I'll turn on the television while you're washing."

She didn't want the television on, now. Didn't he know that? She wanted him to throw her down on the bed and make mad, passionate love to her, Indian lance and all. Disgusted with her silly fantasies, she wheeled into the bathroom, slammed the door and turned on the shower full tilt, letting the sharp shards of water beat some sense into her head.

Once she'd washed and shampooed, Allie felt better. Wiping away the steam, she stood in front of the mirror, glancing at her reflection. Instead she saw Reeve. Reeve naked, standing with just the towel around him, chest bare, feet spread apart in an aggressive stance, all authoritative male. Reeve on his great white stallion. She could remember thinking several days ago that he would bring a woman pleasure. In his arms, a woman would feel like a woman.

Oh, hell, she thought, jerking open the bathroom door. Enough waffling. She wanted to be that woman.

Room service had arrived. Although Reeve hadn't started eating, he was sipping coffee and watching a television news program. He'd pulled his jeans back on, but his feet and chest were bare, like she'd imagined.

He glanced at her. "Hi. Feel better?"

"Much." She leaned against the doorway wrapped in the towel.

"Food's here."

She nodded. "Anything about us on the news yet?"

"No. I imagine if there's anything, it will be on the late news tonight."

"Good." She went to flip off the set and turned to him. "Reeve?"

He glanced at her, obviously puzzled. "Yes?"

"What did you mean a few minutes ago about showering with you?"

"Nothing. Don't you want to watch TV?"

I want you to make love to me.

"No." Allie was almost certain he was lying. Though he had denied that he had meant anything by his invitation, his complexion had turned dusky. Did men flush? She flushed, too, as she said, "I might have done it, you know."

"That's the last thing you need, Allie," he said gruffly, purposely moving away, across the room. God, he wanted her. Every moment he had spent with this woman it had been harder and harder to keep his hands off her. She was warmth and light and life all rolled into one. Passion and fire. Need. When he'd kissed her in the desert he'd wanted to take her right then and there, cart her off on his horse like some savage and keep her with him forever. And he wasn't sure how much longer he could resist. Now she was standing there in that damned towel, warm and damp from the shower.

"Why?" she asked. She'd been puzzled by that comment before. He'd made it in the desert, and she hadn't pressed. Now she wanted to.

"Why what?"

"Why is that the last thing I need?" She hated to be so bold, but she needed to know. She *had* to know. Tomorrow might be the last day she saw him. He might be harmed or worse.

"It just is, Allie."

"Because we'd make love?"

At last he turned back to her. Her hair was wet, and tiny tendrils fell to her shoulders, all curly and blond. The towel barely covered her breasts. "Yes."

"What's so bad about that?" Allie could barely talk she was so embarrassed. She was acting like a wanton. Yet she persisted. "Reeve?" She moved closer to him. "Reeve, do you remember the other day when I asked what you said to a woman you made love to?"

"So, Allie?"

She peered at him, looking all needy and sensuous and warm. "Reeve? Could you talk dirty to me?"

For a moment he didn't speak; he just stared at her, raking his gaze down her body, the towel barely masking the soft curve of her breasts, the lush roundness of her hips, the triangle at the juncture of her legs. How much more could he take? God, he didn't want to hurt her. He was a mercenary. A soldier of fortune. Perhaps not in body anymore, but in spirit. He didn't want a woman to complicate his life. He didn't want to complicate a woman's life, particularly not this woman's. "Allie," he murmured huskily. "Don't do this."

She licked her lips. She could see the passion reflected in his blue eyes. He wanted her, too. She could also see the agony, the struggle. "Please, Reeve?"

"God, don't beg."

"I want you," she said, moving even closer. She laid her hands on his chest and stroked him. She could feel his heart thud loudly, and she gazed longingly into his eyes.

"This isn't right, Allie."

"Why not?" She took his hand and placed it under her breast, letting him cup the fullness. Her nipple peaked against his palm as she thrust toward him, tempting him. "Love me, Reeve."

"How many?" he asked hoarsely, holding back.

At first she was confused. "How many what?"

"How many men have you had?"

"One." Placing her hand behind his head, she started to pull his lips down to meet hers. The space between them grew shorter and shorter. "Only one. Does it matter?"

"No."

"It doesn't matter to me, either."

"Allie, I can't give you anything," he murmured just before their lips met. "I can't make promises."

God, how he wished he could.

"I don't expect any," she whispered back. "All I want is the pleasure of being with you, now."

"Lord," he groaned.

"Don't fight it, Reeve." Standing on tiptoe, she pressed herself into him. The contours of their bodies fit perfectly, as his hardness met her soft curves. "Kiss me."

With a deep, husky moan, Reeve gave in and pulled her into his arms, pressing his mouth to hers. God, he'd wanted her for so long, so badly. It was all he could do to hold back so she would get some pleasure out of it. Passion exploded between them like the heat of the desert. They reached for each other hungrily. Allie ran her hands through the dark hair that had fascinated her for so many days, then across his stubbled cheeks, along his neck, over his shoulders, down his arms.

Burrowing his fingers in her hair, too, clutching her to him, he deepened the embrace, all the while pushing her toward the bed. Arms and legs entwined, lips and bodies pressed together, they stumbled across the room and tumbled onto the nearest mattress. Kissing with an almost savage intensity, they rolled around on the bed like lovers possessed. Allie kept entwining her hands in his hair or raking her nails across his back, pulling him ever closer, wanting him, needing him. Their breath was hot and hard, coming fast.

Reeve was ready for her instantly. She could feel him pressed against her thigh, and boldly she placed her hand on the front of his jeans.

"Wait a minute," he muttered.

Standing up, he unzipped his pants and shed them quickly, along with his underwear. Allie was already naked, having lost her towel when they tumbled onto the mattress. She delighted in the feel of him next to her. With hardly a pause, he drew her back into his arms and kissed her again.

There was no gentleness between them as the desire they had fought for the past week sizzled to the surface. Allie couldn't say who was the aggressor. Pressing closer, she opened her lips to his thrusting, exploring tongue and savored the taste of him. The small gesture seemed to excite Reeve even more, for he kissed her harder and harder, dragging his lips along her body, branding her with kisses. She met him touch for touch, kiss for kiss, caress for ca-

ress. She felt love and rapture, and her entire body ached
with the need of him.

They didn't speak; all they could do was gasp for breath
as, almost roughly, he nudged her leg aside and plunged inside her. The moment was so pleasurable that she moaned
and arched against him. "Reeve."

He rested his head on her chest. "Oh, God, Allie. Hang
on."

Slowly, he started moving. And then faster. And faster.
Harder. Thrusting into her. Driving her on. It felt so good
she wanted to cry. She gasped and arched toward him over
and over, meeting him, needing him, seeking. In all her life
she'd never experienced anything like this before, the joy,
the pleasure, the hurt of loving and being loved.

"Reeve!" she cried out at the end, clutching him as
spasms racked her body.

The moment had to have been explosive for him, too, for
he gasped with pleasure as satisfaction surged through him
in giant waves. Allie could feel the intensity of his climax,
slight thrusting movements inside her. With a sigh of ex-
haustion, he collapsed on her, burying his head in the curve
of her shoulder. "Oh, Allie."

They lay entwined still joined together.

After a few moments he shifted his weight. "Are you all
right? Am I too heavy for you?"

"No, you're fine," she answered, still thrilling to their
lovemaking. Never, never had she felt anything so intense,
so rapturous.

"Here." Reeve moved completely off her and rolled her
over in his arms, hugging her next to his body.

"That's fine." She rested her head on his shoulder as he
smoothed back her hair. It was damp from sweat.

Leaning down, he kissed her forehead gently. "How was
it for you?"

He had to ask? Allie didn't quite know what to say. Okey
doke seemed a bit pale. *Pretty good, fella? Damned good,*

in fact. Reeve Chandler made love like he made war, with every fiber of his being.

"I'm sorry if you didn't climax," he said when she didn't speak. "I couldn't hold back any longer."

"I didn't expect you to."

He frowned at her. His expression was so puzzled. "Allie, are you having regrets?"

"No," she said. "Oh, no. No regrets."

"Then what's the problem?"

She turned away, uncomfortable. "There's no problem," she said. "I'm just not used to being so open about my response to a man."

"Why not? We've shared a lot the past several days." And they'd been open about their feelings the entire time. Placing his hand on her chin, he turned her back to face him. "Did you climax, Allie?"

"Yes," she murmured, turning red.

"Did you enjoy it?"

She flushed darker. "Yes."

"Had you ever climaxed before?"

"Reeve!"

"It doesn't matter." He gestured to the room-service cart. "Are you hungry? The food's here. Though it's probably cold." Swinging from the bed, he handed her a covered platter. "Chicken, I believe."

"Not anymore," she said.

He frowned at her. "Pardon me?"

"I'm not chicken anymore." She swung her legs off the bed, too, and reached for his shirt, slipping it on. Smiling, immensely pleased with herself, she took the plate and began to eat.

"You know, Allie," he said, watching her for several long moments. "I have a hard time figuring you out."

"There's nothing mysterious about me, Reeve," she answered, lifting the cover on the food and digging into the crispy fried chicken. "I just feel good." Rapturous, more precisely.

While they ate, Reeve flipped on the television. The national news was on now. The entire half hour passed without word of them. Of course, considering the crisis on Capitol Hill, and the scandal rippling through another television ministry, she doubted they'd even garner a mention. What were a couple of killers in comparison to sex and sin?

Later Allie took another shower. Reeve was lying in bed with the lights out when she came out of the bathroom, but he wasn't asleep. He kept watching her, yet not saying anything. The only light in the room was reflected from outside.

"Want to watch television?" Allie asked. "I'll turn it back on."

"No."

"Want something else to eat?"

He shook his head. "It's late. We should go to sleep."

"Did you hear the coyote?"

"What?"

Moving beside his bed, she slipped in beside him, still wrapped in the towel. "Did you hear the coyote?" she repeated, snuggling next to him. "I did. He's howling for his mate."

He laughed, actually chuckled huskily.

Of course Reeve made love to her, this time gently, leisurely, as if they had all the time in the world, bringing her to the brink of fulfillment and back so many times she thought she would go mad in his arms. Finally he allowed her to crest the wave; he rode the swell with her. Allie felt as if she had died and come back to life, but it was a pleasant experience. One she wanted to repeat over and over.

Afterward, when her heart and breathing came back to normal, she lay in his arms, resting her head on his chest. "You know," she said thoughtfully. "When I get back to Chicago, I think I'm going to design another line of lingerie."

"Two lines?"

She nodded. "I'm going to call this one Satisfaction."

He looked down at her as though amused by her statement. "Really?" he said dryly. "You're just full of yourself, aren't you, Allie?"

She was full of him. And she was deliriously happy. She smiled. "Very."

"You like to talk a lot, you know."

"You already told me that—a long time ago." Just a week. A mere week.

"Did I? Okay," he said, "so tell me, what's the line going to look like."

She smiled again and leaned back in bed, stretching her arms languidly over her head. "Uhmm. Let me see. I think it's going to be red. With red bows."

"Why so plain?"

"It won't be plain." She glanced at him. "I intend to use see-through fabrics."

"Oh," he said as she lowered her arms and rolled back onto his chest, all in one motion. She tangled a finger in the silky matting of black chest hair, drawing circles. "Reeve, you know they make risqué underwear for men?"

He laughed. "I wouldn't be caught dead in risqué underwear, Allie."

"No, I suppose not," she answered. "But you look good in classic white." She kept twirling her finger around in circles. Finally she traced along the scar she'd noticed the first time she'd touched him. "What's this from?"

"It was a long time ago."

"From what, though?" She pulled back and grinned at him. "Was it a girl? Reeve, were you fighting over a girl?"

"No."

"Then what?"

He scowled. "It's self-inflicted, Allie—to prove my bravery."

She stared at him. "You cut yourself to prove that you were brave?"

"It used to be an Indian tradition. Long since abandoned. Or at least modified."

"A good thing." She flopped back down, resting on him. It was so comforting to hear his heart. "Reeve, did you ever see that movie with the Indians—I believe they were Apache—where they bury the settlers in the sand and spread honey on their heads for the ants to eat?"

"Where'd they get the honey?"

"I don't know. Aren't there bees in the desert?"

"Actually, yes, there are bees in the desert. They gather nectar from the cactus flowers. But that scene sounds grotesque."

"It was. When you first kidnapped me, I thought you were going to do that to me."

He nearly choked in amazement. "What? Why?"

"I have a vivid imagination."

"Obviously. Allie, the American Indian has been cheated by the white man, nearly annihilated by the government and betrayed by his own brothers. Lands have been taken, legends lost, a way of life destroyed, but they have never been more maligned than by the movie industry."

"I'm sorry."

"You didn't do it. Actually it sounds like a fairly decent film. And the Indian torture is accurate, too, nice and subtle."

There was nothing subtle about this Indian. "Reeve, Danhi called you Wòòdii. Is that your Indian name?"

"Yes."

"What does it mean?"

"Runner."

Another irony. He was certainly doing that now. She lay there a moment just thinking. He moved her hand from his chest and brought it to his lips, kissing it. "Allie, that tickles."

"Oh." She readjusted her body, but she couldn't figure out what to do with her hand. Finally she placed it back down. "I won't move."

"What's the matter, can't you sleep?"

"No."

"Frightened?"

"No," she said again, truthfully. "I'm all wound up. You know, I did think you were savage, Reeve. You scared me so."

"I don't anymore?"

"Sometimes you still do," she answered. The situation scared her. She knew this idyllic moment wouldn't last. It would die tomorrow. Suddenly she feared Reeve getting hurt. She didn't know if she could live with that. "Will you hold me, Reeve?"

"Sure." He turned her to her side and circled his arms around her. "Want to hear about my ranch?"

She laughed. "Don't tell me. You have horses."

"That's right," he said, realizing she was mocking their earlier conversation. He probably deserved it. She was mighty spirited, this Miss Martin. "But you haven't seen mine."

She turned her head to him quickly. Her whimsical fantasy of him had resurfaced. "Reeve, what color is your horse?"

"Chestnut."

"You should have a white horse."

He laughed and turned her back over, so he could enfold her more closely in his arms. "Go to sleep, Allie."

They'd spent so many nights together, said so many good-nights, but none like this. She wanted to cherish it. She moved closer to him and closed her eyes. Yes, he needed a white horse. A great white stallion. And a war lance.

"Good night, Reeve."

Chapter Eleven

"Allie, it's time to get up," Reeve woke her early the next morning. Dreary gray came in the windows. "We have to go."

Disoriented, she sat up in bed and pushed her hair back. "What time is it?"

"Around five. I want to get out of here before too many people start milling about," he went on as he handed her the clothes she'd washed out the night before. "We'll catch breakfast on the road."

"How are we going to get to Denver?" It had just occurred to Allie that they didn't have any transportation. They could hardly take the Jeep.

"I'm going to steal a car from the parking lot downstairs."

Allie didn't doubt that he knew how. Dressing hurriedly, she washed and then followed him out of the room and down the stairs, walking on the cement as quietly as he did. She still wore the moccasins he'd made for her, and she crept around soundlessly in them.

"Did you pay for the room already?" she asked as they rounded the last step and headed into the parking lot.

"Yes. Last night."

"Don't we have to go to the office to check out?"

"Most motels have express check-out these days. If you don't have any charges, all you have to do is leave the key on the dresser."

Reeve stopped beside a small, brown nondescript car. It wasn't even a late model. As he walked up to it, he glanced around for anyone who might be observing them. "This one looks good."

"It's little," Alanna said.

Reeve nodded. Reaching into his pocket, he pulled out a long, nail-file-like contraption and slipped it into the key lock. The moment he made contact, an alarm went off, blaring loudly in the predawn quiet.

"Damn!" He jumped back, grabbing her and running before anyone could see them. "There wasn't a sticker in the window. Of all the cars in the world, why the hell is that one rigged?"

Allie couldn't resist. Following behind him, she whispered dryly, "So someone doesn't steal it."

"The damned thing is junk," he whispered back.

Reeve kept crouching and running, pulling her along. They could hear footsteps as several people headed toward the car. In the early-morning silence the alarm sounded loud enough to wake the dead. Ignoring it, they wove in and out of vehicles. Finally Reeve paused near another plain-looking car. "We'll take this one."

"What if it's rigged, too?"

"Our luck can't be that bad."

Allie wasn't so certain. "What if someone sees us? There are people over there."

"They're trying to shut off that alarm."

"Aren't they worried that someone tried to steal the car?"

"Those alarms go off all the time. I'm hoping they'll think it's a false alarm."

As he worked on this car, Allie peeked over her shoulder at the crowd of people that had converged around the little brown car. A police squad car had cruised up and a blue-clad cop was climbing out.

"Reeve, the police."

"Don't worry about it."

"But that's a cop over there."

"Come on, Allie." He'd gotten the car door open; he held it, waiting for her to slide inside.

Suddenly Alanna paused. Call it crazy, stupid, boldness in the face of danger, she had to know. "Reeve, do you really think I'm sexy?"

"Oh, hell, Allie."

"You didn't answer me when we were in the desert," she said. "Do you really think I've got a nice body?"

Reeve stared at her as though he was certain she'd lost every marble she might have once possessed. "You ask the damndest questions at the worst times. Lady, I think you've got a great body. Hell, I think you're balls-out sexy, but we're trying to get away."

"Thank you." She was pleased—no, delighted—and she leaned up on tiptoe to kiss him.

But he just shook his head in disbelief. "Allie, will you get in!" he urged her. "We have to get away!"

She couldn't help being happy. Laughing, she slid across the seat.

"Shh," he warned, starting the car by reaching under the dash and twisting some wires. "Don't draw attention to us."

To her mind they were conspicuous enough. But a part of her wanted to cry out, let every person in the parking lot know that Reeve Chandler thought Alanna Martin was sexy. And that they had just stolen a Chevrolet Caprice. "It's air-conditioned," she remarked. "And it has a tape deck."

"Don't get comfortable. We're going to ditch it before we get to Denver and steal another one."

"Why?"

"The police look for stolen cars."

Right at that moment they went past the police cruiser and the crowd of people circling the brown sedan. The alarm had been shut off, and the policeman was writing out some kind of ticket. The owner of the car would have to pay for shrilling out a false alarm. He glanced up at them as Reeve drove by.

"Smile," Reeve said to Allie, realizing she'd made eye contact with the policeman.

Allie did, but she'd started to tremble. Why had she been fooling herself last night? And this morning. Acting stupid, as if they were a couple of lovers without a care in the world. She'd actually joked with Reeve, and this was serious business.

"You're doing fine," Reeve said from beside her.

"Oh, God," she murmured back as he placed his hand over hers, giving her courage.

The moment stretched endlessly. They drove out of the lot and onto the highway. Allie was afraid to look back. She sat paralyzed, her back ramrod straight.

"Is he following?"

"No."

"Why not?"

"He doesn't have a reason to follow."

"But surely they found the Jeep."

"That doesn't mean they know it's us driving away." Reeve gestured to the dash. "Why don't you turn on the radio?"

She sat stiffly.

"Allie, move!" She jumped at his command. "Look, put in a tape and relax," he said in a softer tone.

"How can I relax with the police chasing us?"

"The police aren't chasing us."

"The Mob then, and the CIA and the FBI." She couldn't prevent the edge of hysteria that crept into her voice. It was as if she had just now realized what they were into. "And the Germans, Reeve, don't forget the Germans." She didn't mention the three men who'd crashed into the wall. Their loss would only enrage their organizations, who would send more of their lackeys to harm Reeve. The thought increased her anxiety.

Reeve glanced at her. "You're losing it, Allie. Pull yourself together."

How could he expect her to just blithely turn on the radio? To just pretend nothing was wrong? Didn't he realize what was going on? There were people chasing them, trying to murder him. Or didn't he care?

"Move closer," he said. "Come on, Allie, put your head on my shoulder."

Now he was treating her as if she were a child. Yet she moved toward him, comforted by his nearness. She sighed. She'd ridden out of Denver in that position; odd that she was starting a return trip to the city the same way.

"All right now?"

"Yes."

"Good. We're almost home free."

"Do you really think the police have found the Jeep?"

"I hope so. Why?"

"I was thinking that if they had, they might have set up a roadblock."

"I'm sure the police figure we've left town after abandoning the Jeep, Allie. Besides," he went on, "it's pretty tough to roadblock a town like Vegas. Too many tourists."

"Are the casinos open?"

"They never close. There aren't any clocks, either, to remind the patrons of the time."

Allie found it hard to imagine gambling when the sun was barely up over the horizon. But then, if there were no clocks, time probably had no meaning in the darkened buildings that were still lit up behind them in the morning sky. Reeve drove north out of the Emerald City into the desert, headed the other way.

THE TRIP FROM Las Vegas to Denver was well over seven hundred miles. But the road curved up into Utah and went directly across Colorado, right through the middle of the Rocky Mountains. They drove all day and well into the night. After they ate dinner, under cover of darkness, Reeve stole another car up near Dillon. It was another midsize vehicle seen commonly on the roads.

Allie had managed to relax some, but she never did regain the high spirits of the morning. They saw an occasional police car along the way, but no one bothered them. So far the Mob was absent, and so was the CIA. The drive could have been the result of a vacation, like so many people they saw on the road, luggage piled up on top of their cars, little kids tucked inside. Yet the closer they got to Denver the more Allie wondered if Sammison hadn't expected Reeve to go back there. Could he have anticipated Reeve's move? So far he'd guessed their every intention.

They checked into a small motel on the outskirts of town. It was built off the highway to catch weary travelers. A small welcome sign beckoned them.

"What name have you been giving?" Allie asked Reeve as they headed toward their room. Though it wasn't late they'd been on the road for a long time, and they were both tired. Their strides reflected their fatigue.

"Mr. and Mrs. John Smith," Reeve answered.

How ordinary. And it didn't even remotely connect to them. Then she supposed that in this instance creativity would have been misguided. "How have you been paying?"

"Cash."

He opened the door and flicked on the light. "Do you want to shower first this time?"

"Go ahead." Suddenly, her fear bursting out of control, she swung around to confront him. "Reeve, aren't you concerned? Don't you want to talk about what we're going to do?"

He shook his head. "No."

She sighed. Whatever had gotten into her this morning had not left. She was feeling so despondent. Frightened. Perhaps it was because she had realized that she was in love with him, and didn't want anything to happen to him.

Allie blinked, stunned by the revelation. *Love? She was in love with Reeve Chandler?* The thought amazed her. When had that happened? She didn't even know him. Yet she felt as if she'd known him forever. She trusted him implicitly.

She glanced at him. He was peeling off his shirt. He pulled both boots off, letting them clatter to the floor, and started toward the bathroom. "How about ordering up a snack?"

She turned her gaze to the accommodations. While this motel wasn't a dump, it wasn't topflight, either, and she doubted that it came equipped with a kitchen. "Do you think they have room service?"

"We can always try. Get me some nachos."

Allie went to the phone. They were going to die, and he wanted nachos. How odd.

Then she shook her head to clear it. She had to stop thinking this way. Nothing was going to happen to them. Yet she was afraid to turn on the television. If they were being hunted she didn't want to hear about it. She tried the front desk, but the manager told her she'd have to go down the street to a nearby shopping center for food. Hanging up, she wandered around the room looking at things while Reeve showered. She listened to the people go by outside, hearing their voices, imagining what they looked like, why they were here.

Perhaps it was the inactivity after all the running they had done or the sudden drop in adrenaline, but Allie couldn't seem to shake her despondency. She glanced at the gun Reeve had tossed on the bed before removing his boots. She could almost forget they were running it if wasn't for the dark metal weapon. Much as she feared it, she had to admit that it had saved her life a couple of times.

Dammit, they could die. Their lives were in grave danger. Worse than before, for now Sammison would really want them dead. Already the lives of at least five people had been snuffed out. She stood up and started pacing across the room. What if she died today? Was she ready for her life to end?

Just then Reeve came out of the bathroom wrapped in a towel. She stared at him. Water dripped from his dark hair and more droplets clung to his chest hairs, glistening in the incandescent light.

He glanced at her. "Something wrong?"

I want to make love with you. I want to lie in your arms like I did that night in the desert, like last night in the motel, and let you protect me.

"Allie?"

She could hardly blurt that out.

He stood in front of her. She looked blond, and sensuous, and frozen scared. "Allie, is something wrong? Did something happen?"

She tried to shake off her spooky feeling. "No, nothing happened. I was just thinking about things."

"Things?"

"Us. Running."

"I see. Scared again?"

"I guess my bravery was short-lived." She stood up. "I'm such a chicken. You know, almost all my life I lived in suburbia. Nothing ever really happened, but I was always scared. My brother would tell me tales about monsters and goblins and the boogeyman. I even hated to go out on Halloween."

"Nice brother."

"He *was* nice," she defended Geoff. "Just mischievous, knowing he could frighten me. It was kind of like the little red dog."

He frowned. "What little red dog?"

Allie sighed. "We had this neighbor who had a little red dog," she explained. "It was the cutest thing. They'd put bows in the dog's hair and brush it and fix it up, but it was afraid. Every time the doorbell rang or someone came over, the dog would just sit there and shake, it was so scared. The neighbor, he'd just laugh. Then he'd go 'Boo!,' and he'd slap his hands, and the poor thing would run. It would run to the bedroom and hide, and he'd say, 'Run, little red dog. Run.'" She paused. "God, I feel like that little red dog. So helpless."

Coming toward her, Reeve took her in his arms. "Come on, Allie. Everything's going to be fine."

Even he had known that she couldn't hold up. Few could sustain this sort of tension, whether city- or country-bred. And he knew she hated to disappoint him.

"Oh, Reeve, I'm so scared."

He held her, stroking her back to soothe her nerves. "Allie, you know I won't let anything happen to you."

She nodded. "Yes, I know."

He kissed her gently.

"Oh, Reeve."

"Don't start crying, Allie."

She shook her head, sniffling. "No, I won't."

"Go get a shower." He traced a line of dirt down her cheek split by a tear. "You're dirty again."

"I always seem to be dirty these days."

"You know, Allie, you are one sexy-looking dame."

She rolled her eyes. She still had scratches and bruises all over her body, and now her entire face was peeling. "You've been in the desert too long." She went toward the shower, but she turned back around. "Reeve, could I call my parents?"

"Why?"

"I've been thinking about them. I don't want them to worry about me."

"I'm sorry, I don't think it's a good idea, Allie."

She nodded understanding. "Okay."

"Did you try room service?"

"They don't have a restaurant here. There's a shopping center down the block."

"Stay put and get your shower. I'll go get us a snack. Want some tequila?" he asked, grinning.

She laughed through her tears. "No. Not tonight." All she wanted tonight was the comfort of his arms.

Pulling on his clothes, he headed for the door. Then coming back, he chucked her under the chin. "Buck up, woman. See you in a bit."

She nodded. After he left, she showered. When she was finished she put back on her shirt—or rather, his shirt—and wandered around the room again. She couldn't say what made her go to the phone. Perhaps she needed to prove that nothing would happen. Or perhaps she needed the security of talking to her family. On sudden impulse she dialed the long-distance operator. She was connected to the number before she could change her mind.

Her father answered sleepily, yet in his authoritarian doctor tone. "Dr. Martin here."

"Hi, Daddy."

"Allie!" He seemed delighted to hear her voice. "Allie, where are you? Are you all right, honey? We've had the police looking all over for you."

She laughed, delighted to hear him speak, too. It had been so long since she'd heard his voice. She was glad she'd called. "I'm fine, Daddy. I'm with Reeve."

There was a brief pause. "That man who kidnapped you? Allie, are you on a first-name basis with him?"

She was on more than a first-name basis with him. "Look, everything's fine, Daddy. I didn't want you to worry."

"Oh, dear, Allie. He hasn't harmed you—bothered you in any way?" he probed, a touch hysterical.

"No, he hasn't harmed me. I just wanted you to know that everything's okay, and you shouldn't worry."

"Where are you Allie?"

"At the Peak's View Motel in Denver. Daddy, listen to me." She had a sudden feeling she'd made a mistake in calling. "Everything's fine. I even took a bullet from his leg."

She could hear some background voices talking, her mother and brother probably. Odd that Geoff would be staying at home. Her father covered the phone for a moment. Then he said, "Okay, honey, that's fine. You say you removed a bullet?"

She nodded even though he couldn't see her. "You would have been proud of me. It's healing beautifully. Is that Mother?"

"Yes. She says to tell you that if you get into trouble she'll defend you, even on Capitol Hill. And Geoff says to tell you that he's looking forward to seeing if your fingernails are broken."

The rat. "They're a mess," she said, glancing at them herself. The once-long, red nails were broken and peeling. "Look, I'd better go." She'd heard some people outside. She didn't want Reeve to come in and realize she'd made the call, particularly not after he'd told her not to. He would be upset. "Don't worry about me. Okay? I'll call you when we get everything worked out. Reeve is going to talk to the FBI in the morning."

"Okay, honey, sounds fine. We love you."

"Oh, Daddy," she said. "When we were kids...it was Geoff who threw that ball through the church window."

"What?"

She broke the connection. Then she went to the television and turned it on. This time, although it was close to eleven at night, there was news of her and Reeve. Their faces flashed on a late-night bulletin. Reeve walked in carrying potato chips and pop just as the photos flashed off and the logo of the Denver-based station crossed the screen dramatically.

"What's this?" he asked.

She shrugged. "I don't know. A news bulletin. It's on next."

He poured two colas and opened the chips as they watched a commercial message. They could have been any travelers, looking at the news. Then the newscaster appeared, a tall, grim-faced man who stared into the camera as if the world had come to an end. "Authorities are still searching the western wilderness areas for the niece of Senator Hack and the ex-CIA agent who has taken her hostage," he said. "The couple was last sighted in Las Vegas where Chandler is suspected in the gunshot murder of newspaper correspondent, Frank Vinees. Both Miss Martin's family and Senator Hack have been unavailable for comment."

They faded into oblivion, replaced by the wife of a television evangelist who was contacting a lawyer, intending to sue the news media for slander.

Reeve handed Allie a glass of cola. "Want some chips?"

She blinked at him. "Reeve, don't you think we should discuss some kind of plan?" She gestured at the television. "They're looking for you."

"In Vegas. And there's nothing I can do about it now."

"Did you call the FBI?"

"No."

"Why not?"

"I'll call in the morning. I don't want to tip off my presence."

"What are you going to do if they don't want to deal with you?"

He glanced at her. "I'm going to go on Channel Four news and tell my story to the nation."

Allie was shocked. "How will you do that?"

"I'll probably have to bully my way in."

He wouldn't have any problems doing that, not if the way he'd bullied her the first few days they'd been together was any indication. Of course, lately, he hadn't bullied her at all. "With a car?"

"And a gun."

Her gaze fell again to the dark blue Colt .45. Tomorrow. Not wanting to think about tomorrow, she turned back to the television screen.

"I brought you something," Reeve said, pulling out a small package from his shirt pocket.

Allie took the green drugstore bag. "What is it?"

"Cream for your face."

She laughed.

"Aloe."

"Why didn't we just take a few plants from the desert?" she joked, but she opened the jar and started to rub the cream onto her thirsty skin. It felt cool and soothing.

"Here." He tossed her some nail polish and a hairbrush.

Allie stared at him.

"I couldn't find a dress."

"Have I been that down that you wanted to buy me a dress?"

"I thought it might lift your spirits."

"Reeve, I'm really sorry for being such a trial to you all this time."

"You didn't do anything, Allie."

"I made things miserable for you in the desert."

"You weren't alone." He laughed. "Actually you've been the least of my troubles."

"I'll bet."

"Will you be glad to get home?"

She hesitated. What an ill-timed question. What was he getting at? "I don't know. Why do you ask? Is something wrong?"

"Everything's fine. It's just that we're almost on the home stretch. And you talked about your parents earlier. I thought maybe you were anxious to see a traffic jam again."

"I can see that in downtown Denver, can't I?" she asked.

He laughed. "Unfortunately, yes. Tired?"

She nodded. "Reeve, I hope your brother is alive and intact."

"So do I, Allie. God, so do I."

Soon after, they went to bed. They didn't say much more. When Reeve reached for her, they made love. Strange, they had made love three times, and each time it had been different. Now their coming together was poignant, tender, as if he was telling her goodbye. But that was ridiculous. They were together. And she loved him.

"Reeve?" she whispered afterward.

"Everything's going to be fine, Allie."

She didn't question him any further. Curling up in his arms, she went to sleep.

ALLIE WOKE EARLY the next morning. Reeve was already up, dressing. She wasn't certain what woke her, a noise perhaps, a feeling of fear. Not having him beside her. As usual, he moved around the room silently, no wasted motions. After he scrawled a note, he checked the chamber of the big gun and tucked it into his boot. Suddenly Allie knew he was leaving without her. He *had* been telling her goodbye last night.

She jumped out of bed. "Reeve, wait."

"Allie," he said, whirling around to her.

"Are you up already?" Pretending she hadn't guessed his intention, she reached for her clothes. "You must want an early start. I'll hurry. Why didn't you wake me?"

He took her pants from her. "You don't have to get up, Allie."

"We're leaving, aren't we?" she said, sitting very still and praying that she was wrong. "I have to get ready."

He didn't say anything for a moment. He'd lain awake most of the night trying to figure out what to do with her, how to handle this moment. He knew she'd be hurt. "Look, Allie, I'm leaving, but you're not."

She shook her head. "That's silly. I can't stay here. Look, give me my pants."

"Listen to me, Allie," he said. "Things are getting too dangerous. I've called the police. I talked to that guy, Younger, who questioned you a few days ago and told him where we are. He's coming to get you."

"Now?"

"In a few minutes. Someone from CIA will probably contact you, too."

"Sammison?"

"No. I told Younger to notify Washington and get somebody official. When they question you, tell them anything they want to know."

Including the fact that they'd slept together? "But why? I don't understand, Reeve."

"What's to understand?"

"Where are you going?"

"I told you, I'm going to see the FBI."

"But the police know where you are. You tipped them off."

"I'll be fine."

"You planned this last night, didn't you?" she accused him. "That's what you were trying to tell me."

"Allie, I'm thinking of your safety."

"I don't want to be safe, Reeve." Her voice shook as she lunged again for her clothes. "I'm going with you," she said when he held on to them. "Reeve, we're in this together. I want to help you."

"The best way you can help me is to cooperate. I want you in police protection, Allie," he said. "Just get dressed before Younger gets here."

"Don't make a joke out of this, Reeve." She was getting mad. "I'm dressing now." He could go ahead and leave. She'd just follow him.

"God, you're stubborn." Shaking his head with disgust, he scooped up her clothes, took them to the shower and tossed them in a heap under running water. "That should slow you down." Coming from the bathroom, he leaned over to kiss her. "Goodbye, sexy lady."

"Don't."

"Come on, Allie." He tilted her chin up. "Give me a kiss."

"Reeve." Tears crowded her eyes. "Reeve, don't go."

He brushed his lips across hers. It killed him to see her hurt. He hadn't wanted to cause her any pain. But now that he realized he loved her, he had to take steps to protect her. He couldn't put her in any more danger. "Take care of yourself, huh?"

"Reeve," she said again as he strode to the door.

He paused, looking back. "You know, Danhi was right. You're stronger than I thought."

But not strong enough to watch him walk out the door. "Reeve!" she shouted, jumping up from the bed as he winked at her and closed it quietly behind him.

"See you later, Allie."

"Reeve!" she screamed.

She could hardly run after him. She was stark naked. By now she was crying. Tears streamed down her face. Wiping them away, grabbing her shirt and jeans, she pulled them on and went to the door. The wet clothes clung to her, cold and soggy.

"Reeve!" she called again, running outside.

He was nowhere in sight. But Paul Sammison stood beside the door. "Good morning, Miss Martin," he said. "Going somewhere?"

Chapter Twelve

A wrought-iron rail circled the second floor of the motel. Beyond the parking lot, a stand of trees shaded the area from the morning sun. Evergreens, mountain ash, and an occasional oak spread their summer leaves. Paul Sammison leaned against the railing and smiled at Allie. "Well, Miss Martin, fancy meeting you here. Enjoying Denver's western hospitality?"

She stared at him in shock. He wore a formal two-piece suit as if dressed for work. "How did you get here?"

"I drove."

She shook her head. Everything was so confusing. "How did you find us?"

"You," he corrected, standing up straight. "I was looking for you, Miss Martin. And I found you. By the way, you're all wet."

"I got caught in a rainstorm," she said, equally facetious. "How did you find me?"

"You've got awfully nice folks." His smile grew wider. "I've talked to them every day this week."

Damn! "My father told you where I was?" She kept staring at him, now in horror. She'd been so wrong to call. Thank God Reeve had gotten away. He didn't have to pay for her mistake.

Sammison moved his head back and forth in mock gravity. "They're very concerned about you. They called right after you did last night."

"It won't do you any good. It doesn't matter that you've found me." Allie crossed her arms under her breasts and glared at him. "You've missed Reeve," she said smugly. "He's gone. He left."

"I know," Sammison answered, his tone smug, too. "I waited, hoping he would leave. And he did. And now I've got you."

Allie frowned. "Me? What do you mean?"

"I don't know how he could have mistaken you for Liz," Sammison went on, tilting his head to one side and frowning at her. "Aren't you a natural blonde?"

This was silly. What did the color of her hair matter? At least he confirmed Reeve's feeling that a Liz Hernandez did exist—or had existed. "Look. What are you here for? What do you want?"

"You, love."

"What are you talking about?"

"Just what I said." He took her arm. "Come on, doll, we've got a long trip ahead of us. Chandler probably called the police, and they're bound to arrive any minute."

"Wait— Don't touch me." Allie pulled from his grasp. "Just what do you think you're doing?"

"Taking you hostage."

She was stunned. "What?"

He smiled again, but it was an evil-looking expression, and he took out his gun and cocked it, right in her face. "Aw, Miss Martin, don't look so surprised. You should be accustomed to being kidnapped by now. This is your second time. And we're going to have fun together."

His eyes raked over her body.

"No," she said, backing away. "No. You're not going to kidnap me."

"Now, now, mustn't get scared, sweetie. Everything's going to be fine."

"Reeve—"

"Will come after you." He grabbed her arm again, this time roughly, twisting it up behind her back. Then he pushed her in front of him down the hall. "Let's go."

It hurt so much, Allie let him push her along. No one was up and around, or she would have screamed. Thanks to Reeve's penchant for getting up early and staying at out-of-the-way motels there wasn't anyone to help. "Look, I don't understand," she finally gasped through the pain. "Why do you want to kidnap me? What good will it do?"

He paused beside a shiny black sedan. "You're the trump card, honey."

"What do you have to bargain for?"

"My life. My job."

"What—how can I help you?"

"Because, Miss Martin, if Reeve Chandler feels about you like I figure he's feeling about you, when he finds out I have you, he'll do exactly as I tell him."

"Which is?"

"To deny my involvement in this whole mess. And to cease and desist."

Allie laughed. "You're joking. Reeve's not going to do any such thing."

"Honey, you better hope he does, or you're going to wish I *was* joking."

"Reeve won't deny your involvement," she told him firmly. "No matter what. Besides, what good would it do? Everyone knows you're involved. You're Curt's boss."

"All Reeve has to say is that he dealt with someone else."

"Who?"

"Anyone."

"He won't do that."

"Yes, he will," Sammison said. "If he wants to see you alive, that is."

"But that's silly. People have seen you."

"No one important."

Allie shook her head. "I'm telling you, Reeve won't rescind his word. His brother is in prison, and he won't stop until he gets him out."

"Well, honey," the tall, blond agent drawled, opening the car door and shoving her inside, "I don't really care anymore if he gets his brother out or if he doesn't. But if he doesn't rescind his word, you're going to be in big trouble, because then I'll have to kill you.''

The threat was ominous, but Allie had heard threats before—from Reeve. From others. And she wasn't about to sit here and let some two-bit government agent who had messed up royally take her captive. The moment Sammison started around the car, she opened the car door and jumped out, heading for the trees at a dead run.

Unfortunately she had underestimated the CIA agent. Catching up with her, he grabbed her by the hair and whirled her around, slamming her against a tree trunk. ''Whoa, honey. Not so fast.''

''Let me go.''

''You're not going anywhere. Hold still.''

''No,'' she said, still fighting. ''I'll never hold still. I won't cooperate.''

She could hear sirens in the distance—police. If only she could last. Sammison heard them, too. ''You dumb bitch,'' he said. ''Always fighting. Looks like I'm going to have to get rough.''

And then he slugged her. Not expecting the blow, Allie's head snapped back like a stretched rubber band and hit the tree. She saw stars and moons and whatever else was in the universe. Then she crumpled to the ground.

''Stubborn broad,'' he mumbled as she passed out. ''Gotta make things tough, don't you? We'll just see how tough you are, honey.''

REEVE CALLED THE TWO FBI agents as soon as he left Allie at the hotel, arranging to meet them at a downtown Denver department store. Then he had to wait until past ten, when the store opened. He had wanted somewhere busy, somewhere where they wouldn't be able to corner him and start shooting. Or arrest him. Since it was a weekday, most shoppers were women with little children who chewed sticky chocolate candy and stared at him curiously.

He held up the watch to the light at the watch counter. He'd been pretending to examine it for several minutes. In the background he could hear the soft chime of bells, the store paging system. There was also the hum of voices as clerks set up merchandise, or customers exclaimed over store bargains. Where the hell were the two cowboys? He was ready to give up when he noticed them. Although they were dressed in suits, he recognized them immediately.

"Are you interested in the watch, sir?" the salesgirl asked him. "We have a sale on them until the end of the week."

Reeve handed back the gold Seiko. "Maybe another day. Thanks."

"If cash is the problem, you could apply for credit at our credit department."

"No, thanks," Reeve answered. "I have a charge."

He strolled to wallets and watched the two men look for him. Finally he stepped up behind them and tapped one on the shoulder. "What happened to your boots?" he rumbled into his ear.

The thin man swung around. "They hurt. Hello, Chandler. Where's the girl?"

"Allie?"

"Your Aunt Kate."

"Somewhere safe."

"We never touched her."

"Only because you didn't get the chance."

The thin man shrugged as though in agreement. "Maybe. What the hell was she doing at the Rustic River Inn?"

"Selling bras."

"Jesus."

"Okay, cut the crap," the other man cut in. "What is it you want from us, Reeve?"

"Help, and a bargain."

He laughed harshly. "Why the hell would I want to bargain with you? I've got two double agents—and I worked like hell to hide their identities and set this spy ring up—and thanks to you, they're dead."

"They got involved with Paul Sammison."

The man sighed. "So did a lot of other people. What is it with you, Chandler? Don't you know when to quit? Why are you carrying this on?"

"I'm a crusader."

"Sure."

"Look, I'll quit when my brother is out of jail."

The man scowled. "We can't do anything for you. We didn't put your brother there, and we can't get him out."

"It's a chance to get the CIA guys," Reeve argued.

He shook his head. "You're in the wrong country, Chandler. This isn't Russia."

A saleslady had been watching them. She walked up. "Can I help you, gentlemen?"

Reeve shook his head. "Just browsing."

"Let me know if you need anything. We have a nice special on key chains today." The girl smiled and moved on. A few moments later a woman carrying a screaming child came to the counter.

She smiled at them, too, halfheartedly. "Take my advice. Don't have children."

The thin man stretched his lips across his teeth. "Yes, ma'am." When the woman turned to the saleslady, he glanced at Reeve. "You know there's a federal warrant out for your arrest."

Reeve nodded. "Yes, but neither of you are going to serve it."

"We should. Look, Chandler," the thin man went on. "We know what you're trying to do, and we empathize with you, but we can only look the other way for a short period of time. We're not about to bite the dust for you or for your goddamned cause."

"My cause should scare the hell out of you both," Reeve answered. "It could be anyone in that East German jail with the government denying all knowledge of their existence. It could be you. Or your kid brother. Or your—"

"But it's not. Go to hell, Chandler, and leave us out of your mess."

The woman had wrapped up her purchase and walked between them, the child still screaming. "He wants his binky," she said, obviously embarrassed.

The thin man grimaced. "Really?" He turned to the saleslady. "Miss? Could I take a look at that gold key chain in the corner?"

The other man turned around, too. "You say you have a special on today?"

The girl nodded. "Ten percent off the regular retail selling price. Today only."

Realizing he wasn't going to get farther, Reeve turned and walked away. He hadn't expected to make much headway, but he'd hoped they'd bite. At this point, the whole venture was messed up. He was too hot a political item, because of all the media exposure due to Allie's kidnapping. Going down the escalator, he slipped out of the department store and onto the street. They didn't bother to follow.

Near the exit a woman cooked wild rice. She had it laid out in little white cups with plastic spoons. "Want a sample, sir?" she asked him. "It's from a recipe in the Denver Women's Guild's new cookbook, *Rocky Mountain High*."

"No, thanks." He'd had enough Rocky Mountain high.

Reeve came upon the agents' car half a block later, parked near a fire hydrant. He paused. It seemed just payment.

Quickly he popped open the door lock and slid inside, and in moments, had stolen a government car, plates and all. No one stopped him. Flipping on the air-conditioning, he drove up the street, thinking. The car started missing. It was a wreck, but what had he expected for government issue? He sighed. He was down to his last resort. Channel Four news. The hour was early, but he wasn't going to get another chance. A squad car passed him, and he thought about Allie. By now she'd be with Zane Younger, under protection. He hoped she had the sense to tell them everything. The nation was going to find out about it in a few short minutes, anyway.

Reeve parked down the street from the Channel Four building and went inside along with a bunch of other peo-

ple. A guard sat at a desk in the lobby. Reeve waited until an
elevator opened, and then he walked past the guard, holding up a card and mumbling something about an appointment. He walked inside the elevator doors just as they
closed.

"Sir!" the guard called. "Come back here, sir."

But it was too late. The doors glided smoothly closed, and
the elevator car lifted off the ground. He was still in a
crowd, and no one paid him any heed, despite the cries of
the guard. If in fact the people with him had heard the old
man. They stood like people usually do in an elevator, well
against the wall but not touching it, not speaking and
watching the lights at the top of the doors as if transfixed.

Since Reeve had been in the building before, he knew
which floor housed the broadcast booths. Several other
people exited with him, going various ways. He waited his
turn to see the male receptionist.

"I'd like to speak to whoever's in charge of the news
broadcasting today," Reeve said when everyone else had
been properly dispatched.

"Do you have an appointment, sir?" the man asked. He
was about thirty, tall and skinny with reddish hair and
freckles. He wore a suit and tie and a pair of horn-rimmed
glasses. From his accent Reeve guessed that he was a Denver native.

"No, I don't have an appointment," Reeve answered,
"but I think he'll see me."

"It's she," the receptionist told him with a tolerant smile.
He shoved his glasses up on his nose. "Today Ms. Hower is
in charge, and she won't see you without an appointment."

Reeve smiled back just as tolerantly, and pulled the gun
from his boot. "I think we'll be able to convince her. Don't
you agree?"

"Sir," the receptionist gasped. "There is no need for
violence."

"I agree," Reeve answered. "And there won't be any if
you follow orders." He signaled toward a door at the back
of the room with his gun. "Shall we?"

The man trembled visibly as he rose from his chair.

"What—what do you want me to do?" the man asked.

"Take me to the news set."

"But the news set is off limits."

"You know, you don't strike me as stupid," Reeve answered, "so please don't patronize me. We're going to the news set, whether it's off limits or not. And then we're going to switch on the power and do a little broadcasting."

"Yes, sir." The receptionist nodded agreeably. "Anything you say, sir."

By that time several other people in the area had noticed what was going on. They all stood terrified, particularly when Reeve swept the gun their way.

"Everyone take it easy," he said, hoping he wouldn't encounter a crusading cowboy anxious to prove his or her bravery. "My friend and I are going through that door." He gestured in the distance. "When we leave, you can feel free to call the police. But please, in the meantime, don't try any heroics. I'd hate to see anyone get hurt."

"Believe me, sir," the receptionist murmured, "I've worked here for a long time. I doubt anyone would be stupid enough to risk their life."

Not trusting them nonetheless, Reeve kept the receptionist in front of him as they streamed through the doorway, yet kept his back from the crowd of people. Everyone was as busy beyond the doors as in front of them. With each person they met, Reeve had to explain that he meant business.

Still things happened slowly. It took him over twenty minutes to convince someone to call for a cameraman and to connect him into a national broadcast. "But it's not news time," one of the producers, an attractive woman in her thirties, complained. "We can't do that."

"Lady," Reeve said patiently. "All you have to do is press a button." Holding the receptionist in front of him, he sat in one of the chairs on the news set. Surprisingly it was plain: a white counter with the Channel Four logo in the background above them.

"The game shows are on."

"Interrupt them."

"This is highly irregular."

Reeve swore softly.

"We're not set up for a news broadcast," she continued to whine. By that time the police had arrived and were waiting for Reeve to slip up. The receptionist seemed even more nervous.

"Please, Betty," the young man said. "Please do as he asks."

"But New York will get angry."

"A lot of people are going to be angry when this is all over," Reeve countered.

"The set is bad," the woman went on. "He's got the chair facing the wall that's not painted and—"

"Would you just do as he says, Betty?" someone asked. "He's got a gun."

"I know." She blustered around a few more moments, obviously at a loss. Reeve tried to wait patiently, but he was running out of patience. He cocked the gun.

"Look, folks, let's get things going."

"Right." A tall man scurried about, moving up a camera. Someone else appeared with a clipboard.

"Okay, you're on," the man said after conferring with a police lieutenant.

Reeve just shook his head. "I'm not stupid. Let me see a monitor. Tune it to NBC."

The policeman shrugged at the other man. Apparently they were at last in agreement. Once they had decided to cooperate, it took only a few minutes to connect Reeve nationally. Realizing that he was going to have to do some smooth talking in order to convince the watching nation that the red-eyed, wild-looking man holding a gun on another man in Denver, Colorado at eleven in the morning was legitimate, he told his story quickly and set his gun down on the counter.

He held up his hands. "All yours."

At that moment, apparently realizing they had messed up in regard to a news scoop, a dozen people beat the waiting police to the punch and rushed up to Reeve, firing questions at him faster than a machine gun. The camera didn't stop recording the action until the police pushed everyone aside, handcuffing him, and then they switched to a national newscaster analyzing the arrest.

As he was led out of the newsroom, he heard the newscaster say sympathetically to the waiting nation, "Apparently for days now, Reeve Chandler has been trying to convince the government of his plight."

Reeve would have laughed had the man not been so serious.

From there he was handcuffed, Miranda-ized, hustled downstairs into a waiting squad car, taken to the police station and booked on several counts, the least of which was assault with a deadly weapon.

Reeve asked about Allie several times, but no one would give him any details. He was hardly in jail at all before a high-level official from the CIA arrived. The man was older, heavyset, balding with gray hair. Reeve knew immediately that he was someone important. That surprised him. He'd expected to get action, but he hadn't expected a personal visit, and particularly not from someone flying directly from Washington, D.C.

"How'd you get here so quickly?" he asked when the man stood in front of the cell.

"I was in Kansas City when I heard the news. Mr. Chandler, I presume?"

Reeve nodded. "What can I do for you?"

The man stood in front of him. "Plenty. Did you have to embarrass us?"

"Believe me, it wasn't by choice."

The man shook his head. "I just wish the country could hear some of the good things we do."

Reeve shrugged. "That's how it goes."

"Mr. Chandler, I want you to know that I had no idea that your brother was one of our agents. Or that he was in jail in East Germany."

"Why not? Aren't you in charge?"

"This wasn't a sanctioned veil."

"I already know that. It was obvious that Sammison had gone solo when he brought in the Mob."

"You're not listening to me," the man said, wiping his brow and fighting back his growing exasperation. "I mean that Sammison was soloing long before your brother got caught."

Reeve looked at the man, incredulously.

He nodded. "That's right. Sammison's pulled off several missions no one ever sanctioned. Your brother's was the latest, the riskiest. Sammison thought that if he got some secret information he'd sent Curt Chandler in for, he'd get the final feather in his cap he needed for a big promotion. And I mean, big."

Reeve lifted a brow. "He wanted Washington?"

The man nodded. "Top circles."

Reeve was glad for small favors. Sammison at least had been stopped before embedding himself in top government circles. The near miss sent a chill down his spine.

"How'd you find all that out?"

"I spoke to a woman named Liz who called me. But whether you believe me or not isn't the point. I just wanted you to know that I've made arrangements for your brother's immediate release. He's being flown from East Germany to Washington right as we speak."

"So he's alive?" Reeve said, struggling to contain his emotions.

The agent nodded. "Yes, very."

"That was quick."

"I've made quicker bargains."

"Who'd you give them?"

"Several spies."

"What now?"

The man looked around the cell. "May I sit down?"

"Please." Reeve gestured to a cot. "Make yourself at home."

"Needless to say, this has been a trying day." The man mopped his face with a handkerchief. "It's hot in here."

"Maybe the government's footing the air-conditioning bill," Reeve remarked.

The other man produced a wan smile. "Mr. Chandler, as soon as your brother arrives in The States, we'll get him admitted to the best medical facility available. He will have the best care possible."

"He's ill?"

The agent nodded, grimly. "They couldn't touch him. He got ill from the drugs they administered to treat the rat-bitten foot. They were waiting for him to recuperate before getting . . . more forceful."

"No gangrene?" Reeve asked, his brow pleated.

"None our preliminary medical teams could detect. But he'll be hospitalized as soon as he returns and be given whatever he needs."

Reeve hesitated. "How do I know you're telling the truth?"

The man shrugged. "You have to take my word for it. The police are dropping all charges against you. If Miss Martin wants to press charges, I'm afraid we can't intervene."

"Who convinced the police to do that?"

He shrugged. "I have far-reaching influence."

"I see. Even with television stations?"

"Are you kidding?" The man shook his head in disbelief. "You've given the news media something to talk about for weeks. You're only a few hours old, and already their ratings have soared." He laughed. "Channel Four is honored that you chose them. I heard on the radio you're being hailed as a national hero."

"I'm not sure that's a compliment," Reeve said.

The man's smile broadened. "When it comes to capturing the sympathies of a nation, it is. Will you come to Washington to see your brother?"

"Probably," Reeve answered.

"When the news reporters find you, please be kind to the agency. You used to be one of us."

Reeve smiled at the man; a person couldn't help but respect him. At least he was sincere. "I'll try not to embellish the truth."

"We're going to find Sammison."

Reeve nodded. "Thanks."

The man held out his hand. "It's been nice meeting you, Mr. Chandler. If you ever want to come back, I have an opening for a good agent."

"No, thanks." Reeve said. "I think I've had enough excitement the past week just convincing someone I needed help. I don't think I'll tackle the agency."

"Take care then. Oh, by the way, where is Miss Martin? Her uncle has been worried sick about her. I imagine that after your news broadcast, he's going to be camped out on my doorstep ready to wring my neck."

"What do you mean, where is she?" Reeve asked. "She's in custody, isn't she?"

The man frowned. "Did you release her?"

"This morning."

He nodded. "I'll ask the desk, then."

But he didn't have to ask. Zane Younger walked into the lockup and paused by the cell. "Reeve Chandler?"

"Yes?" Reeve glanced at the young man he'd spoken to early this morning.

"Listen, Chandler, we've got a little problem. I hate to tell you this, but Miss Martin is not in custody."

"Where is she?" Reeve asked.

"Gone."

"Gone?" he echoed.

"When we got to the motel this morning, she wasn't in the room. She wasn't outside, either."

"Damn!" Reeve swore. "Sammison's got her."

Chapter Thirteen

Allie regained consciousness in the car. At first she didn't know where she was, then it all flooded back: Reeve leaving, Sammison coming, her getting knocked out. She blinked a few times, staring at the silver radio buttons, yet not really seeing them.

"Well, I see you're awake." Paul Sammison glanced down at her.

The charade was over. She sat up, moving her jaw gingerly.

"Hurt?"

"Yes."

"You need to learn to cooperate, Miss Martin."

"You can't get away with this," she said. "This is crazy. Someone will catch you."

"Really? The way I see it, I'm already washed-up. I've got nothing to lose and everything to gain."

She glanced at him. "You're mixed up in the Mob, aren't you?"

"Let's say I have a few investments."

"Did you tell them to kill Reeve?"

"They were willing to help."

"The police are going to find you," she said. "Or the CIA. You've gone too far."

"Don't count me out yet, lady," he answered. "Remember? I've got the ace up my sleeve."

Allie didn't say anything more. She looked around at the landscape beyond the car windows. In the past few days she'd been all over this state, and several others, too, and still she found elements of her surroundings alien. "Where are we?"

"Don't worry about it."

Seven days ago she wouldn't have cared. Now she needed to know. Call it curiosity, survival, instinct. The mountains were to her right, to the west of the city. That meant they were traveling south. "We're going to Colorado Springs, aren't we?" she said.

"Not quite. But where we are going is a nice little place. You'll see when you get there."

"Then what are you going to do?"

"Contact Chandler."

Allie frowned. "But how?" she asked. "Where? Reeve left the motel."

"He'll come back."

"Don't count on it. I told you, he's gone. He left."

"And I told you, he'll come back."

Although it was painful, Allie shook her head. "He went to do something about his brother. He thought the police were coming for me."

"And they'll tell him you're missing. You've underestimated yourself, Miss Martin. I've watched you, and Reeve Chandler is in love with you."

"When? When did you watch me?"

"In the desert. And since he's in love with you, being such a hero, he'll want to rescue you."

"That's as ludicrous as your kidnapping me," Allie said. "Reeve Chandler is not in love with me."

"Really? Then why would he turn you in to the police just when he could use you the most?"

Allie didn't have an answer for that. She still wasn't sure why Reeve had abandoned her that morning. She wondered where he was, what he was doing, if he had made any headway with the FBI agents.

"We're almost there." Practically midway to Colorado Springs, Sammison turned the car off onto a smaller highway, and then onto a paved road, that dwindled to a gravel road, which finally, several miles later, became a rutted path. They kept going west, into the foothills of the mountains, bumping along on bad springs for miles.

"Where is this place?"

The area was desolate, yet an occasional military jet flew overhead, high above them. Allie could hear the high-pitched whine as the planes glided by. "In the mountains."

"Is it a building?"

He laughed. "Not quite."

Bouncing around another hill, they pulled in front of an old abandoned mine shaft. She'd heard there were claims up here, but this one was in such an out-of-the-way spot, she doubted anyone could find it even knowing the location. Yet they were here.

Sammison got out of the car and went around to her side. He opened the door and swept his hand out wide. "Welcome to Shangri-la."

Since she didn't have much choice, Allie stepped from the car and stood looking at her surroundings. Once she'd sworn to Zane Younger that she wouldn't set foot in these mountains. Well, here she was. All she needed now was for Patsy, the old man with the pick, to step out.

"What are you going to do with me?"

"Tie you up. We'll wait a while. Then I'll make my call. Just relax for now."

They waited several hours. Allie sat with her back to a wooden beam and stared at the rugged peaks that surrounded them. The sun was hot, beating down on her face. Compared to Arizona it was cool here in the mountains, yet she was hot. The terrain was already rough, and it wasn't even considered *the* mountains. Funny, she hadn't really been to the desert, and she hadn't really been to the mountains, and she'd suffered through them both. Since her hands were tied, she couldn't wipe the sweat that beaded on her forehead.

She glanced at Paul Sammison. He was sweating, too. Apparently it was time; he got to his feet and smiled at her. "Well, here we go. Don't go away." As if she could, she thought. "I'll be right back."

"Aren't you using the car phone?" she asked.

"Yes, I am, but then I'm going for a ride. The car's nice and air-conditioned."

At that point Allie didn't care anymore. All she wanted was him to go and get this over with. Her head ached, and her mouth was dry. She was back to square one. "Fine."

"What's the matter, Miss Martin?" Sammison stood in front of her. "Spunk all gone?"

After he had hit her, she had decided that it was useless to fight him. He was physically stronger and he would use it liberally to subdue her. He was mean. She would have to wait and bide her time and plan her escape. "Yes."

"Good, that makes things easier for me. Shall I tell Reeve you said hello?"

"Whatever."

"I'll tell him you miss him. How's that?"

"You know," she said, his arrogance sparking her defiance, "even if it does mean that you'll kill me, I hope he doesn't deal with you."

Sammison arched an eyebrow. "I guess your spunk isn't gone, after all, Miss Martin. Or may I call you Allie?"

"Call me anything you wish."

"Good. Well, since you don't care if you live or die, maybe I ought to let you wait a day or two before I tell him where you are. Just so you can ponder it. What do you think?"

She shook her head and glanced away, at the mountains. "I don't really care."

"Aw, too bad. Would you care if I kissed you?"

She glared at him. If she had to kill him, she wouldn't let him touch her.

He laughed again. "I see that got a rise out of you. Too bad I don't have time for a little caress. And more. Tootleoo.'' He waved. "Don't get lonely now. And watch out for the snakes."

Allie would prefer snakes and scorpions any day. She watched him get in the car and drive away. No, she hadn't lost her spunk. And even though she was tied, she didn't feel helpless, thinking of all the things she'd done when she was with Reeve. She could do this, too. The moment he was gone she started wiggling her fingers, working at the bonds that held her hands. After all, Paul Sammison deserved a little surprise for when he returned.

If he returned.

REEVE GLARED AT Zane Younger in absolute fury. "Where the hell have you been?" he thundered. "What have you been doing all morning? Why didn't you tell me Allie was missing?"

"I've been trying to find her."

"Damn." Clutching the bars of the cell, Reeve glanced at the man from the CIA. "If you're right, and I am free to go, get me the hell out of here."

"I'll take care of Sammison."

"Not if I find him first."

The man studied Reeve a long moment. Then he nodded. "Guard," he called.

Reeve was released seconds later. Zane Younger accompanied him from the Denver police station. "Do you really think Paul Sammison has kidnapped Allie?" the detective asked.

"Yes," Reeve answered. "Now all I have to do is figure out where the hell he's taken her."

"Where are we going?"

"Back to the motel."

Younger nodded. "I figured that would be a good move. I took the liberty of having a recorder put on the phone there. We'll be able to monitor any calls."

For once Reeve appreciated the help. "Good thinking."

"When do you think he'll call?"

Reeve shook his head. "I don't know. We'll just have to wait."

Which was not an easy task. Reeve paced the room restlessly for several hours, waiting for the phone to ring. How he wished there was something else to do, but he didn't have a single other solution—except strangling Sammison with his bare hands. And he couldn't do that until he found the man. All he could think of was Allie. Allie being mistreated by Sammison, Allie alone. Why had he left her this morning?

Zane Younger watched him pace back and forth. Finally his curiosity got the best of him. "What happened between you two out there?"

Reeve glanced up sharply. "Who?"

"You and Allie."

"What do you mean by that?" Reeve stared angrily at the cop.

Younger held up a hand. "Don't worry, I'm not about to say anything derogatory about her. I just wondered how you two managed to get along. From what I've seen so far, you've both got lousy tempers. But you don't have to answer. Just the look on your face, and I already figured it out."

Reeve turned his anger to the phone. "If he doesn't call soon, I'm going looking for him."

Younger sighed. "He's making us wait on purpose."

"I know." But knowing didn't make it any easier for Reeve.

When the phone finally did ring, it startled everyone in the room. Yet they all sprang into instant action. The man monitoring the call put on his headphones and waved. "Just keep him talking long enough to get a fix on his location."

Reeve nodded understanding. Zane Younger went to stand by the sophisticated tape recording system to listen, and a host of other cops jumped to their feet. Reeve placed his hand on the receiver, waiting for it to ring a second time. Then he snatched it up.

It was Sammison. "Chandler? I see you've gone back to the motel. Having a nice time?"

"Cut the crap, Sammison. Where is she, and what do you want for her?"

"Who? What do you mean, Chandler? What's going on?"

"Don't play stupid with me, Sammison. I want Allie back and I want her back now."

"You can't always have what you want, you know. I didn't get what I wanted—you dead."

Reeve swore. "Dammit, Sammison, where is she?"

"You seem upset, Chandler." From the sound of his voice, Sammison was enjoying himself. "That's unfortunate. I guess you're just going to have to stay upset, because I'm not going to tell you where she is. I'm going to keep her for a few days. Just enough time for you to deny my involvement in your brother's case."

Reeve laughed, but it wasn't a sound of humor. "That's ridiculous. You know I'm not going to do that."

"A pity. You know," Sammison answered, "you and your girlfriend both sound like broken records. That's what she said, too. But I believe it can be done. Try it. Or else she dies. Oh, by the way, you don't have to trace my call. I'm using my car phone."

With that he broke the connection. "Dammit!" Reeve swore again and slammed down the receiver. He turned to the man running the tape recorder. "Did you get a fix on the location?"

The man's expression was apologetic. "If it was a car phone, we won't be able to pinpoint a location."

Reeve started pacing again.

"What do we do now?" Younger asked.

"Wait." Reeve swung around. "But I'm not about to play his game. Rewind the tape."

Younger's forehead wrinkled in a frown. "Did you hear something?"

"Yes." Reeve thought about the call. "Yes, I did. I only hope I can figure out what I heard."

They played the tape several times. Reeve could make out the sound of the car air-conditioning. In the background there was a whining noise. It was faint, but it was there, almost far away. An echo in the air, like a sonic boom.

Suddenly he knew. "That's an airplane," he said, jumping up, "an air force jet. He's got her near an air base."

"What the hell good does that do?" Younger asked. "There are tons of air bases out there. I swear we have more planes per capita than people."

In a way, Younger's statement was true. In addition to the Air Force Academy and Peterson Air Force Base near Colorado Springs, there was Lowry Air Force base, the largest base in the United States, just outside of Denver. Other military installations ringed the area, as well. Added to Stapleton Airport and Arapahoe County Airport, planes were a common sight in the sky. And a common sound on the ground.

"But there's only one airfield close enough to the mountains to make that kind of echo," Reeve said. "It's a top-secret base, and if I know Sammison, that's where he took her."

"If it's secret, how do you know about it?"

"I used to work for the CIA." Reeve started out the door.

Zane Younger paused, surprised by that revelation. Then again, he thought, it figured. Reeve Chandler was the CIA type. Tall and bold and flaunting danger in the face. "What are you going to do?" he asked, walking quickly to catch up.

Reeve paused and turned back to him. "Simple. I'm going to find her. And then I'm going to go f her."

"Does she know how much you care about her?"

Reeve shook his head. "No. But if I find her, I'm sure going to tell her." He didn't even ask the detective if he could use the car. He just clattered down the steps, got in and started the engine.

Younger got in beside him. "By the way, you're not talking about NORAD, are you?" he asked. "It's near here, and I know not too many people know about it."

"The supreme headquarters of the nuclear defense system?" Reeve asked. He knew it was built half under ground, somewhere between Denver and Colorado Springs. The personnel were on full-time alert. But he shook his head. "No. This is a small base. Just a few planes. It's squeezed between a couple of mountains for security. There's no access except a single dirt road."

"How do they land a jet?"

"Very carefully. It's near an old abandoned mine. That's how I know about it."

"How does Sammison know about it?"

"We worked together on a case. It was our rendezvous point. We were flown in and out of the country from there."

"Nice."

Reeve glanced at the young cop. "I know it seems wrong, but some secrecy is necessary for security reasons."

The cop nodded. "I guess. Until someone goes bad."

Reeve agreed. "Actually, in spite of all you hear, that's a very unusual outcome." Maybe the CIA man was right, he thought. Maybe Americans should hear the good things the agency accomplished. But that would undermine their effectiveness. No solution in sight, he just kept driving.

"Wonder why he'd pick the mine?" Younger asked after a few moments. "Considering you know about it."

"I'm sure he didn't count on my hearing the planes." Reeve shrugged. "But maybe you've got a point. Maybe he picked the mine because he knew I'd remember—and come."

"A confrontation?"

"Actually it's about time," Reeve confirmed. "He's hated me for years. You don't have any jurisdiction out here, you know."

The detective glanced at him. "Neither do you."

"I don't have a job that I could blow."

"I messed up with Miss Martin when she first came to town," Younger explained. "I'd like to make amends."

Reeve glanced back at the man. "Just so that's all you intend."

Younger smiled. "You're a lucky man, Chandler."

Reeve nodded. "I know."

He knew the road so well he could have driven it blind-folded. Once out of the city, he pressed on the accelerator, pushing the car to the limit. Then, at a small crossroad, he turned off the road and headed toward the mountains, away from civilization.

They drove for several more miles. Knowing sound traveled, he stopped the car well before the mine shaft. "Are we leaving the car here?" Younger asked when Reeve shut off the engine and opened the door.

"No sense giving away our surprise. If in fact we have a surprise."

"What do you want me to do?"

"Just stay quiet and cover my back."

They crossed several hills and scaled some rock outcrop-pings. Reeve crept up quietly, Younger behind him. It had been a few years, but as far as he could remember, the mine was just around the next hill. Crawling on his belly, he peeked down the overhang. But he couldn't see anything. Behind him, Younger whispered, "Are they there?"

Reeve nodded. He could hear them moving around. Or rather Sammison moving. The man's shoes made a hollow sound on the rocky soil as he walked back and forth in front of the shaft. "Yes, they're here."

"Look, let me radio for help," Younger said. "I'll call the state police. Wait for me."

"Just tell them to stay on the perimeter unless they hear gunshots."

Younger nodded and crawled back down to the car. The hardest thing Reeve did was wait. Now he could hear Allie talking. He would have recognized her voice anywhere, the soft, slight husky tone. She sounded tired. She'd been through a lot lately. But she'd held up, after all. Sprawling across the cliff, he tried to decide how to best go in. If she was tied, as he suspected she was, he couldn't very well bar-rel forth shooting. He could spring from the overhang like a mountain lion and surprise Sammison. Either way, Allie

would be in danger. Damn, he loved her—and now she wa
in more danger than ever.

When Younger came back, Reeve signaled him down
"Let's go around. I want to see where he's got her tied. Are
you with me?"

The detective nodded. "All the way."

Perhaps it was from the days she'd spent with Reeve
perhaps it was merely a survival instinct, but Allie wa
growing attuned to her surroundings. It was getting dark
The sun was setting in the west. The planes had stopped a
few hours ago. Situated near the entrance to the mine, now
she could hear water dripping from somewhere deep in
side. A footstep on the roof. A pebble rolling down the sid
of the mountain. Someone was out there. Someone look
ing for her?

In the hours she'd spent sitting, she'd managed to work
her hands loose. Yet she held them behind her as though
they were tied. Even when Sammison had come back with
food and water, she had pretended she was helpless, letting
him torment her with a few drops of water at a time or a
morsel of food, the threat of rape. He was enjoying him
self. No wonder he'd betrayed Reeve. The man had no con
science, or fear, or sense of justice.

"What kind of mine is this?" she asked after a few mo
ments, hoping to cover the new sound she'd heard: foot
steps on the ground behind the shaft.

"A gold mine."

"How did they get out the gold?"

"Dynamite, I guess. Picks." Sammison sat across from
her, closer to the dark entrance. A few rotten old board
shored up the chasm. Most of them had fallen. "Why?"

"I just wondered."

"Might even be a few dynamite charges left down in
there. Want to do a little mining?"

"No."

By now Allie was certain that it was Reeve's scrambling
she heard. She could sense his presence, and her heart be
gan to pound with foreboding. If he had come to rescue her

she had to help him. But what if he wasn't there? What if it was wishful thinking? Not wanting to tip off her suspicion, yet wanting to let him know she knew he was there, she said to Sammison, "Did you hear the coyote?"

"What?" He frowned at her.

"Did you hear the coyote?" she repeated louder.

"There's no coyote."

"I'm sure there is. I heard it."

"You're cracking up, lady."

"Maybe," she said. "Are you going to call again?"

"Chandler?" Sammison nodded. "Yes, later. I'll let him stew a while. If he wants you, he'll be ready to bargain by morning."

"What if he doesn't?"

"Then I guess I leave you to rot, and then I hightail it out of the country." He jutted his head in the distance. "That's why I chose this place. There's an airfield close by. I've got a few friends there who will fly me out."

"Not if Reeve catches you first," she said, and suddenly she threw herself forward and started rolling down the hill. "Reeve!" she shouted. "I'm untied."

Allie's heart did flip-flops. If she was wrong, she was dead, for Paul Sammison would start shooting. But how could she have been wrong about the man she loved?

"Dammit, Allie," Reeve said, jumping out in front of her, his weapon already drawn, "that was stupid."

Caught by surprise, Sammison didn't have his weapon out, but he drew it quickly and stepped back into the mine shaft, shooting all the while. Reeve hit the dirt and fired back.

"Get the hell out of here, Allie!" he called as he rolled behind a beam. Bullets rang out like firecrackers on the Fourth of July. Allie could see tiny beams of fire in the gray twilight.

"You're a dead man now, Chandler," Sammison called. "I'm going to kill you."

"You won't get away with it," Reeve answered. "We've got you. Throw down your gun."

"The hell I will. If you want me, you're going to have t
take me."

Allie couldn't see the action from where she had ende
up. Scrambling to her feet, she ducked behind a rock an
tried to watch.

Zane Younger touched her shoulder. "You all right?"

Surprised, Allie gasped and swung around so fast that sh
almost knocked him off his feet. "Oh, God, you scare
me," she whispered.

"You all right?" he repeated. He'd crept up to her fro
a nearby outcropping of rock.

She nodded. "I'm fine. How did you find me?"

"If I didn't know any better, I'd say faith."

"What?" She frowned.

Younger nodded toward Reeve. "He recognized the j
planes in the tape recording. But I think he would hav
moved heaven and earth to get to you. I thought he wa
going to kill me when I told him you were missing."

Allie turned around to watch the man she loved creep u
on the man who had kidnapped her. She would have move
heaven and earth to get to him, too. But what was going t
happen now? Sammison went deeper into the dark cavern

"Give up, Paul," Reeve shouted. "Throw down you
weapon, and we'll talk."

"Sure."

"You know I won't cross you," Reeve said.

"Yeah. You're always honorable, Chandler. But you se
either way, I'm a dead man. And if I have to die, I'm no
going to let you capture me and do it by degrees." A volle
of fire followed. "Don't come any closer."

Reeve rolled along the ground dodging bullets withou
shooting. In the distance they could hear the police sirens a
the state police closed in.

"Give up, Sammison," he said. "It's over."

"You should know it's not over until it's over," Samm
son taunted. "Come on, Chandler. Come get me. I've g
a little surprise for you."

Hunched over, determined to bring the agent out, Reeve made his way toward the mine shaft. Occasionally he would shoot, but Allie could tell he aimed wide of the mark on purpose. Whether Sammison actually knew about the old dynamite charges or had just inadvertently mentioned them, and had decided to kill himself rather than risk capture and prosecution, she wasn't certain. But just as Reeve reached the entrance, suddenly, along with the sound of diabolical laughter another shot rang out, and the entire shaft exploded.

"No!" Allie screamed into the dust and dirt that blew through the air. She could see Reeve fall over from the force of the blast. "No!" she sobbed, starting forward.

Zane Younger held her back. "Stay here."

Allie twisted from his arms as a second explosion rocked the ground. After all that they had been through, to have Reeve die because of her would be the ultimate irony.

"Reeve!" she screamed, rushing to him and falling on her knees beside him. Flying rocks and debris had cut his face, and he lay on the ground stone still. She couldn't tell if he was breathing or not. "Oh, God, Reeve, answer me." She slapped at his face. "Reeve, dammit, wake up."

Younger tried to pick her up. "Allie, come on. Listen—"

"No." She twisted away again. "Reeve Chandler!" she said ominously. "Damn you, wake up."

He opened his eyes. "You know something, Allie," he groaned. "You talk a lot."

"Reeve." She practically fell on him, kissing his cheek, his hand. "Reeve, are you all right?"

"I'm fine. What are you so upset about?" He frowned at her. "And why the hell did you put yourself in jeopardy by rolling down that hill?"

"What did you expect me to do?" she answered testily, his anger rattling her ire. "Wait until you came charging in on your white horse?"

"I don't have a white horse."

"Well, you should."

He paused. "Allie, why are we arguing?"

"I don't know," she answered.

He ran a finger down her cheek. A dark bluish bruise marred her complexion. "Did Sammison do this to you?"

She nodded. "Yes."

"If he wasn't already dead, I'd kill him."

"He was just trying to get me to cooperate," she said.

"You do have a stubborn streak."

She glanced toward the mine shaft. Smoke still belched from the entrance. "I'm sorry he had to die."

"So am I, but he made that choice. To elude capture, he fired into an old cache of dynamite stored inside," Reeve mumbled. "We found it years ago, and buried it in case the explosives came in handy. I guess he dug them up, figuring they had."

"He may have wanted to lure you inside, and then use them, Reeve," Allie said, not wanting Sammison to sound too noble.

Reeve nodded. "I'm sure he wanted both you and I trapped inside, so he could detonate them. Knowing his mind, he wanted to bury us alive, then flee the continent."

Allie grimaced and lowered her head pensively. "Reeve, do you think the mob will still try to kill you?"

He shook his head. "It's all over, Allie," he said in that low stirring voice. "Without Sammison, the contract's off."

By that time the state police had arrived and surrounded the shaft. "Everything's fine," Zane Younger told them. "Let's get a car in here for Chandler and Miss Martin."

"Sure thing."

An officer scurried away. Allie didn't move from Reeve's side. He sat up gingerly and felt his head. "Got any aspirin?"

"Sure. Right in my back pocket."

He grinned at her jeans and shirt. "You know, Allie, I saw this great dress in a store window today while I was in Denver. It's red, and it would go super with that underwear you've got on."

"Lingerie, Reeve. We call it lingerie."

"Who's *we* Allie?"

"The fashion industry, and women."

He laughed. "Kinky stuff, anyway."

She blushed. "There's nothing wrong with you at all."

"You're right," he agreed. "I feel great. Say, aren't you tired of those jeans yet?" He eyed the pair she'd thrust herself into in the desert grove.

"Actually I've gotten attached to them," she answered.

"Why?"

"Can't very well take you home to meet Danhi in jeans," he said, shaking his dark head.

She paused, her heart racing a thousand miles an hour. "What do you mean, take me home to meet Danhi?"

"There's this animal called a cow, Allie. It's got a tail and four legs. In a way, it kind of resembles a horse."

"So?"

"I know you've seen a horse. I just wanted to familiarize you with a cow. I've got a few dozen head of them on my ranch. I've got a couple chickens, too."

"Any scorpions?"

"Occasional. They don't get inside, though. I do have a garden. I grow a little corn. Make some meal out of it for fry cakes. Sometimes I have trouble with snakes. I have to beat them back, like you wanted to do in the desert. I've got some coyotes, too. And the ranch house is pretty nice. There's this room with a skylight—" he gestured with his hands "—that would make a great place to draw designs. That is if a certain boss would let a certain employee work long distance."

"And if he doesn't?"

"Maybe she could open her own company?"

Allie licked her lips nervously. "Are you asking me to visit you, Reeve?"

"No. I'm asking you to come live with me and be my woman." He smiled at her. "Hell, I'll even marry you."

She arched an eyebrow at him. "Really? A confirmed bachelor like you? I thought I was irritating."

"You are. You're like an itch. But it's a nice itch, and I've just discovered that I can't live without it. So what do you think? Can a city girl live in the desert?"

"I thought you lived in the mountains."

"It's just a short jaunt to the desert. Is that a problem?"

She laughed. "I don't know. What would we do?"

He shrugged. "Argue. Make love. Go camping."

"I hate the heat. We'd have to have air-conditioning."

"I thought you were getting used to it."

"In small doses," she said.

"Okay. I'll buy a generator tomorrow. I thought we'd get a little red dog—"

"I'm not afraid anymore, Reeve."

"I know. God, Allie, I love you," he said huskily, pushing back the stray wisps of hair that always fell in her face. "I thought I wasn't going to get a chance to tell you."

She laughed again. "Oh, Reeve, I love you, too." Suddenly she sobered. "What about your brother?"

Reeve's rugged face broke out in a grin. "He's fine. He'll have a bellyache for a time. Got ill there. But he'll be okay. We could go to Washington and visit him—"

"He's back?"

Reeve nodded. "He's on his way home."

"Oh, Reeve, you did it." She smiled proudly, grazing his cheek with a kiss. "You got his release. You've got to be pleased."

"Actually I'm just relieved. I'm glad it's over."

"So am I. I do have one request, Reeve."

"Then you'll marry me?"

She nodded. "Yes, I think so. As long as you're willing to buy a generator."

He laughed. "Allie, I think you're enjoying this little adventure."

"I think you're right. Reeve, when exactly is your brother due back?"

He shrugged. "Tomorrow, maybe. It's a long flight."

She nodded toward the mountains. "Want to go for a hike?"

He studied her. "Got any water?"

"We'll make our own."

"How about cornmeal?"

She stood up and hitched up her moccasins. She wanted nothing more than to be alone with him in the wilderness. "I'm sure we can find something to eat. You never did get around to making rattlesnake stew."

"What about notifying your parents? Your uncle?"

She smiled at him and held out her hand. "We can do it all in the same day. Right now, I want to show you what I've got in mind for that line of lingerie, the one called Satisfaction?"

He smiled and took her hand. "Allie, I can hardly wait. I might have a few helpful hints—from the male point of view, mind you."

"Do you have any other suggestions?"

He mused a moment. "Things don't have to be a hardship," he said. "There's a motel up the hill a ways. They have a few cabins. I think they even have a hot tub."

"What are we waiting for?"

Zane Younger stood there staring at them. "Hey," he called, "what about the car?"

Turning, Reeve grinned at him. "Bring it back tomorrow around three. We'll have checked out by then."

The detective nodded. "Yeah, tomorrow."

Reeve winked at Allie. "Let's go, sexy lady. We've got some designs to work on." Clasping her hand, he guided her up the mountain.

HARLEQUIN SUPERROMANCE BRINGS YOU...

Lynda Ward

Superromance readers already know that Lynda Ward
possesses a unique ability to weave words into heartfelt
emotions and exciting drama.

Now, Superromance is proud to bring you Lynda's tour de
force: an ambitious saga of three sisters whose lives are torn
apart by the conflicts and power struggles that come with being
born into a dynasty.

In *Race the Sun, Leap the Moon* and *Touch the Stars*, readers
will laugh and cry with the Welles sisters as they learn to live
and love on their own terms, all the while struggling for the
acceptance of Burton Welles, the stern patriarch of the clan.

Race the Sun, Leap the Moon and *Touch the Stars* . . . a
dramatic trilogy you won't want to miss. Coming to you in
July, August and September.

The Welles Family Trilogy

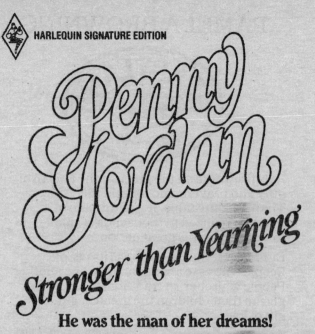

Penny Jordan

Stronger than Yearning

He was the man of her dreams!

The same dark hair, the same mocking eyes; it was as if the Regency rake of the portrait, the seducer of Jenna's dream, had come to life. Jenna, believing the last of the Deverils dead, was determined to buy the great old Yorkshire Hall—to claim it for her daughter, Lucy, and put to rest some of the painful memories of Lucy's birth. She had no way of knowing that a direct descendant of the black sheep Deveril even existed—or that James Allingham and his own powerful yearnings would disrupt her plan entirely.

PAMELA BROWNING

...is fireworks on the green at the Fourth of July and prayers said around the Thanksgiving table. It is the dream of freedom realized in thousands of small towns across this great nation.

But mostly, the Heartland is its people. People who care about and help one another. People who cherish traditional values and give to their children the greatest gift, the gift of love.

American Romance presents HEARTLAND, an emotional trilogy about people whose memories, hopes and dreams are bound up in the acres they farm.

HEARTLAND...the story of America.

Don't miss these heartfelt stories: American Romance #237 SIMPLE GIFTS (March), #241 FLY AWAY (April), and #245 HARVEST HOME (May).

HRT-1